ABANDONED

John David Jacobs (signature)

J.D. Jacobs

Outskirts Press, Inc.
http://www.outskirtspress.com

978-1-4787-8638-2

Cover Photo © 2017 J. D. Jacobs. All rights reserved - used with permission.

Outskirts Press and the "OP" logo are trademarks belonging to Outskirts Press, Inc.

PRINTED IN THE UNITED STATES OF AMERICA

Credit to:

Ralf Schuster: editing assistance and much needed advice

Renae Carpenter of Carpenter Creations: photography and editing of the author pic and front cover

Mauro Halpern: back cover image of bird

To my parents and my sister, for having to hear about this made-up story for over 5 years.
Thank you for being patient and encouraging. Love you

1

Intro

HAVE YOU EVER looked at yourself in the mirror and been absolutely clueless with the person looking back at you? Or maybe perhaps you recognize who it is looking at you, but you've grown to hate him? You hate the look he gives you, hate the fear that drowns his eyes, hate the way he carries himself. That's how I feel right now. Everything about this Jaden Foxx kid who I share the same reflection with, who continuously mocks my every move, infuriates me.

I watch myself lift my hand and rub my fingers across my face, feeling the jaggedness that subdues it. I pull my left hand back and punch the mirror, shattering the glass and throwing shards into my clenched fist. I give out a scream of pain. A scream that I've let out far too often. So often that I can't even feel the pain anymore. The blood running down my elbow reminds me that, in fact, it is still there.

But the mirror is still in tact. I can still see myself through the cracks of the broken frame, meaning that burst of anger accomplished basically nothing. I can't bare to look at myself anymore. I turn around to the mattress that lies on the floor directly behind me and throw myself down on it. I need a break. A break from myself, or maybe a break from reality. I shut my eyes to search for my escape, and after a few seconds, I begin to revisit my past, revisit the journey

I've experienced.

So what better way to start then from the beginning. . .

⸺※⸺

Finally, Saturday afternoon. It took long enough, but this week is finally over. I walk through the front door of my house, and head straight towards my room. As I make my way across the house, I notice my dad sitting in his chair in the living room next to the fire.

"Hey, Dad," I greet him. He gives a somewhat dull response, resembling a groan. I stop in my tracks for a moment to see him staring straight into the fire. He looks agitated, bouncing both of his legs up and down and gazing in the flames as if he has lost something in the fire and is looking for it.

"What's wrong?" I ask him from across the room.

"Oh, nothing," He replies, still staring into the pit.

I can easily tell that something is wrong. I walk up behind him and ask again.

"Okay, tell me what's the matter?" I ask, with enough concern in my voice to tell him I'm serious. He turns his head away from the fire and looks at me.

"It's nothing," he tells me. "I'm just thinking about your mother."

A lump rises in my throat. This isn't a subject that I'm too fond of talking about, so I remain silent and keep my hand on his shoulder. After about a minute I take my hand off, grab my keys and head out the door.

"Wait, where are you going?" Dad asks me, sounding disappointed that I'm leaving.

"It's Scarlett and Ryan's birthday," I tell him. "I asked you earlier if I could go out to eat and bowl with them and you said it was okay."

"Oh yeah, sure, that's fine," he says, clearly having forgotten about it until now. As I leave the house, a part of me wants to stay and comfort him a little more, but what really can I do?

I get in my old, baby blue truck and drive towards Ryan and Scarlett's house to meet everyone. They should be there, as well as Terra and Cody. I'm really excited about tonight, considering we haven't done anything like this in awhile. I really do have a pretty good group of friends. Very diverse, in my opinion.

First, there is Cody, who has been my best friend since kindergarten. Actually, he was my only friend throughout elementary school, which is quite weird, considering how different we are. Cody being one of the few African American kids at our school, and me being the whitest kid in the city. Cody being an all-around athlete, and me being the kid who was cut from the JV baseball team at age fifteen. Cody standing a good 6'3", 6'5" if you include his flattop, while I stand a whopping 5'9". Cody and his family being well off in terms of money, while me and Dad sat comfortably on the bottom-half of the middle-class. It's funny how complete opposites like us couldn't have been more destined to be each other's best friend.

Then there's Terra, one of the few African American girls at my school. She and Cody hit it off from an early age, and ever since elementary school, they have always been together. She has long dreadlocks that sweep at her lower back, and she's had braces for as long as I can remember.

Ryan and Scarlett are fraternal twins that moved to Westwood my Eighth grade year. When they moved to Westwood, everybody loved them – well, everybody loved Scarlett. Cody and I became friends with Ryan first, and eventually, Scarlett began hanging with us, too. Scarlett has always had people lining up to hand her whatever she wants, but I guess she feels more comfortable in our group instead of being worshipped by a flock of jocks. Ryan, however, is completely the opposite of Scarlett.

Honestly, Ryan is weird and nerdy, which made him and me

click immediately. The first time he came to class, he was wearing a Star Fox shirt, which just so happens to be my favorite video game franchise. When I told him I liked his shirt and introduced myself to him, he thought it was the most insane thing in the world that there was a guy with the last name Foxx who liked Star Fox, so he gave me the nickname Starfoxx and it's stuck with me ever since. As we grew older, I sort of kept my nerdy side hidden from everybody other than Ryan, while Ryan embraced his nerdy side.

Ryan is tall and skinny. Well, perhaps scrawny is a better description. He knows more than anybody else that he's going to make it in like on his brains, not his muscles. He has shaggy, shoulder-length hair and spends his spare time working with computers. I'm not exactly sure what he does with them, but whatever it is he does, it's too complicated for me. He enters Stage IV Nerd whenever he starts messing with software, so I stay away from all that.

But then there's the stunning Scarlett Avalon, the girl of my dreams. Simply put, Scarlett is the girl that I always wanted to end up with, but I've always been too scared to do anything about it.

I remember first seeing her when they moved here. I thought she was the most beautiful thing I had ever seen. Even in middle school she was gorgeous. Since I've known her, Scarlett always had long, curly, blonde hair, always wore bright red lipstick, and always wore scarves. That was her thing. She was a cheerleader, so of course other guys were chasing after her. Despite this, Scarlett and I are very close friends, and I haven't really understood why she likes being around me more than she does other, more established and much less awkward guys. I guess it is because I was one of the first guys she met here. I can't really think of any other reasonable explanation.

But anyway, that is our group of friends. As I pull up to the Avalons' house, I see them all waiting for me in the yard.

"Took ya long enough," I hear Cody yell at me once I step out of the truck. "How many times did the truck break down on the way over here?"

"Only twice," I say, patting the hood of my truck. I've been driving that old, rusted truck for two years so I'm used to the jokes by now.

"The question we all want to know is when ole Ant is going to give you an upgrade," Ryan says to me, referring to my dad in the nickname we gave him. "That truck is about twenty years past its prime."

"I've been asking Dad for a new one for two years now," I reply. "I'm telling you. Ole Ant is strict when it comes to spending money, especially when it's being spent on his only child."

"Alright, let me go get the keys," Scarlett tells us as she turns to head inside her house.

"No, no, no, Princess Avalon, you're not driving tonight," Cody fakes an absurdly atrocious British accent, holding his hands out to signify a change in plans. "Since it is yours and Sir Avalon's date of birth, I would be glad to escort us to the finest eating establishment and bowling alley this side of Westwood." He gives a facetious bow, which is answered by Ryan throwing his jacket over the face of our new unconvincing chauffer. All of us then walk towards Cody's brand new, sharp gray sedan that makes the rest of our vehicles look like trash. One thing about Cody is that he and his family have always had a lot of money, and they have never been scared to flaunt it.

Terra takes the front seat as the twins and I sit comfortably in the spacious backseats. With Scarlett sitting next to me, I look over at her and talk to her for the first time of the night. "You know, I would drive us tonight, but I couldn't because my truck–"

"–Is a piece of crap," Cody humorously interrupts me with a remark that he tries to wave off as an abnormally loud cough.

"Don't feel too bad," Ryan assures me from my other side, "at least you have a vehicle to yourself."

"Yeah," Scarlett chimes in, "our parents are making us carpool until Christmas. I'm guessing that's when Ryan will get his own vehicle and I can have the SUV all to myself."

"You say that as if it's a good thing," Ryan comically remarks. "I hate that thing, it's terrible to drive. Plus, it doesn't fully brandish my masculinity." He gives a smirk that ensures he's being sarcastic.

"Oh, and the car you're looking at will?" Scarlett blatantly returns. She then turns to the rest of us in the car. "Just guess what kind of car he wants."

"I'm gonna guess," I ponder for a good joke, "he's gonna drive back and forth to school in the Millennium Falcon."

"Nah, man," Cody corrects me, "that's too mainstream. He's just gonna put a motor on his gamer chair and use his PlayStation controller as a steering wheel."

"Yeah, but that's also bad for the environment," I reply. "I know, he's going to single-handedly save the planet and get one of those electric cars that runs on double-A batteries."

"Or, if all else fails, he might just get himself a Flintstone mobile and Yabba Dabba Doo himself to school."

"Nah, that involves running. You know Ryan doesn't do physical activity."

"Wow, you guys are just so funny," Ryan interrupts mine and Cody's back and forth jabs at him, sounding unamused and a tad bit offended.

"Actually," Scarlett tries to say between laughs, "one of those guesses is right."

"Sweet, dude, you're getting the Millennium Falcon?" I ask Ryan as Cody and I burst out laughing at the same time.

After Scarlett gets done giggling at my remark, she continues. "He's wanting to get an electric car."

We all give our sign of disapproval, as Cody and Terra throw boos at Ryan. "What?" Ryan tries to defend himself. "Nothing wrong with electric cars, they're eco-friendly. Plus, who's going to be the one laughing when all of you are filling up every weekend and I'm running free with my electric car?"

"Uhh, pretty sure everybody who sees you driving that thing is going to be the one laughing," I give my input, and the car erupts in laughter.

After a few more jokes at Ryan's terrible life decisions, we eventually reach Rochester's, the one and only restaurant in the city of Westwood. Why we only have one restaurant is beyond me. We have thousands of people, even have a giant superstore, but only one place to eat. I've always found it weird that Westwood, despite being the decently sized city it is, only had one food joint, but it is what it is. Gourmet burgers are delicious so that's a plus, at least.

We take our seats on the largest table; a round booth in the corner of the building that we always sit at when it is rarely open. After a few minutes, a middle-aged, unappealing waitress comes to our table.

"Welcome to Rochester's, may I start you all off with some drinks?" the woman dully recites to us.

"Yes, but first," Cody begins as he throws his arm around Ryan. "It is this fellow's and that madam's birthday today."

The woman gives Cody a lackluster scowl, then turns to Scarlett. "May I see your ID, madam?"

The group remains silent as Scarlett fiddles around in her purse for her ID then shows it to the woman. After giving a simple nod, the woman takes our drink orders and informs us that she 'will deal with all that birthday stuff after the food comes out,' then walks away.

"Well, then," I turn to the group, "I think somebody is a little upset that it's not their birthday."

"Terra and I came here two weeks ago and she was our waitress, and she was God-awful," Cody begins with his rant on our waitress. "First off, I wanted sweet tea and she gave me unsweet..."

"Oh, dear Lord, how is this lady not in jail," I interrupt him.

"No," Cody adds on, acting like I didn't say anything, "but then she got Terra's order wrong completely, and when we told her she did, she told us 'well that's tough.' They were right at closing, so she wouldn't go back and replace her order, which sort of pissed me off."

"To make things even worse, it was a veggie burger," Terra informs us. The entire table outbursts in a groan at the thought of poor, innocent Terra having to unjustly eat a veggie burger.

"Exactly," Cody goes on. "Like, if you hate your job so much that you're just gonna be a complete drab, then why work it? Nobody likes a giant stick in the mud."

"Well if there was a stick in the mud right now," Ryan comments, "I'd pull it out of the mud and poke that mole on her nose with it. Did you see that thing? I don't want that thing anywhere near my food."

As we all burst out in laughter, I can tell that our behavior is bothering our waitress, who peeks over at us from across the building and slowly makes her way towards us to get our orders.

We all place our orders and continue talking. Well, all of us except Terra. Terra has remained rather quiet the whole time.

"Terra, are you okay?" I ask her from across the table. "Or are you afraid that if you say anything that you'll be punished with the veggie burger again?"

"No, not that. I don't know," she answers me. "I've just suddenly started feeling bad."

"Well, do you want me to take you home?" Cody sincerely asks her.

"Yeah, I really think you might have to," she tells him. Cody, clearly having not expected her to say yes, follows her as she leaves the booth and hands me a fifty as he passes by.

"Oh, Cody, you shouldn't have," I tell him with a grin on my face.

"Chill out, man. It's for our bill. It shouldn't be more than $25, so you better give me my change back," he tells me.

"You're coming back, right?" Scarlett asks him.

"How else are you guys getting home?" He beams at us as Terra tells me goodnight and wishes the twins a happy birthday. "Plus, I got three asses to kick in bowling, starting with you Foxx, so you better give me my money back." They then walk out the door with Cody embracing Terra as she coughs into her fist.

"Wonder what's up with her?" Scarlett expresses her concern.

"I don't really know," I reply. "There's some bug spreading around lately. Hopefully she'll be okay. But what I want to know is how the birthday duo is doing, I haven't had a chance to ask you two all night."

"I'm alright, I guess," Ryan tells me. "I got the new Army Front video game from my aunt and uncle in Nebraska. It came with the–"

"–the expansion pack with three new maps and the updated sniper rifles?" I finish his sentence as the nerd inside of me is released.

"Yeah, the maps are okay, but the scopes on the snipers are the best thing yet. You've got to come over tomorrow and play it."

"I definitely will. Do I need to bring my headset or are we–"

"Wow, okay, sorry to interrupt the geek squad," Scarlett playfully breaks in our engaging nerd talk that was a completely different language to her, "I believe it's my turn to answer the question. I'm good and all, but I'm a little irritated at my parents."

"Why?" Ryan and I both insist at the same time.

She hesitates for a minute, surprised that we don't know what she's talking about. "Ryan, does it not upset you that Mom and Dad won't let us go anywhere outside this city for our *18th birthdays*?" The emphasis she puts on the *18th* informs me that she is genuinely upset about this situation. "We're stuck eating at the same restaurant and bowling at the same place that we have been our entire lives."

"I mean not really," Ryan calmly tells her. "The bowling alley is always fun, and I'm fine with Rochester's. I mean, they have yet to spit in my food. However, Ms. Mole needs to chop that thing off before she serves my food."

"Ahem." All three of us turn to see our waitress approaching our table carrying a large disk that holds all five of our plates of food. "What, these two had to leave the party?" she asks with no interest whatsoever as to where they went.

"Yeah, they had to run home to get some stuff," I tell the lady.

"Well, what a shame," she scornfully sneers. "I'll be right out with your birthday sundaes. I'll try not to drop my mole in it, just for you." She throws an acerbic look to Ryan as she heads off back to the kitchen.

"Okay, I'm definitely not eating that sundae anymore," Ryan nervously declares. "I'm honestly too afraid to eat this burger."

"Well, if you won't, I'll be glad to," I say, poking my fork towards his plate before he swats it away.

We down our food quickly and wait for Cody to walk through the doors any minute, but he doesn't. When the waitress comes with their sundaes, we pay our bills and tell the lady to bring back to-go boxes. She gives a negative sigh and leaves.

"Okay, she's seriously asking for, like, a negative tip," Scarlett complains.

"I'm not leaving one," I tell her. "We can make Cody leave one since he hasn't come back to get us yet, but I'm not that mean of a person."

We box up Cody and Terra's food and wait for him to return, but after fifteen minutes, the waitress kicks us out of our tables. As the cool, October air contacts our thick jackets once we leave, we sit at the outside tables of Rochester's and call Cody numerous times, but he doesn't answer any of them.

"Well, what do you guys wanna do?" I ask the twins after the twelfth unanswered call. "Do ya'll want to sit here and wait on him some more or do ya'll just want to go ahead and walk to the bowling alley?"

Scarlett looks down at her watch. "It's already 11 o'clock. The alley closes in an hour so we can't wait here much longer."

"To be honest, I don't even know if I want to bowl anymore," Ryan confesses to us. "Cody killed the mood. It's all his fault."

"I think you just don't want everybody to know that you still have to use the guard rails," I jokingly jab at him.

"I can bowl perfectly fine without the rails," he unconfidently corrects me.

"Yeah, we believe you," Scarlett says with little belief in her voice. "What did you score last time we didn't put them up, like a 40?"

". . .38," Ryan ashamedly admits.

"Well, I'm totally okay with calling it a night," Scarlett says as she begins walking toward her house. Their house is a good three miles away from Rochester's and to get there, we will have to walk down my neighborhood, which directly borders the outskirts of Westwood. "Besides, a few of the cheerleaders are coming over tomorrow so I don't want to be too tired when they do."

"Oh yeah, I forgot that Scarlett Avalon has more important friends," I kid at her. I then look over at Ryan. "I guess we're just the odd ones out, huh?"

"Speak for yourself, Starfoxx, they're going to be at my house," Ryan boasts. "But, then again, that doesn't mean they will have anything to do with me. I still wish you would give Zoey my number, Scar."

"Oh my God, Ryan, she still has a boyfriend," she groans, as it sounds like she's told Ryan this a million times. "And, no, Jaden. The cheer squad always has some kind of party for each girl's birthday. Honestly, it sucks being the youngest of the senior cheerleaders, so I'm ready to go ahead and get my birthday over with."

"Yeah, not me though," Ryan tells me. "I'm spending all tonight and all day tomorrow playing the new Army Front gam. . ."

"Ryan, I swear you've talked about nothing but that stupid game all day," Scarlett snaps at him.

"Look at her! Scarlett Avalon, angry. Who would've thought?" I joke with her, giving her a wide smile as she counters with a smaller one of her own. Scarlett is always cheerful, so it's fun to pick on her for being irritated at something for a change.

"I think you're less mad about my awesome game and madder about Mom and Dad not letting us go off to Roaksville," Ryan tells her.

"Well. . ." she begins but quits as she knows he guessed correctly.

"Well if it's that big of a deal to you, I'll take you to dinner somewhere further off than Roaksville, if you would like to."

Wait. Did I just super-casually ask Scarlett on a date? Oh dear God, I think I just did. Everything was going fine, too, and I just had to screw it up. I look over at Ryan to see his reaction, but he hasn't given my statement any extra attention. I mean, I want to, I've always wanted to take her out, just me and her, but I didn't expect it to slip out so easily. Oh God. What if she says no? What if she—

"Yes, please do," she strongly responds. I don't think she viewed it as a date when I suggested it, but I surely am. "I just want to get out of this town just for a little bit."

And for the rest of the walk, a smile rests happily on my face.

We pass by Terra's house shortly after. With Cody's vehicle parked there, we decide to ignore it and deal with Cody ditching us next time we see him. My house is close by to Terra's, but the lights are off, and I don't want to wake Dad up by getting his car and driving us.

Forty-five minutes later, we finally reach their house. By this time, the clock has passed midnight.

"Well, guys, I'd love to stay and chat, but I have a brand new video game that's calling my name," Ryan tells us as we make our way to my truck.

"Wait a minute," I tell him. I reach in my truck and look for the presents I got for Ryan and Scarlett. I find Ryan's first and grab it.

For Ryan, I got him a shirt displaying the logo of Army Front, which I hope his aunt and uncle from Nebraska didn't already give him. I hand him the present first, and he seems happy with it.

"Oh man, this shirt is really awesome! Thanks Jaden!" He extends his hand, but I know it's not for a simple handshake, but for our personal handshake that we had come up with years ago. After a few seconds of a bunch of random hand motions, he heads inside. "I'll see you tomorrow, Jaden! Don't do anything too crazy on your way home!"

"I will just because you told me not to," I yell back at him as he walks through the door. I then turn my head towards Scarlett to see her smiling at me.

"I swear you guys are seriously the biggest nerds on the planet," she says to me with a soft laugh, having cooled down from her earlier anger.

"What? I can't help it," I defend myself. "Besides, we have had that shake for four years now. We can't break tradition."

I give her an identical smile, and for a moment, I can't keep my eyes off of her lips. But after a few seconds, I snap out of it.

"Oh, yeah. And for you. . ." I say as I search my truck for her gift. I find the long, slim box under my seat and hand it over to her. "Happy birthday."

I watch as she throws the poorly wrapped paper off the box and opens it. Her eyes widen in awe, and she looks at me for a brief second like I had just given her the best present she had ever received.

She takes the golden scarf out of the box and bundles it around her neck. "Jaden, this is absolutely beautiful." I can tell she is genuinely happy, and that brings a broad smile to my face.

"I thought, you know, you could always need another one," I proudly tell her.

She looks up at me with joy in her eyes. "Thank you so much, Jaden!" She reaches over and hugs me tightly. I love the feeling and embrace it as long as possible until she eventually let's go of me.

"This is so beautiful!" she admiringly claims. "How did you know I needed a gold one?"

Honestly, I noticed that I never saw her with that specific color. I know she wears all sorts of different colored scarves, but I had never seen her wear a gold one. I don't want to sound weird, thought, so I just tell her, "I just got one I thought you would like. Just try not to strangle your parents with it since you hate them now." Well, so much for not sounding weird.

"Oh my gosh, I don't hate them! I'm just mad that they treat me like I'm still fourteen," she tells me, not finding my remark weird at all.

"They only treat you like that because Ryan actually still is fourteen," I cheer her up.

"That may be true, but still," she says with a fading laugh. "I can't wait to graduate and move out of this house and out of this city. I know graduation is still seven months away, but I'm really looking forward to being on my own. I've already been accepted at Kentucky, I just wish I could go ahead and move up there."

"Really, though, other than horses and really good fried chicken, what does the state of Kentucky have that Mississippi doesn't?" I inform her on the important facts that will definitely change her mind. "Besides, you can't move too far away because then you will have a new group of guys to adore you and you'll forget about little ole Jaden Foxx," I tell her as I throw my biggest pair of puppy dog eyes I can attempt to pull off.

"Quit it," she smiles at me and gives me a light push. "Don't throw that crap at me. You know I'm not going to forget about you. There's plenty of people here that I want to forget, though. Like that creepy kid who kept staring at me in history class today."

"You mean Creepy Peeper Pete who's been staring at everybody since first grade? Nobody is going to forget him; he's going to be in everybody's nightmares. Actually, it's rumored that the further you move away from Westwood, the more likely chance you are to wake up in the middle of the night with him staring at you."

"Dang, I guess I'll have to go to Ole Miss then," she shrugs her shoulders and accepts her fate.

We both laugh, but I'm sure neither of us are laughing at the joke. She might just be giving me one of those sympathetic, 'wow-this-poor-kid-just-won't-go-home' laughs, but I, on the other hand, am giving her a 'my-God-you're-so-gorgeous-please-don't-leave-me' laugh.

"Jaden," she begins with a smile, "really, thank you so much for the scarf!" She leans in to hug me, and as she does, I consider whether now is the time for me to do something. Should I make a move? Is now really the right time to? Not now. It's too risky. She lets go of me before I have time to reconsider myself and heads inside.

"You better not forget, either." She orders me.

"Forget what?" I ask.

"I can't believe you already forgot. You have to take me somewhere far from this place!" she reminds me before she opens her front door.

"Oh yeah, I won't forget. I'm ready for it!" I perhaps-too-excitedly call back to her. "But I can only afford to make it to Roaksville, maybe the Alabama line if I have a full tank, so if your far away is, like, Paris, then I'm gonna have to back out."

I give her a grin and she laughs, then gives a short pause before continuing on a more serious note. "Be careful on the way home, Jaden."

"I'll try my best," I say as I give her a wave goodbye.

I continue standing there in her driveway, watching as she walks in. I don't guess I will ever have the nerves to tell her how I feel. A part of me kicks myself, because I can't ever pull up the guts to do it, but then again, another part of me knows that, if I were given the same opportunity again, I still wouldn't do it – it's too risky. What if she doesn't like me back? I wouldn't want to ruin such a great friendship.

But that will change. I promise to myself that whenever Scarlett and I go on our 'date', I'm going to make a move. I mean, if she shoots me down and things between us get awkward, it's not like she's going to be in Westwood forever. Like she said, she's going to Kentucky after graduation, which is in seven months. I can handle seven months of awkwardness.

I get in my truck and crank it up, still thinking things over. If I make my move, I don't think she will reject me, though. She has to like me back. I mean, she agreed to go on a date with me. I am taking Scarlett Avalon on a *date*. That sentence alone has to tell me something. And, she also got me a birthday present a few months ago, too. I look down at the leather rope around my neck with the shark tooth dangling from it. I was honestly surprised when she gave me a present, but I was glad she did. It has to be a sign that she feels some sort of affection towards me, right? Or is it just solely friends with her?

I'm overanalyzing everything; worrying too much. What is meant to happen will happen. I just need to worry about making it home without falling asleep.

I return to the house, which is dark and quiet, just as it was when we passed it a while ago. I head straight to my room and get in my bed, falling asleep shortly after . . .

I'm lying in my bed, and the first thing that enters my mind is whether I'm in a dream. I can't really tell. My vision is blurry, and my surroundings seem as if I am, but it feels like reality. I can't really decide, so I just remain lying in my bed, hoping that if I'm awake, I will go back to sleep.

Right at that moment, I hear the muffled sound of my door

slamming open, and I spot my Dad running in at me. What is he doing? I begin to sit up, but an invisible force pushes down on me, keeping me from doing so. It feels like I'm strapped down to the bed.

Dad places his hand on my elbow and squeezes it. I can't really move my head to see what he's doing, but after a few seconds he aggressively starts pushing me into the mattress. "C'mon son, wake up!" he commands me, with a concealed and distant sound to his voice. I look straight at him and begin to say something, but no words come out. I can't even open my mouth. He puts his other hand on my opposite shoulder, and continues to drive me down in my bed.

"Jaden! Please, wake up!" His echoed screams are turning into muzzled wails as I can see his eyes begin to water. He keeps shaking me, rocking me up and down on the bed, hoping to wake me up.

The odd thing is, I'm looking straight into his eyes, and he's staring right back at mine. He must know I'm awake.

Wait a second. I have to be dreaming. None of this would make sense if I were awake. Who am I kidding? This isn't a dream, this is more like a nightmare. I have to wake myself up somehow.

While Dad is shoving me, I notice my arm flail up towards him. I'm shocked, as my arm seemed to swing without me even controlling it. Dad pauses at my reaction, not sure whether to be happy or not by my sudden movement. Then, suddenly, I see my opposite arm swing at him. Dad backs away just in time to avoid my hand, but I am left paranoid. Why am I doing this? I didn't want to swing at him. I can't even decide if it was meant to hit him or to just shoe him off of me. Either way, I've decided that I'm ready for this nightmare to be over.

Dad steps down off my bed and intently eyes me, as if this were the last time he would see me. I can barely see him wipe the tears from his eyes as his body shakes in what appears like both sorrow and anger. I'm trying my best to move, to speak, to tell him I didn't mean to swing at him, but to no avail. No matter how hard I try, nothing works.

"Oh, Jaden," he bawls to me while he's crying, "I love you so much. I'm sorry, son." He softly rubs my forearm, then turns towards the door and walks through it, closing it behind him. Where. . . where is he going? I continue lying there, waiting for him to come back in. He isn't leaving me, is he? I wait for him to come back, but he never does. . .

2

The beginning

MY EYES SHOOT open. I look around my room, looking for my dad to be close by, but he isn't. I then make sure that I'm capable of sitting up, and after I do, relief overcomes me. It was all just a bizarre nightmare. I'm not sure if it woke me up or I slept on after it happened, but either way, I'm just glad it was a dream.

I look over at my clock. 6:30 A.M. No way I can go back to sleep right now.

I feel the need to go look for him and talk to him, perhaps tell him about my dream. And I better do it before he leaves for work at the hospital.

I quickly spring up out of my bed and rush out of the room to see if he has left yet. After searching through the house, I realize that he has already left. Dang it! I should call him. Maybe he's on his way to work, and I can get in touch with him before he starts his shift. I dial his number but get no answer. That's understandable, he must have already started working.

I go to fix myself breakfast. I guess cereal will do, considering that's all we have. I reach in the fridge to get the milk, but once I start pouring it out, I find out that the milk is spoiled, and it comes out very lumpy and putrid. I could've sworn we bought milk last week. Besides, the expiration date says it's good for another two weeks.

Oh well. It's no big deal. I will just call Grandmother, see if I can go to her house and eat breakfast there. She won't mind. She loves cooking for me, anyway. I call her, but I get the same empty ringing I got earlier. Well that's rather odd. She always answers her phone. She must still be asleep.

I'll just wait until Grandmother calls me back. I sit down on the couch and turn on the TV to pass the time. Nothing. A blank, white screen. I try to change the channel, but it won't let me. It's like the satellite was completely turned off. I get up and head outside, thinking that maybe I can find out what's going on with the satellite. But as I open the front door, I find something completely different. Something I had no intentions on finding.

Looking out into the neighborhood, I'm met by the sight of chaos. The only real way to describe it. Absolute chaos. Clothes, jewelry, picture frames, furniture, all scattered across the street. Nearly every door on every house is slung open. Windows are broken, and as I look down the rows of houses, I can't find one that isn't shattered. I run out to the middle of the street and stand in horror at what I see. Everywhere. There is stuff thrown everywhere.

I begin to panic. What's going on? Why is everything like this? As I scan my surroundings, I find something sticking out from everything else. It takes a minute for me to capture what it is, but when I do, I wish that I hadn't.

A body.

I sprint over to the body, which is facedown into the asphalt road. After a few unresponsive shakes, I can tell that the person is dead. I stand up as a shriek of terror exits my mouth. What happened? What do I do? The only thing I can think of is to call the cops. I run back to my house, grab my phone, and quickly dial 911. *Bzzz. . . Bzzz. . . Beep.* No response.

What? How can there not be anybody answering? I call again, desperately needing somebody to pick up on the other end.

Bzzz. . . Bzzz. . . Beep.

That's when the reality hits me. I drop the phone to the floor, and my heart follows it.

I'm alone.

No. That can't be. There's no way. That doesn't even make sense. I try to convince myself these things, trying to think of any reasonable explanation as to what is going on. Maybe. . . maybe the phone lines aren't working. Yeah, that might be it. I take off out the door, and give out one long yell for help. For anyone. But I get no answer. I'm screaming to myself.

This can't be happening, it can't. I yell as loud as I can again, hoping I get a response this time, but I don't.

I start trotting down the street, giving out a plea for help every few houses. Every house looks the same: open doors, smashed windows, and the occasional holes in the side of the house facing the street. Everything is cluttered. Destroyed.

My trot turns into a full out sprint as I'm now hopelessly wishing for somebody to yell back at me. I keep on running, determined not to stop until somebody replies. Please, somebody, please.

I reach the outskirts of downtown Westwood. I've ran twenty blocks to be greeted by the sight of a ghost town. Total abandonment. The whole city is a wasteland. No color to it, no life to it, nothing but pure silence. I give one last shout for help and give a pause in hopes that someone in the city heard me. I wait, and as the seconds turn into minutes, I realize that the cry falls to deaf ears. Or, in this case, nonexistent ears.

What. . . what is going on? I keep asking myself this question aloud as I head back to my house, hoping somebody will overhear me and answer it for me. My mind is racing with so many questions, but it seems that that specific one is the only one to escape my mouth.

What is going on. . . as I walk back to my house, I become

terrified with what the answer may be. I mean, it doesn't make sense for everybody to up and leave overnight. Where is everyone? Is everyone okay? Oh, God. I think back to the body I found earlier today, and try to come to grips that the latter is probably false. What had happened to everybody? I want to know but I'm not sure how I'm going to find out.

I look up and down my street. Houses lined up on each side of the road with a spacious, identical yard separating each house from one another. There is about thirty houses on each side of my street, with an additional two streets parallel to mine, all looking the same. They all stretch out in a straight line, starting from downtown Westwood and running into the main road, Highway 4. The three roads connect about twenty times from my house to the city limits of Westwood, making this lonely walk seem longer. After each intersection I pass, I look down to see if the parallel roads are any different, but they, too, have come to the same fate as my street.

It's hard to believe how much everything looks differently than it usually does. The houses appear as if nobody has lived in them in years. The yards are filled with personal belongings, looking as if they were simply tossed out of a car. But what catches my attention the most are these wooden crates that appear randomly on the porches of different houses. I have absolutely no idea how they found their way here. My curiosity gets the best of me, and I walk up to one on the porch of a nearby house to inspect it.

The crate is about three feet wide, three feet tall, and looks like it was used from old scraps of wood. The lid to the crate is nailed shut, and there's no way I'm going to pry it open with my hands.

The crates are definitely strange, but I forget about them and continue walking back to my house. Investigating these random crates isn't my top priority at the moment.

What is going on? I begin to ask myself the repeated question again. I keep replaying it out loud, but it's pointless. Where is everyone? Where are they? I can feel my head begin to ache at all the things that have been thrown at me in such a short time.

I piercingly yell the repeated question as loud as I possibly can, as a way to release my frustration. I hear my echoes talk back to me, and I view them as a form of company.

Not entirely sure why I keep repeating that same exact question out loud. Maybe it's because I view it as the most important question. Maybe because I feel its answer is the only one I can take.

I don't really want to ask if everyone is okay, because I feel that they're not. I mean, with a body lying in the street, it's alright to worry about how it got there.

Speaking of the body, I'm getting closer to my house, and I can see the body in the distance, still in the same position as I left it. I really don't want to, but I have to see who it is. I'm pretty sure that I will know the person, but I just hope that it isn't somebody important to me, especially my Dad. I've already seen enough close relatives of mine die to last the next thirty years. I really don't want to have to go through another one.

As I inch closer to the body, I notice that it is not Dad, thankfully. I get to the body and look it up and down, seeing if I can tell who it is that's face is waiting to be turned over. Wearing khakis and an orange flannel, nobody specifically comes to mind, so I reach down, grab his shoulder, and flip him over.

I see the face of the town's barber, Mr. Lawkins, looking back at me. The face I see, however, is more than I expected, and I feel my stomach turn when I first catch glimpse of it.

His face has turned completely pale white. Blood has spewed from his mouth, and has dried up overnight. The feature that I find the most disturbing, however, is his eyes, which are wide open, staring straight ahead. The eyes look so...I can't decide. They just look as if there were some magnificent stars in the sky they were gazing at. But at the same time, they look as if there is some ghostly silhouette right over my shoulder.

I can't dare to look at him any longer. I flip him back over and walk back to my house. It, too, has smashed windows that I failed to notice earlier, but unlike the others, the door is still intact and none of our belongings were thrown out from it.

I step inside the house. I can't believe how normal it looks, in a time where nothing is the same. Even if everyone were to come back tomorrow, there's still Mr. Lawkins's body out there to account for.

I honestly don't know if I can take anymore of this right now. I look at the clock and discover that it has only been two hours. It feels like it has been an eternity.

This is all a dream. It has to be. It's just a realistic dream, just like last night. I'm still asleep. I walk in the living room and lay down on the couch, staring at the ceiling. As I wait to wake up from my dream, I lean over off the couch and vomit on the floor. This isn't a dream. This is real life. I'm left here with no clues, no answers, and honestly, I'm terrified. I don't know what to do. The only thing I feel I should do is lie here and pretend like it never happened. Inside my house, I'm in my own little world, and right now, I need to get as far away from reality as I can.

This is it. This is my life now.

3

Westwood

I'VE BEEN SITTING in the porch swing at my house for hours now, thinking this whole thing through. I'm really surprised that I'm not hungry yet, but I really don't care. I guess this whole thing made me lose my appetite. I don't really know how long I have been sitting here, but the sun slowly descending hints to me that it has been at last six hours.

It's been an awful lonely six hours. I've had nothing to look at but the sight of bedlam on the streets. Not even noises are affiliated with me. Except for the intermittent sound of the porch swing rocking back and forth, there is no other sound whatsoever. Not a single bird chirping, not even the sound of a breeze blowing through. Total silence. And honestly, it has done nothing but frighten me even further.

Is this me? Just sitting here, stuck between afraid and depressed, wasting my life away on a swing? I have to find some answers that are somewhere in this city. Or maybe I don't need to find answers, maybe I just need to find something to get my mind off of things. I can sit here all day and worry my ass off, but it's not going to help anything. I need to do something.

I hop off of the swing, trying to motivate myself to do something, but not knowing exactly where to start. Without a sense of direction,

I turn around and walk through the front door of my house, hoping to find Dad sitting in his chair, staring at the fire. But sadly, he's not.

I walk over to the mantle above the fireplace and look at the pictures that sit on top of it. There's a family photo of us five: Grandmother, Pawpaw, Dad, Mom, and me. I'm about five in this picture. I have to admit; I was a cute little joker when I was little. I can't get over how happy all of us look. We didn't know what the future had waiting for us, we were just happy to be together as a family at that moment. That's really one thing people take for granted: family.

I focus my attention to my mother. I remember the day she died. I was seven years old. October 17th.

It was a regular day at school until I was suddenly called to the office. Confused as to what they needed me for, I walked there to see Pawpaw sitting in the lobby. His face was stiff, trying his best to not have any expressions. I instantly knew something was wrong, so I asked him what the matter was. He avoided my question and told me to follow him. As soon as we got in his car, I asked him where we were going, and this time, he gave me a response.

"Jaden," he began with a solemn voice. "Jaden, your mother was in a car wreck, and she is in the hospital right now. I came to take you there to see her."

"Is, is she okay?" I stuttered.

"She. . ." he stopped, thinking his response over, trying to think of the safest reply to tell a seven-year-old kid. "We're not sure."

Neither one of us said anything on the rest of the way there. Since I was so young, I had this assumption that everyone turns out fine when bad things happen to them. People just die when they get old. However, mom was only 34, so it wasn't her time yet.

When we got to the hospital, Pawpaw told me to sit down in the waiting room as he rushed to the emergency room. The only other person in the room was Dad, who was still in his scrubs. I guess when he found out about her wreck, he got as far away as he could so he wouldn't have to see her so badly injured.

His head was in his hands, and he was glowering at the ground, as if it were the floor's fault for her wreck. He looked up when I came up to him, and once he saw me, he pulled me in by my arm and hugged me. I could hear him crying on my shoulder, which was enough confirmation for me. Mom wasn't going to make it.

A few minutes later, Pawpaw and Grandmother walked out from the emergency room with a doctor right behind them. Grandmother was torn apart, crying uncontrollably to the point where Pawpaw had to hold her up. Pawpaw was trying his best to stay calm, but I could see the devastation in his eyes.

"Anthony," the doctor said to my Dad, "I'm incredibly sorry. She —"

"Please don't say it," Dad interrupted him with a crack in his voice. "Please, just leave us be."

The doctor gave a slight nod and exited the room. Dad fell back to his seat and cried heavily in his palms as my grandparents went to comfort him. I couldn't come to the realization that Mom was gone forever. It didn't really hit me until her funeral, which is still by far the worst experience of my entire life.

I remember everything vividly. She was beautiful. Her long, black hair that I had played with numerous times just lay there, still. They had put her favorite ruby earrings on her, the same ones she had on when she died. I'm sure she would've loved that, those were her favorite. Even the coffin was eerily beautiful, with wooden flowers sketched gracefully on the sides. The thing that really stuck with me, however, was the earrings. I couldn't handle the loss of my mother. My life was void of a figure that couldn't be replaced.

It's funny how your mood, your mindset, can change for an eternity with just a simple action. The last three words I said to my mother that day weren't "I love you", which I wish so dearly that they were. Instead, they were "see you later". I planned on seeing my mom later that day, what reason would I have no to? I left the book open, only for it to be slammed in my face an hour later. If I learned anything from her wreck, it's that life doesn't always go the way you want it to. Even when you have a plan for the next day or the next month or the next decade, something is going to tear you apart. It simply depends on how long it takes you to sew yourself back together.

I've been stitching myself up for the last eleven years, making it a little bit easier to get over her death. I suppose it's the void of a mother that effects me the most today, but I'm getting better at accepting it. Dad, on the other hand. . . I don't think he ever really stitched himself back up.

Dad had quit drinking about two or three years before the accident, but after her funeral, he went back to it – this time, heavier than before. When he got drunk, I remember him throwing books, smashing plates, and breaking whatever he could get his hands on. He would also yell and hit me, and since I was the only child, I received all the backlash and blame. I soon became terrified of him, and would stay at my grandparents' house for weeks on end.

Never getting the assurance I needed from him really hurt me. Never being told, "Hey, son. It's going to be alright." I needed that from him, but I never got it. And since he never told me, I just assumed that everything wasn't going to be okay, that life was never going to be as good as it was before.

I can't really blame him. To him, this was just the same song, different chorus. Both of his parents had died before he was twenty-five. He has a sister who lives far away from us, but they weren't really close. And now, he had lost his wife. He had every right to give up. But at the same time, he also had every reason not to, because I was still with him. I was the only one he had left. And now he was shunning me, and that really hurt me.

I thank my Grandparents more than anybody for helping me get over her death. I know it was hard for them, as well, considering Mom was their only child. And, eventually, they got Dad to crawl out of his sulky hole. He quit drinking around my 8th birthday, which was the following June. He started back to work at the hospital regularly. He started to become the dad I needed months before.

I'm not entirely sure what happened, but I'm almost certain that Grandmother and Pawpaw had a sit down talk with him about his behavior. Neither one of my grandparents would come out and tell me, so I just assumed they got his life back on track. I would've loved to know what they told him that caused such a sudden change. I'm sure it included the fact that, although he had lost almost everyone in his life, he did still have me. And if he kept staying withdrawn from me as he used to be, he would lose me as well.

Whatever they said, it worked. Dad became more active in my life. We became a lot closer. We realized how much we needed each other. From then on out, life was practically normal.

I feel a tear start to roll down my cheek. If the loss of Mom wasn't bad enough, now there's Dad. And the worst thing is that I don't even know what happened to him. He may be lying on the streets, dead, just like Mr. Lawkins. Or, for all I know, he may be in another city, which could definitely be an option. I'm really hoping that is what happened. For some oddball reason, everybody is just out of town. I know it is unlikely, but that's the hope I'm clinging on to.

I look down the row of picture frames on the mantle and go to the next one, which is a picture of Pawpaw and Grandmother side by side.

Both of them had taken care of me when I was little. I would constantly stay at their house, and they were more than excited to have me. They even bought clothes for me specifically for when I went over. Pawpaw would tell me all sorts of stories about his time when he was young. Grandmother would always have some kind of pie waiting for me.

I always found it weird that I had given Pawpaw a name but never called Grandmother anything more childlike. I was too little to remember why I never called her anything different, so, when I was about eleven, I asked her. "Well," she responded with her strong smile that I had come to admire, "it's because you told me that 'sometimes the simplest things in life mean more than you think, and they don't need any changing to it'."

Of course, I was too young to think of anything that complex. She probably just reworded how she thought I had felt, or maybe she was trying to teach me a life lesson at an early age. I'm not sure, but that was one thing she was good at. Words.

Pawpaw died about a week ago. I was heartbroken, but the experience with my mom had led me to be resilient. The death surprisingly affected Dad more than I thought it would have. Grandmother was emotionally unstable. But as Grandmother had to suck it up and be strong for me whenever Mom died, I had to do the same for her. I guess that is when she sat down and realized that it was his time to go. They were both aging. Besides, death happens to everybody eventually.

Eventually? That makes me wonder if everyone might be dead. It's a terrible thought, but a possibility.

No, that can't be it. If everyone were to die, then how come I didn't? Besides, if so, where are all the bodies?

I think about where Grandmother might be. I do hope she is okay, but I can't help to think that she didn't make it. What if everybody did leave and go to another city? Her mobility was starting to become limited. She could move around the house fine, but she always wanted me to go get her groceries. I don't know if she could have made it out safely.

I then think back to the realistic dream I had this morning.

What if it was real? What if Dad really did go in my room and tried to wake me up. What if . . . what if that's the reason I'm left here. Because I didn't wake up.

Oh lord, here I go again, worrying myself to death. I've got to find something to do to get my mind off of things.

I walk out the front door to the house, and I'm greeted by the same pandemonium that unpleasantly welcomed me this morning. Nothing has changed. As if I was planning for things to be different.

I begin walking towards downtown Westwood, thinking of what I can do. In the city limits, there are plenty of businesses, so maybe I can find something there that will help me out.

I'm still leaning on the theory that everybody is in a different town, and the only way to find out would be to drive to the nearest city. I have nearly every affordable car model in existence at my disposal, so I don't have to take my raggedy, old truck. Wait now. That gives me an even better idea.

I can get a motorcycle. I leck yeah. I've always wanted to drive one, but Dad always thought it was too dangerous for me to ride. And here's my chance.

There is a motorcycle dealership in the city that I can get one from. Oh yeah, this is perfect. I will have hundreds of bikes to choose from. Not saying I will know how to drive one, but I can learn quickly. It's not like I need to know any rules or laws anyway.

So I guess that's that. I will just head to the dealership and get one as soon as I get into the city limits, which shouldn't take long.

I look at the houses I pass by as I make my way down the street, wondering what caused such destruction. Did somebody come through and trash the place? Or did the owners do it themselves? I'm not sure why they would want to destroy their own homes, but at this moment, I'm not sure about anything.

As the silence begins to penetrate my eardrums, I start talking to myself out loud to help comfort me. I start to say everything that

I see, giving myself something to listen to. A book, a broken mirror, a chair. Yet, after I run out of things to say, I am revisited by the silence. I decide to give up on talking to myself. It's better to embrace the silence at once than have it keep returning to me.

I notice the sun starting to fall. It doesn't seem late at all, but no matter what the time is, I just need to get the motorcycle and leave before it gets dark. I should have more than enough time to do so, I just don't want to have to wait until tomorrow.

I pass by the last house at the end of the rows and begin to walk into the city limits of Westwood. Filled with devastation, I look around at the buildings that walk beside me and replace all the houses.

I see the burger joint that we went to yesterday, Rochester's. The tables outside have been knocked over, and even the umbrellas are torn up. I pass by it and look at the next building, which is a convenience store. The windows are smashed, and numerous accessories are scattered throughout the gas stations.

That's a good sign. It looks like people were rushing to get all that they could so they could get out as quickly as possible. The abandoned cars that fill all the parking lots support the theory, but makes me wonder what people left in. I just wish I knew.

I look down the road to see what stores are nearby. I see the hotel, the bowling alley, the school, the hospital, and then I see the huge sign with the name Retro's Motorcycles spelled out on it. There it is.

But as I walk by the bowling alley on my way to Retro's, I find it strange that it appears relatively normal. Every other building I passed by had broken windows and doors, while the bowling alley remains seemingly untouched. I walk up to the front doors of the building, which are sealed shut and tightly locked. I jiggle the handle, hoping my limp grip will magically send the doors open, but of course it doesn't.

I'm left puzzled as to why this building, out of all the other buildings, seems perfectly intact. Maybe this was the only building that locked its doors whenever whatever-this-is happened. The fact that the front doors to the alley aren't glass is definitely a factor, as every other nearby building had a mainly glass door. I walk away from the door and investigate around the corner of the building, trying to find a way in. If it's this intact on the outside, it must be the same on the inside. And if so, this would be the first normal building I've found yet.

I find an old metal door near the back of the building with a deadlock bolting the door together. However, I notice that the lock has the key that unlocks it still in the key slot, so I twist the key, take the lock off, and tug on the rusted handle. The door barely comes ajar, and I tug the door the rest of the way open with a little force.

I look into the dark shadows of the bowling alley, still perfectly set up and in place as if the people running it were still working there. I marvel across the giant room as I make my way in the building and close the door shut behind me. The carpets look thoroughly vacuumed, the pins on each lane are still standing up and in position. It is a little unsettling at how dark and bleak the place seems, however, as it feels like nobody has stepped foot in here for ages.

I inspect every aspect I can as I make my way to the front of the building, with my faint footsteps on the carpet serving as the only noise. The tables are wiped clean, chairs tucked in nicely under them, the bowling shoes are properly in order. Absolutely nothing is out of place, which is very odd. What made the bowling alley so special from the others? After seeing absolutely nothing but destruction throughout the city, I'm astonished at how protected this place was. I don't know if it was the tightly locked front doors or the lack of any windows but whatever it was worked.

I pass by the first lane on my way to the front door and decide for it to be my destination instead. The only thing missing are the glow-in-the-dark neon green lights that suffocated the alley every

Saturday night. I grab one of the bowling balls off the rack beside me and slowly approach the lane, deciding that getting my mind off of the situation at hand would be for the best at the moment.

It bothers me that the screen above me isn't on, and yeah, it's a lot warmer than it usually is in here, but that doesn't keep me from bowling a strike. I imagine a giant 'X' flashing on the screen as I throw double fists in the air like I just won some tournament. I wait for my ball to return, but then remember that the power is out so that ball is gone forever and these pins aren't going to stand themselves up. Luckily for me, there's 19 more lanes with pins calling for me to knock them down and I'm sure there's more than 19 bowling balls in here.

I slide over to lane two and grab another ball, this one heavier. I keep my same motion, sling the ball down the lane, then *bam,* another strike.

"Money, baby!" I yell out. I quickly step over to the next lane, grabbing a different, this time the same weight, ball off the rack. "Let's go turkey hunting, boys."

I roll the ball down the lane and watch as it collides into the pins. All but one falls over. "Ah, dammit," I curse at myself. "I was really wanting some turkey." Immediately once I finish the sentence, I decide to commit the bowler's number one penalty, but before I do, I look around to make sure nobody catches me in the act.

I run down the lane, trying my best not to slip, and kick the lone pin down once I reach it. "YEAH! TURKEY!" I run back up the lane, yelling at my miraculous feat. "I am unstoppable. Bring your best." The wall I'm staring at while I say it doesn't seem to have it's best to bring me, though.

I go to the fourth lane and decide to spice things up. I grab a bowling ball and chunk it overhanded towards the pin. The ball lands loudly halfway down the lane, and proceeds to knock two pins over. I granny-roll the ball down the fifth lane, and after a full minute, it rolls off in the gutter. I throw a chair down the sixth lane, but it doesn't even make it to the pins, and I flip the pins on the seventh lane the bird, hoping that me teaching them a lesson would make them fall over.

I run out of different ways to knock pins over by the time I reach the fifteenth lane. I look behind me, proud of my own little destruction that I've made in only twenty minutes ago. But I've grown bored of the lanes, and decide to look around in here for something else to occupy my time.

I stumble across the arcade, which is shut down entirely due to the lack of power. It was a small arcade, only two little motorcycle simulator rides, an air hockey table, the worst deer hunting video game in existence, and a prize-grabber machine. I could never win anything out of this thing, the claw was always too dangly for me to judge. But now, I think my luck is going to change.

I look into the machine filled with crappy stuffed animals that nobody would actually pay for but would pay to win. This thing has conquered me so many times over the years, but now is my time to come away victorious.

I reach over for the plastic rifle attached to the deer hunting game, snatch it out of it's attached socket, and slam the stock of the fake gun through the glass of the prize-grabber machine. Glass shoots out over the pile of stuffed animals, but that doesn't keep me from reaching in and throwing every stuffed animal in the machine out.

I give off an evil laugh as every cuddly duck, every fluffy little troll, now belongs to me. I grab the pile of stuffed animals and run over to the sixteenth lane, throwing the animals down it. Most of them don't even make it halfway, but a few of them barely knick the pins.

But just as the excitement came to me, it leaves just as quickly, and I'm suddenly reminded of the fact that nobody is here to stop me from doing this mainly because nobody is here. No matter how hard I try to get my mind off of things, the fact that nobody is in this town and I still have no idea why that is haunts me.

I leave the bowling alley and walk back down the heated streets that are occupied with random debris and notice that the sun is still slowly making its way to the horizon. As I walk towards Retro's, though, the sign of our school, Westwood High, comes into sight, with the words "Home of the Giants" proudly showcased across it. I make my way across the front lawn - which is filled with books - and onto the front steps of the building.

It's funny to think that I would normally be back here tomorrow. The building is completely deserted, even to the point where it looks creepy. Then again, it always had a spooky aura around it. Especially in Coach Witherspoon's fourth period biology class.

I suppose that's one upside that I've found so far: no more public high school education. I would say that I would never have to step in this building again if that were the case, but here I am, literally about to step in the building.

I push the front doors open as they give a loud *creek* that sounds like something from a scary movie. The sound echoes through the desolate hallways, filling them with the only activity.

The halls are ransacked to the point where I can't even see the floor tiles. Many of the lockers have been slung down on the floor, lying in a sea of papers and desks that would make last year's senior prank look like a kindergarten April fool's joke. The school is destroyed, but instead of having a sense of confusion or terror of the unknown cause, I feel warmth. A strange happiness. The sight of this school in this state is rather beautiful to me. I don't necessarily care about the reasoning behind it at this point, I just sort of wish I could have been a part of it.

I know this isn't what I should be thinking, considering I found a dead body outside and that whatever happened here was probably not out of joy. But still, I enjoy the sight of it.

The front office is nearby, so I head to it before I start checking out the halls and classrooms. I open the office door and see that it, however, isn't as damaged as the halls are. Although the receptionist's window is destroyed, the rest of the office hasn't been touched.

As I investigate everything, I get to the intercom. Out of curiosity, I flip the switch up to see if it still works. Surprisingly, a dim, red light flashes on, and a low buzzing noise emits from the microphone. I lightly tap the microphone, hoping to hear something in return, but I don't.

"Testing . . ." I unconfidently say into the mic. My voice is suddenly thrown across the school, and I can easily hear a hoard of Jadens yelling "testing" back at me.

Oh, this is so cool. I can't believe this thing still works. Hearing my own voice from the halls and classrooms makes it seem a lot less creepy to be in this building.

"Is there anybody in here?" I ask into the microphone. I wait for someone to shout out from the halls at me, but I hear nothing but my own voice fading away. "Anybody here? . . . Hello? . . . Helloooooo . . ."

I didn't really expect a response, but it was worth a shot. If nobody was out roaming the streets when I was out there, then it's rather unlikely they'd be in the school.

I should turn the intercom off and leave but decide to have a little fun before I do. "Ahem . . . Good morning students, faculty, and staff," I buoyantly call into the microphone like our principal, Mrs. Armstrong, did every morning. "First off, I want to congratulate our very own Jaden Foxx for being awarded the prestigious 'Average Man of the Year', an honor given to the one teenager who is ranked number one nationally at being mediocre." That's a reasonable award I could get. Don't want to get too carried away with myself.

"Also, we would like to congratulate Cody Goodwin for making it one full day without being a humongous tool. Well deserved by him." Oh, man, if Cody was here, he would be hysterical right now. If only he were here . . .

"And, uhm . . ." as the possibility that Cody may even be dead enters my mind, I hastily turn the intercom off.

I leave the office and begin heading towards the front door to leave when I hear a loud slamming noise come from the hallways around the corner. The sound frightens me at first, as it sounded like somebody had picked up a locker and thrown it on the ground, but the fright leaves as I'm reminded that the sound means that somebody is here. Somebody is here!

"Hello?!" I yell as I make my way down the hall and towards the sound. I don't wait for an answer, I just keep running.

I turn the corner at the end of the hallway and look down the perpendicular hall that the noise came from. I see a group of lockers being pulled away from the wall at the very opposite end of the hall, but I don't see anybody pulling it out. I slowly walk down the hall, trying not to make a sound so I don't disrupt whatever is going on.

Suddenly, the group of lockers falls to the ground with force. Once the lockers hit the floor, I see a silhouette of a person standing behind them.

"Hey!" I excitedly blare out, waving my arms at the person. The person doesn't react to my yelling, as he remains staring down at the lockers at his feet, so I begin running towards him. "Hey, please help me! I have no clue what's going–"

The person's head then suddenly snaps up at me. The person is too far away for me to identify any features about them, as the only things I can really tell about the person is that he is a tall and apparently strong man. But the person's actions stagger me.

The person vigorously bashes his head on the lockers below him. I stop and watch as he repeats the process over and over, each slam more violent than the one before it. The slams get so intense that I start to wonder how he is still conscious and not covered in blood yet.

The repetitive head slams send an unnervingly loud noise through the halls that causes me to step away from the person. I begin flinching in anticipation of each loud thud, not wanting to see the man's skull bash open. As I switch dramatically from excited to disturbed, the person stops it's bashing and looks up at me. From my distance, I can't see a single drop of blood marked on it's face. Actually, I can't even see any eyes or a mouth on it. I'm sure if I get closer I might can see some blood on it, but I do not want to get anywhere close right now.

And, as if he read my mind, he immediately disappears before me.

4

The wall

OKAY. NOW IT'S time for me to get a motorcycle and get the hell out of here.

I turn away from the scene and sprint down the halls and out of the school. What did I just see? It couldn't have been a regular person; people just don't disappear out of freaking thin air. And also, people just don't bash their head into a locker over and over without bleeding!

The more I relive and think about the incident, the faster I run away from the school. I head towards the motorcycle dealership, Retro's, all while looking back occasionally to make sure that the suicidal ghost isn't following me.

I slow my pace down as I make it into the assumed safe-zone of Retro's parking lot. The sign above the entrance is still perfectly intact. Panting and sweating profusely, I walk through the wide-opened, used to be automatic, front doors, pretending to forget everything I just saw.

The entire spacious showroom is filled with all sorts of bikes, ATVs, and mopeds. Many of the motorcycles have fallen over, but a few are still standing. I remain standing still, trying to gain my breath, all while being amazed at the amount of motorcycles in here.

I walk down the aisles of motorcycles, hoping to find one with the keys already in it. I find one on the front row with the key on the seat, as if begging for me to take it. The bike looks absolutely flawless – dark blue, extremely shiny, handlebars jacked way up. It's just a beauty. But for a guy who knows nothing about the subject, that's not saying much.

Lying on the seat along with the key is a blue helmet. I feel no need in wearing one, so I knock it to the ground, sit down on the seat, and crank it up. *Vrum.* The motor sounds amazing. A giant smile appears on my face as I rev the engine and feel the whole bike shake. *Vrmmmm.* My entire body vibrates with the bike, and I kick the stand out from underneath it, eager to put this thing on the road.

I twist the throttle with my right hand, and the bike shoots off across the floor with me on it. I quickly engage the brakes, trying to stop from running into another bike. Okay, maybe I should just push the bike out of the building. It may be harder to drive than I thought.

I push the bike outside, jump back on it, and twist the throttle again. I only know a few things about driving motorcycles, and that's how to make it go, how to make it stop, and how to switch gears. Hopefully that will be enough to get me to the nearest city.

I thrust myself on to the main road and head back as if I'm going back to my house. The nearest city is Roaksville, which is about a good forty minutes away. I should make it there by nightfall. I shift up gears and gain speed as I hit the road.

Wow, this feels so great. I feel so free, nothing can stop me. The air streaming through my hair makes me feel like I'm soaring above the streets.

All the objects in the street make the ride difficult, and constantly having to avoid random furniture prevents me from going as fast as I want, but I'm fine with that. I'm not in any big hurry. The sun still won't set for another hour or two.

I pass by my house to the left of me, looking back at it as I go by.

Maybe that will be the last time I see my house. It doesn't look like civilization is ever coming back to Westwood, so it very well could be. I turn my head around and see something approaching me in the distance.

As I get closer, I see that it's not coming to me, but me to it. I'm not entirely sure what it is until I get two houses away from it.

It's a wall. A silver, towering wall that stands about fifteen feet tall greets me from the distance. What? A wall? Better yet, how do I keep from driving into it? As I near the wall, I jerk the bike to the right so I won't crash into it, and run parallel with it, examining it as I go.

What is this? Why is there a wall? A better question may be, how did a wall get up overnight?

I look back on the road every few seconds to make sure I don't hit anything, and as I do, I see that the wall stretches on for miles. I focus most of my attention on the wall, and what it is doing there. Is it there to keep me in? Or maybe to keep something out? Does it surround the neighborhood? Or even the entire city?

Right as all these questions are fluttering through my head, I come across a message written across the wall in big, red letters.

ROT

The end of the T drifts across the wall, as if the person who painted the word there was being dragged away from it. At the base of the end of the T lies the person who wrote the word; pale, stiff, and lifeless. The dead body catches me by surprise, and I jerk the motorcycle away from the wall in fright.

The motorcycle cross over a huge bump, and the bike starts spinning out of control. I must have run over something. The bike swerves across the road as I try to regain control.

Suddenly, I hit another bump, and this time I'm thrown off the bike. I land hard on my left leg, and my shin slams painfully into the ground. As I recover from my fall, I turn over on my stomach to see where the bike is. I watch as the bike rapidly drifts across the street and heads towards the wall. It's going fast enough to crash into the wall, but it doesn't look like it will become too damaged to drive. It should just bounce right off of—

BOOM

Instead of hitting the wall and bouncing off, the bike slams straight into it, causing a great, thunderous explosion. I immediately turn my head away from the unexpected explosion, but as I begin to wonder what had just happened, I suddenly feel heat. A lot of it, growing hotter and hotter. Oh god, the heat.

The heat coming from the explosion slaps the right side of my face, and I quickly roll back over to keep it from hitting me even more. I clamp my hand up to my face as my cheek becomes scorched by the fire. The pain keeps growing. Growing. Oh dear god. I can hear the flesh melting as I let out a roar of pain. Oh, please, please, stop.

The heat feels as if it is seeping through my skin, and the pressure I put on my face becomes stronger. I form a somewhat fetal position and hear a few agonizing moans escape my mouth as I roll around, trying to find away to cease the burning.

Tears start streaming from my eyes. I have got to find a way to stop this, I have to. I open my eyes and look around for anything that may help. I see a swimming pool a house over, but as I stand up, my leg gives out from underneath me. The impact on my leg must have been more than I thought. I try again to get up, but a rush of intense pain sends me back to the ground. My only option is to crawl, so I begin crawling to the only source of relief I can find.

I am eventually able to get myself back up without using my left leg, and I hop one-legged over to the pool and plump down next to it, submerging my face in the cold water. The burn seems to grow stronger, causing additional moans to exit, but after a while the heat slowly seems to subside. I continue dipping my head in the cold water multiple times, each time feeling more relieving than the one before.

As I pull my head underwater and become relaxed enough to open my eyes, I see a person floating against the corner at the bottom of the pool. A scream of horror escapes through a surge of bubbles, causing me to snatch my head out of the water and send myself feet away from the water's edge. I then rip my shirt off and push it to my face, deciding that I'm not going back in the water.

I remain sitting for half an hour with the shirt now stuck to my face. My head wails in pain, and I feel as if I may pass out any minute, but I don't. I look down at my pants and see that a huge stain of blood has spread out on the entire lower half of my leg. I don't want to look at my leg right now; I'm afraid to see how bad it is. As the sun falls, my disposed body becomes cold, and I peel the shirt off my face to cover myself. As I do, I see a huge circle of blood across the shirt. All this blood... This must be worse than I thought. I must be in worse shape than I thought. However, as bad as these injuries are, I can't help but feel soothed by the cool night air brushing across my burned cheek.

I haphazardly go to stand up, but the brief inactivity on my damaged leg causes me to fall back down again. As I concentrate on standing up by relying mainly on my uninjured leg, I take a quick glance into the scene in front of me. The motorcycle made a much bigger impact than I had assumed, as a huge chunk of the wall is now missing. A colossal mushroom cloud levitates above the sole fissure in the wall, with smoke forming at the base. The charred remains of the motorcycle lie scolding close by the opening. As I remain overwhelmed as to what had just happened, I notice a blur run across the streets and into the smoke. A blur that resembles a person.

A person! Somebody is here! My body is enlivened by the sight of another person, and I begin hobbling after the person, frantically yelling as I do.

"Hey! Excuse me!" I joyfully call out, alleviated to finally find somebody. Through my excitement, I apply pressure on my injured leg. I ignore the immense pain because I'm far too determined right now.

I'm then reminded of the person I saw in the school earlier. What if this person I just saw is just like that person? Do I want to chase after this person?

I have to. This person can help me out, too, because I need it right now. I finally reach the opening that I saw the person run through, with smoke still pouring out from the damaged wall and adding on to the enormous cloud above my head. As I get closer to the gap, I realize that the smoke isn't just any regular smoke. Instead, the smoke appears . . . green? Green smoke?

I get within arm's reach from it and put my hand in the arcane smoke. No heat, nothing; it seems totally harmless. I call out to the opposite side of the wall, but I don't get a response. As I look through the smoke to find any moving object, I instead see something much worse.

I see about ten bodies lying on the ground, spread out from one another, and face down. No telling who these people could be. The sight frightens me, but even though I want to make sure that there isn't anybody I know lying dead in the street, I still want to find the running person.

I pull my arm back and limp through the green smoke. However, as soon as I inhale the smoke, my legs lock up and I fall over backwards, and before I hit the ground, I black out.

5

Faceless

I WAKE UP to the sight of a charcoal black sky and notice that the sun is almost completely out of sight. As I go to stand up, I make sure I stay as far away as possible from that green smoke. It's both dangerous and mysterious, which doesn't make for a good combination. I'll have to forget about the person, since the smoke is preventing me from going through the wall. Plus, the last thing I want is to be out here in pitch black darkness. I need to get back to my house quickly.

I get back on my feet and feel a wave of pain overcome my left leg. I totally forgot about my injuries. Along with my leg, my entire right cheek has gone numb, and it doesn't even feel like it's there anymore.

I begin to stumble back to my house, but my leg is starting to become too much of a burden. I'm not sure if I can make it back to my house, even though it's only a street over from the wall. All I know is that I just need to get out of this darkness.

As I'm gimping back down the street, I hear something come from the outside of the wall. A long howl pierces the night air, sounding like a howl from a coyote. Wait . . . there are coyotes? No humans. No other animals. But *coyotes*?

I hear the howl again, and this time a second one joins it. I start to get frightened, which is stupid, because I know coyotes don't attack people.

The howls start to become more frequent, and I hear them gradually getting closer. With my limited mobility, these coyotes seem like they're going to make it to me before I can get anywhere.

As soon as that thought crosses my mind, I hear a yipping come from directly behind me. As I turn around, I see a coyote creeping up on me from a few yards behind me. This coyote is very big and muscular, resembling more to a wolf. Of course, that is impossible. There aren't any wolves in Mississippi, or not that I'm aware of, anyway. Foam is overflowing from its mouth, indicating that it has rabies. This beast looks dangerous, and I'm afraid it's going to catch up with me any second.

It locks its eerie eyes with mine and inches nearer. I begin to slowly stagger backwards, keeping eye contact with the beast the entire time. I'm afraid that it will jump at me if our eyes unlock from each other. I have to fight the urge to do so, because I want to get a good look of this meaty creature. From my peripheral vision, I can tell that there is something unordinary about it. Something unique. There's got to be some reason for it to still be here, and maybe its appearance can give me a hint.

I avert my gaze for a split second to check its body out. I was right. This thing is different.

Not only is this thing bigger than regular coyotes, it has something unusual about its fur. Instead of the dark gray I was expecting, its fur is a light purple, a lavender shade mixed in with gray patches. I know that there aren't any purple coyotes, but I'm not entirely sure about wolves. The more I examine this creature, the more I start to believe that it isn't a coyote. Except for the location, this thing appears like and is acting exactly like a wolf would.

But purple fur? I've heard of gray and red wolves, but never purple. Then again, my eyes may be tricking me, because it's getting pretty dark.

I just need to get away from it. I turn around to see what's behind me, hoping the wolf doesn't attack me while I'm checking. There's a house about a hundred feet away from me, and I can make it there if I could run perfectly fine, but that's the issue. I'm just going to have to slowly walk backwards to that house and hope the wolf doesn't attack me.

I look back at the wolf and notice that a second is trailing the first one, mocking its actions. This second one is shaped differently than the first wolf, but is still abnormally muscular for it's size. I'm going to have to move fast or both of them are going to get a hold of me. I stumble over a glass cup at my feet and reach down for it. I throw the cup at the feet of the closest wolf, sending glass flying on its feet and belly. I take that as my cue, turn around, and power-walk to the house.

The first wolf flinches, but the other reads my move like an open book and darts at me at a great speed. I look down, hoping to find something that can distract it from me, and the only thing I see is a foldable chair. I reach down and pick it up, but as soon as I turn around to throw it, the wolf is already mid-air, about to land on top of me.

I swing the chair, hitting the wolf square in the face and sending it to the ground directly in front of me.

As the second wolf falls, the first one recovers and growls at me. Okay, I'm going to have to run, despite how much my leg hurts. I start to run, gritting my teeth in pain with each step.

I finally reach the house, and I walk up the steps of the front porch and into the wide open front door. As soon as I touch the door, I hear the wolves' feet hit the wooden floor of the porch right behind me.

I slam it shut, and just in time. Both the wolves collide into the door, making a thud noise. I quickly place my back against the door to try to prevent the wolves from breaking in. I hear them clawing on the door, barking at it just like any regular house dog would. After a few minutes, though, they give up.

I separate from the door, lock it right behind me, and limp over to the window to make sure that they leave. I catch a glimpse of them as they return through the hole in the wall.

Well, that's not fair. How come I get knocked out by the gas but they don't? Well, then again, they somehow get to share the pleasure of being the only two living things left in Westwood, so I wouldn't really call them the lucky ones.

The opening in the wall now leaves me vulnerable to anything outside the wall. The purpose of the wall might be to keep something out from the city. Maybe the wolves are being kept from entering the city. Or maybe there's something even worse out there, maybe a group of bears is waiting to maul me apart outside the wall. I need to get out of this city, but I guess I can get to that tomorrow. That is, if my leg lets me.

I turn around to face the house that I will call home for the night. It's a nice, quaint little house. I reach the living room, but when I flip the light switch, the lights don't turn on. Please don't tell me that the power is out. I can't do that. I need light. Heck, I need some noise, too. It's far too quiet. I walk down the dark hallway, looking for a bathroom I could use to clean myself up with. I'm in desperate need for a medical kit, or at least a few hundred band aids.

I then think back to the figure I saw running through the gas. Had I seen correctly? The figure just ignored me, disappeared be a better term. A part of me wants to believe that that person is just like me, left in this city with no clue as to what's going on. But another part of me thinks that that person is just like the person I saw in the school. It acted very strangely, practically ignoring me, then disappeared in thin air. I don't feel like the two living people I've seen so far are anything at all like me.

I can feel myself starting to become scared of not only the dark but the quiet. I can actually feel the loneliness. The complete absence of people. The feeling of being alone.

I hate it. I need light. I need something. I go into one of the rooms down the hall and flip on a switch, hoping the light turns on. Luckily, it does, and a huge sigh of relief exits me. Oh, how I'm glad to have light.

Looking around the room, I see that I'm in a small bathroom. Perfect. I run across it and turn on the shower, adding some needed noise.

I walk back over to the sink and look in the mirror, expecting to see something terrible. What I see is far worse than I had envisioned, and my stomach turns at the sight of my own appearance.

The burn is much more severe than I thought. There's no longer any skin on my right cheek, leaving a strong reddish-pink of exposed flesh. It looks terrible. The burn nauseates me, and I can't help but to pity myself. My face doesn't even look like me.

I'm extremely lucky that the burn neither reached my eyes nor my mouth. I put my hand on the injury, but jerk back. The burn is really tender, and doesn't even feel like my cheek anymore.

I place my finger on the outside edge of it, with half of my finger on the burned area and the other half on the part that didn't get singed. I gently run my finger right below my ear, where part of the lobe had been burnt as well. I slowly lag it down the jaw bone and to my chin, where the barely noticeable beard I had is now cut in half. I then take it from there, up around my mouth, away from my nose, and to my right eye. My eye...

The iris of my eye is light purple. I check the other eye and find out that it is a lilac purple, as well.

I'm paralyzed by shock at first, but then I think that I might be seeing things. I turn the water to the sink on and splash my eyes, hoping it clears my vision. Nothing. They're still purple. Okay, okay.

Now I know things are messed up. I have always had green eyes. I really want to know what is going on. How did they become purple?

This is really starting to worry me. Why? Maybe . . . I don't know. Maybe my eyes are just out of whack, and I'm seeing things. I rub both my eyes to clear up my vision, but once I regain focus, I see that they are still purple. The same lavender color I saw on the wolves a few minutes ago.

What does this mean? What is it saying? Is it trying to tell me that I'm connected to them somehow? But how? None of this is making sense. None of it.

Maybe . . . maybe one of the wolves bit me without me realizing. Maybe it's some kind of mutant animal? I don't know. Anything is possible at this point.

Eh, that sounds too unlikely. Let me just calm down and think for a minute. Maybe . . . maybe it was the gas. Yeah, it could be the gas. Both of the wolves and I had walked through the gas, and all three of us have something purple. The gas changed the color of their fur. The gas changed the color of my eyes. Yeah, that is a more logical explanation.

As absurd as it sounds, I can't decide which bothers me more: the giant burn mark or the color of my eyes. I still haven't checked my leg out yet, either, so I'm not done with the unveiling of my ugliness quite yet. I take my blue jeans off and throw them on the floor.

There's a pretty good-sized scratch going from my knee to my ankle, but my shin looks like it absorbed most of the impact. I should look for some kind of ointment to put on it that might help. I also need to put something on my burn. I'm almost positive that there's a gel for treating burns, but I don't remember what it's called. Before I do that, though, I need to get in the shower.

I strip down and get in the hot, steaming shower. The water feels refreshing as it settles on my back. I keep my face away from the water, but the vapor from it seems to ease the pain.

This feels good. Here's another place I can just pretend that everything is back to normal. I lean up against the shower wall, leaving the water to pour on the top of my head. I clear my mind of everything. I will have plenty of time to ask myself questions once I step out. But right now I'm just concerned about one thing, and I find that out after a few minutes. The gel is called aloe vera.

I milk the hot shower as long as my injured leg will let me, which is right when my fingers begin to prune. I step out and decide I need to find some new clothes since mine are drenched in blood. I'm sure the people who lived here wouldn't mind, anyway.

I walk over to the room across from the bathroom, which appears to had belonged to a boy who was about eight. None of these clothes will be able to fit an eighteen-year-old, so I exit it and go to the next room. However, I'm met with the same predicament, except for this time, it's a girl's room.

Actually, the girl's clothes are much bigger than the boy's clothes, and her clothes might actually fit me, as sad and depressing as that sounds. I walk to her closet and try to find the most masculine shirt she owned but give up after deciding I'm not trying to impress anybody. I randomly rip a shirt off the clothes hanger and hold it out in front of me before I put it on. Sweet, a royal blue shirt with a bedazzled picture of a dolphin on it. That's pretty manly.

I put the shirt on, all while cursing my parents for giving me the genes to be as big as a thirteen-year-old girl. In my defense, I think it has less to do with the fact that I'm 5'9" and more to do with the fact that this is a big ass thirteen-year-old girl.

Whatever, the shirt fits perfectly, and I hate myself because of it. Wouldn't it be great if I ran into Dad and all my friends in Roaksville, and they saw me rocking this shirt? I think they would just send me back to Westwood to be myself and reconsider my decisions.

I walk further down the hallway until I reach the master bedroom that signifies the end of the hall. Of course, a master bedroom, where the parents sleep. I can't believe that I didn't let the high possibility of a grown man living in this house cross my mind, but I don't let it stop me from yanking the dolphin shirt off of me and limp over to the closet to see what the dad has for me.

The dad looks as if he was about my size, so I have no problem finding clothes that I can wear. I pick out a yellow, long sleeve shirt and another pair of jeans.

I look around the room. Maybe there is something useful in here I can use. As I'm searching through everything, I spot multiple pictures of the family together. One of the pictures standing on top of the night stand grabs my attention, and I pick up the frame. The two kids, looking as happy as they could be, with their two parents, who looked as if they couldn't be more proud of their family.

I immediately think of the picture of our family sitting on the mantle back at the house. In a way, this family sort of went through what we did. All happy, then suddenly being ripped apart by a tragedy. I know the pain. It was a terrible pain ten years ago, and that was only my mom. This entire family being ripped apart *all* at once?

I think about how terrible of circumstances that is, but then I realize that the same has happened to me right now...

As I examine the family picture closer, the mom catches my eye as someone who looks familiar. After a few hard seconds of pondering, I realize who it is she resembles. Sandra. She must be Sandra's sister. Ugh. *Sandra.* A terrible woman. Even though it's not all Sandra's fault, she is still someone I strongly despise.

When I was about five, Dad was caught cheating on Mom with another nurse who worked with Dad. That woman was Sandra. I didn't know her; I just knew what she looked like. I remember right when Mom found out. She was both angry and heartbroken, but there was nothing she could do about it. When she tried to talk to Dad about it, they would end up arguing and fighting. Dad would get angry at Mom and become violent, which is a scene that a five-year-old shouldn't have to witness. Whenever they fought, I ran to my grandparent's house across the street. I'm positive there was physical abuse involved, but I'd like to think that there wasn't.

Anyway, they were on the brink of divorce when Pawpaw and Grandmother had a talk with them. My grandparents were by far the wisest people I knew. When it came to difficult situations, they knew how to solve it. They somehow talked them into staying together. I have no clue how it worked, but my parents forgave and started loving each other just as much as they did before my dad was caught cheating.

Either that or they were really good actors.

Didn't ever hear much about Sandra after that. I was surprised Dad never went back to her once Mom died.

This woman has to be related to Sandra, probably her sister. She looks way too much like her. Come to think of it, I guess these people may have actually minded if I took their clothes, but oh well. Who cares.

I decide to look for medicines to treat my injuries. I go back to the bathroom and search through the drawers for anything that looks useful. I mean, her sister was a nurse. She's bound to at least have some ibuprofen.

I find some kind of cream that's meant for deep scratches and rub it on my leg. I'm pretty sure that aloe vera is kept refrigerated, so I go to the kitchen to check for some. Luckily, I find a tube of it, and slowly pat it on my face. The cold gel feels soothing against my wound, and it seems like it instantly starts healing it.

I realize that it's getting late, and I decide I should go to bed. I can leave for Roaksville tomorrow morning. Well, I'm not in any rush. I can rest a day and then go the day after. However, if I do decide to stay an extra day, I'm going to make sure I rest in my own bed. I would go home now if I was certain that I wouldn't encounter those wolves again.

I walk back to the master bedroom, turn the lights off, and get in the bed. I look over at the clock on the wall. 9:27. It feels much later than that. Hard to believe that twenty-four hours ago my friends and I were all happily eating at Rochester's and everything was normal. No telling what the next twenty-four hours have in store for me.

I kick my shoes off and lay my head down on the pillow, trying not to touch my injured face. I fall asleep within a minute . . .

I open my eyes and see that I'm lying down in a completely new environment.

"Where am I?" I ask myself as I sit up and look around for any clues that might help me answer that. I'm sitting on the same bed I fell asleep on, but I'm now in the dead center of a giant room that looks about the size of two gymnasiums placed side by side. There isn't anything on the ground or on the walls. The only thing that meets my eyes is bleach white. The ceiling, walls, floor, all combine to form an infinite, pure white blur that makes it hard to distinguish them from one another.

The brightness from all the white hurts my eyes at first, so it takes me awhile to adjust. When I finally do, I get up off the bed and walk around. There's got to be a way out of here somehow. As I take my first steps, I hear the echoes of my own footsteps travel throughout the whole place. After a few seconds, the room falls back to complete silence.

This place is too quiet. Far too quiet. I get the feeling of loneliness again as I'm reminded about walking through the house a few moments ago. At least I have plenty of light this time. Perhaps too much light.

I take a few more steps and let out a yell, just to see if someone else is in here. After a few silent moments, I conclude that I'm alone yet again. Yelling for somebody but not getting a response. Where have I heard that one before?

I take a few more steps when I eventually do hear a response. I can't make out what is said at first, so I stop and listen for it to repeat itself, and it does.

"How could you?" I hear the voice of a woman. "How could you do this to us?" I can almost feel the misery in her voice.

"Ma'am, what are you talking about?" I reply back to the woman that I don't see, confused on what it is she is talking about.

"You know what you did, you monster! You were our last chance, and you failed us!" Anger has replaced the misery in her voice from earlier, and I feel somewhat threatened now.

"Ma'am, I promise you, I have no clue what-" I get interrupted by another voice yelling at me.

"You betrayed us!" I hear the voice of an older man bellow at me from the opposite side of the room. I turn to look for him, but I see nobody. It's as if the walls are the ones yelling at me.

"Killer! You're a killer!" I hear a different man yell at me, but I still cannot find the culprit emitting these harsh statements.

"Please, I don't know what you're talking about! I just want to know how to get out-"

"Shut up! Just shut up, you murderer! You selfish, good for nothing, murderer!" A much younger lady voices her opinion at me this time. The screams are starting to get louder. It seems like they're not just echoing, but more like jumping off each wall and ricocheting at me.

Several other screams start pouring in at me, and they combine into each other to where I can't understand any of them. I hear the occasional "coward" or a "murderer" from the group, but the thing is, I hear all these shouts at me; yet, I still haven't seen anybody. I begin to walk back to the bed. Yelling back at them is pointless.

As I get closer to the bed, I see a woman start walking towards me from the other side of the bed. The woman is wearing a short, blue dress. She looks about my age, maybe a little older. I guess she's the one who called me the "selfish, good for nothing murderer." I walk towards her, as if to meet her halfway. However, when I get close enough to her, I stop in my tracks. What I see is just. . . Terrifying.

The woman. The woman has no face.

I squint at her to make sure my eyes aren't deceiving me again, and they're not. The woman has no face and is still walking towards me. No eyes, ears, or mouth, with the only thing on her head being her hair. As I turn around to run away from her, a group of people walking my way greets me from a few feet away. These people are just like the lady behind me: faceless.

The combined yelling just keeps getting louder and louder. I turn around to go back, but the woman has company now, as another group traps me from the other side.

The voices keep rising. Keep growing. It's a cluster of incoherent words that are impossible to understand. The sound of the combined cloud of words keeps growing louder, and my ears are starting to ache. I don't know what to do. I can't run away from them, there's far too many of them.

I look up. People in business suits, people in overalls and straw hats, people in elegant dresses, people in black drapes. People in all sorts of clothing, all yelling at me with mouths that don't exist. All surrounding me, preventing me from leaving, as if there was a way for me to. The only thing I can think of is to sit down, close my eyes tight and shut my ears. Maybe that will get rid of the voices.

I do this, but it seems like they know I'm trying to cut the sound out, so they just start screaming even louder. The people are slowly encasing me, and all I can do is sit here.

As the voices plunge through my head, I let out a scream in return to theirs, except mine is filled with distress. I throw my arms over my head, hoping that this will save me somehow.

I can feel the people getting closer and their yells growing louder. I don't know what it is they want with me or what they're planning on doing, but I hope whatever it is, they just do it quick.

The voices continue rising as the faceless people all reach out to grab my arm. My heart is beating uncontrollably in anticipation as what they're going to do with me. But as the closest hand gets within an inch from touching my arm, they stop. Every single hand quits moving in at me and pauses. The faceless people stand completely still.

And then the voices die out, all at once. Every yell, every word, gone away. Everything has fallen back to silence. I'm not sure what to do or to think. I just continue sitting there, staring back at the people's nonexistent faces.

Complete silence. Not a sound. It's so quiet my ears start ringing. I'm even more terrified now. I'm waiting for one of them to jump at me or to grab my arm. I'm just waiting for something to happen. As the apprehension builds, I'm too afraid to look at them. Their motionless bodies are far more frightening than their moving bodies. I duck my head back under my arms and shut my eyes.

"Please. Get it over with," I whisper to them.

No reaction.

I sit up in the bed, sweat pouring down my neck. It was all a dream. A terrible, horrifying dream.

6
Chance

I stare out into the darkened room, gasping for breath. I look down at my shirt and notice that it is drenched in sweat. I quickly take it off and toss it on the floor, with my heart still beating franticly. I glance at the clock on the wall. 4:25 AM. There's no way I can go back to sleep now.

I get out of the bed and skip over to turn on the lights. I flip them on, but I hesitate on turning around. It's as if I can feel hundreds of faceless bodies right behind me, staring at me without any eyes. But gladly, there's not any.

I can worry about the dream later. All I know is that I need to get out of this house, but where will I go?

It's still pitch black outside, so if I'm going to leave, I should find a flashlight. I check throughout the master bedroom and the kids' rooms but don't find one. I walk around the house some more and find myself going back into the bathroom.

I walk in and flip the lights on. I had forgotten to put on a shirt after I threw the sweaty one on the floor. I look at myself in the mirror, to see if my appearance had changed overnight. Actually, it sort of did.

My face is starting to scab over now. It still looks hideous, but after a few hours, my face is somewhat improving. It's still hard to get over the purple eyes, but I try to ignore them.

The feature that grabs my attention the most is the necklace I have on. I forgot I was even wearing it. The shark tooth is still in place as it was when I got it from Scarlett earlier this year.

Scarlett. I guess the saddest part is that I never had a chance to tell her how I feel. That I never had a chance to take her out like she had wanted me to. By all means, I'm no catch, and she probably wouldn't have had mutual feelings towards me. But the fact that I will never know now is what eats me up.

I mean, who knows? Maybe she did like me. I mean, girls followed Ryan around, and I have yet to figure that one out. Maybe it was because he was so smart, but I think it was his shaggy hair that did it. Whatever it was, it worked.

Cody really was a cool guy. He was hilarious, athletic, and tall. But he had never tried with any other girls. He always had his mind set on Terra, and her only.

And then there was me. I didn't play sports like Cody did, but I was semi-athletic. I wasn't as smart as Ryan, but I made mid-B's consistently. I was by no means as attractive as Scarlett, but I never considered myself to be some hideous troll. I guess I was just an even mixture of all my friends.

I always had self confidence with how I looked, except for when it was dealing with Scarlett. The name itself sounds so graceful that it would intimidate any man.

Scarlett Avalon. Whenever that name was mentioned, people knew they were talking about THE Scarlett Avalon. The prettiest girl in the entire state of Mississippi. The most flamboyant cheerleader in the entire county. The girl who everybody wanted their own daughter to grow up and be like. And here I was, the regular Average Joe, best friends with her.

I couldn't confess my love to her. Our friendship was something I cherished, and it was far too much of a risk to tell her. I didn't want things between us to get awkward, because if they did, then the same would happen to our group, and I couldn't lose that. I couldn't lose the friends I have.

And now here I am, staring at a shark tooth in the mirror, having done exactly that.

I walk out of the bathroom and limp back to the master bedroom to find another shirt. Once I get there, I bend down to get the damp shirt on the floor, which now feels like a wet rag. As soon as I touch it, I'm reminded about the nightmare that I wanted to avoid until it's actually daylight.

As I grab the shirt, I see something sticking out from under the bed. I pick it up and discover that it is a pocket journal.

I stand back up with the journal in my hand and sit on the bed. The journal was left open to a page with something written all over it, and without anyone to tell me otherwise, I begin reading it.

The paragraph starts in the middle of the page and is written sloppily, with the sentences drifting off of the lines:

"I don't know what to do anymore. I try to keep a strong head for my family, but I can't even convince myself that we have a chance anymore . . . My brother went yesterday, died right in front of his kids. His wife took the kids and they left before things got even worse. It's hard, but I'm afraid that I will have his same fate. I want to take the family with me, but I'm afraid they won't make it. The man was right. Westwood is done. And so are we."

I stare at the pages for awhile and reread it multiple times. I grasp on to every word, to try to get the meaning of each. This is the first evidence I've found that slightly explains what caused all this, but it still doesn't tell me everything.

From reading it, I can gather that, apparently, something incredibly deadly had driven people out of Westwood. But where did they go? It has to be Roaksville, that's the only place within a fifty-mile radius that makes sense. If everybody left, Roaksville would be the only city big enough to shelter that many people. Hopefully that was everybody's mindset: when things got bad in Westwood, go to Roaksville.

It seems all I've done the past 24 hours is ask questions that I cannot answer, so finding this pocket journal makes me feel better as to what happened to this place. However, if everyone is in Roaksville, I still have a lot of questions to ask them. I come up with an idea and begin searching around for a pen. After finding one, I look for a blank page in the journal, which is easy considering there isn't anything else written in it.

I'll just sit here and think of as many questions as possible that I can ask everyone once I get to Roaksville. It gives me something to look forward to, at the least.

I begin with the simplest one and go from there.

1. Why did everyone leave?
2. What happened?
3. Why am I the only one here?
4. How did wolves make it through?
5. Why are there wolves?
6. What's the green gas in the wall?
7. Why is there a wall?
8. Why are my eyes purple?
9. Why was everybody dying?

Those nine are the only ones that pop up out the top of my head. I know I have more, they're just not coming to me at this moment.

I read over the list. I may can answer why my eyes are purple, but that just adds to the 'what is the green gas' question. It's a cycle that seems to want to add on to itself.

I look over at the clock. 5:15 A.M. The sun should be starting to rise in about a half hour. I guess watching it rise would be enjoyable.

I stand back up and go back to the closet to find another shirt. A blue, long sleeved shirt seems to work. I put it on and begin to head out the bedroom door. I put the pen and journal in my back pocket and mentally prepare myself for the darkness that awaits me in the hall.

I turn the light off behind me, surrounding me in a black area. I don't know why I turned them off. Not like anybody is going to pay the electric bill. I just look at the ground, trying my best not to imagine a faceless figure standing directly in front of me.

I get to the front door and open it. The sky is still black, but has a dark blue tint to it. To the left of me is the wall, with green gas still pouring out from the hole and adding on to the smoke cloud above it.

Where am I off to now? I guess I should get somewhere high and watch the sunrise. There aren't many tall buildings around for me to climb up on, however. I could always go back home and get on top of my house, but I'm not sure if I'm physically capable of doing that.

I look around the neighborhood for anything tall. I notice all the wooden boxes I saw yesterday, now I just need to figure out a way to use them. The boxes are about four feet tall, and I suppose I could make a set of stairs from the boxes and climb on top of a house, but since most of the houses are either two or three stories tall, I would need a bunch of boxes for that.

As I look around for something else I can get on top of, the only object I can find that is suitable is the wall. Not a good idea. Definitely not a good idea. But honestly, where else is a better place to go? Back in the dark houses and secluding myself is the only other option. The wall seems dangerous, and I'm not entirely sure how safe it is, but since the only treacherous part is spewing out from the opening, I suppose that it should be sustainable as long as I stay away from that part.

But still, I'm not too wild about the idea of lying on top of the thing that exploded yesterday. I don't *know* if it's just the gas that is dangerous and not the wall, I'm only assuming. Nonetheless, I'm going to have to come in contact with this wall in some shape, form, or fashion in order to get to Roaksville.

Across the street, I see a wooden crate on a house's porch, just like I had seen the day before. I hobble over to the porch and walk up the steps. I haven't really understood the placement of these boxes yet, as I think it's pretty weird for a box to randomly be sitting on an empty porch. As I'm scouting out the porch, though, I notice something through the open doorway and inside the house.

At first, I don't know what it is, but once I creep closer, I find out that it's an arm peeking limply from behind the door.

I flinch at the sight but decide that it's best not to examine it, since this house didn't belong to anybody important to me. Maybe I can convince myself that I was just imagining it.

I pick up the box, which is much lighter than I had expected, and carry it over to the wall. I drop the box about a fifty yards to the left of the opening and push it against the metal structure. The box is tiny compared to the wall, and there is no way I can reach on top with one box. If I want to make the stairs I was considering earlier, then I will need at least five more crates: one column of three, one of two, and then the last is just one. I don't know if I can physically lug that many boxes to the wall, but I'm going to have to try. These boxes aren't all that heavy anyway.

I walk from house to house, picking up boxes and taking them to the wall. Most of them feel like they're empty, but a few seem to be filled with lightweight items. I would still like to open them up just to make sure. There has to be some reason for these boxes, right?

As I'm lugging the boxes around, I wonder what I'm going to do once I'm on top of the wall. I will watch the sunrise but what after? Do I want to jump to the other side and head towards Roaksville already? It's a good forty miles away. Plus, once I go over, there is no coming back to Westwood unless I go through the green smog.

I stack the boxes up like I had planned and drag myself up them. With my left leg still hurting, it's a struggle to squirm on the four-foot-tall boxes, but I do it and eventually reach the top of the wall. At first, I was worried about how much room there would be on the top, but there is a good three feet for me to lie down on.

I hesitantly sit down on the metal peak and look out across the top, glad that the wall didn't explode once my butt hits the steel. The wall extends what seems like thousands of yards on both sides of me, so it must be surrounding the entire city. I turn my head to the outside of the wall and see that it looks surprisingly beautiful. All the trees look so extravagant, with their leaves in all shades of green. The few houses I see on the other side aren't damaged, and it looks like people may still be living in them. Everything looks so calm, as if nothing outside of Westwood has been touched.

I then look along the wall so I can get a better view at this mysterious object. I gently rub my fingers across the top of it. Little, tiny holes envelop the entire façade of the structure, and they feel smooth across my fingertips. As I sit in silence, I hear a low humming noise coming from underneath me. Confused, I place my right ear to the wall and hear a hollow *swoosh* throughout the inside. Oh yeah, I forgot it's normal for a spontaneous wall to make noises. Whatever is making the low humming noise must have been connected to either the green smoke, the explosion, or both. Of course, that doesn't make me any more comfortable, but the sound itself is oddly consoling.

With the green smoke cloud behind me, I lie down and look up at the starry sky as a light blue emerges from above my feet. I can see the crest of the sun as it turns every part it touches into an orange blush. I guess this whole "apocalypse" isn't so bad after all, minus all the deaths and destruction. It makes me appreciate what I took for granted. Things such as sunrises, friends, family, and life.

I hope my family is okay. If everybody in Westwood did relocate to Roaksville, I hope Dad and Grandmother made it safely. I'm really worried on whether Grandmother could even have made the trip, though. I'm not sure how much more she could've gone, considering her age. If everybody was in a big rush as it appears they were. . .I just hope they didn't leave her behind.

I'm then suddenly reminded of what I found yesterday. I sit up and look down from the wall to the ground on the outside of the wall. I see all the bodies that I had spotted yesterday, all face down on the main road.

My heart jumps at the sight of them, but my mind remains calm, somewhat expecting them the whole time. I get a better view from the top and find out that there are many more bodies than I had expected earlier.

About fifteen or twenty bodies are spread out across Highway 4. As terrifying as it is to me, I still should get down and go check them out. I think it over for a second and decide that I won't jump down quite yet. Once I jump down, there's no way back in other than through the gas. Whenever my leg has healed and I'm ready to go to Roaksville, then I will. Besides, those bodies aren't going anywhere anytime soon.

I lie back down and look back at the sky. Clouds are starting to become visible as the sun is slowly beginning to reveal itself.

As the sun's rays lightly tap my face, I'm suddenly reminded about my dream I had earlier. I run it through my mind to seize every detail about it. The faceless people. The clothes they wore. The white room. I'm sure it didn't mean anything, but I just found it strange that I have a nightmare two consecutive nights when I hadn't had one in a long time.

When I was little, I used to have nightmares every other week. Every time I would have one, Mom would come rushing into my room and sing to me to calm me down. After she had died, I would just imagine her singing to comfort myself.

The image of the faceless people is still etched on my mind. How they yelled at me and surrounded me. They tried to grab me, even had me in their reach, but then they suddenly stopped.

Just reimagining it gives me goosebumps. The nightmares I had when I was little we're always about somebody getting killed or something terrible happening to me or my family. Things that could actually happen. But with faceless people? I'm not sure how I should interpret that.

As far as I know, there may not be any interpreting. It may have just been a random nightmare, which is what it most likely is. I'm over-thinking things, I know I am. All this extra time on my hands has me thinking stuff that shouldn't be thought about.

I don't really like all this extra time. I don't like examining every aspect in my life just because I have nothing else to do. I have learned more about myself in the last twenty-four hours than I have the last five years, which isn't a good thing. Instead of learning about myself, why can't I learn about what's going on? I'm just adding on to questions I already have.

I really need to leave Westwood. I don't think staying here is going to help anything; I need to try to find other people. There's obviously nobody in Westwood, so I'm wasting my time here. I stand up on top of the wall and pace back and forth, trying to convince myself that my leg is good enough for me to make it to Roaksville. The automatic wince that escapes me after every step is enough evidence that I can't make it at this moment.

I sit back down and pull the journal and pen out of my back pocket and begin writing. I start numbering across the top of the paper, and go all the way until ten. This will be how I keep track of the days I spend alone. I put an X over the one, and put one dash over the two to signify that I'm still in that day. Hopefully I won't have to cross out many more numbers.

I should number further on, just in case. As I sit there and number to thirty, I hear something in the distance. I tone my ears towards the direction the sound came from, hoping I'm not just hearing things.

I hear the sound again as it gradually gets louder the longer I listen in on it. It sounds just like a helicopter, hovering this way. I stand up and look around, but I don't see anything. I know I'm hearing correctly; I just don't know wher–

There it is! To my left, I see a helicopter protrude from the horizon, heading towards Roaksville. I begin to briskly limp down the wall, jumping and waving my arms, hoping to get the pilot's attention.

It's not flying that fast, so I have a decent chance to catch the pilot's eye. I start yelling at the helicopter, hectically jumping around for it to see me. They have to. I mean, I'm the only thing on the ground that isn't either dead or completely still.

I run down the wall some more, hoping to get as close to the helicopter as possible. It's pretty high in the air, so the closer I get to it, the better.

As the helicopter begins to pass over me and to my right, I begin to believe I missed my chance. How could they miss me? No, they haven't missed me yet. I have to catch up to them somehow.

I begin full out sprinting on the wall, ignoring the pain in my left leg. I have got to catch their attention. This is my chance. This is my chance to find somebody, to ask them what's going on. Maybe they're going back to where everybody is, or they could be searching for any survivors. They've got to be looking straight down at me. Maybe they're just ignoring me.

I start jumping around, waving my arms as the helicopter flies away from me. Please, please turn back. I need to . . .

As I'm jumping up, I land on my right leg awkwardly, and slip. My right foot rolls off the top of the platform, and I collapse from all the weight being put on my left foot. I try to regain my balance but fail to and fall off on the outside of the wall. As my body topples to the ground, I cover my face with my arms to protect the burn.

I hit the ground with a loud thud, and the impact knocks the breath out of me. I roll around on the main street where I landed, clutching my stomach to help gain my breath back. As I gasp and groan loudly for air, I hear the helicopter flying away, without any sign that it is turning back. Along with my deep pants, I listen to the helicopter fading away into silence.

I missed it. I missed my chance.

7

The outside

I CONTINUE LYING face down on the ground for a few seconds to regain my breath. After I do, I try to stand up and look around. Immediately, my left leg gives out from under me, and I fall back down. Oh my God, my leg is killing me. I try once again to stand up, struggling as my feet finally hold me up. With my leg throbbing with every second I stand on it, I realize just how vulnerable I am right now. If those wolves came out right now, I wouldn't stand a chance. I need to get back in Westwood, but the only way for me to get in isn't exactly my favorite option. I hobble down Highway 4 towards the green gas opening, looking at the bodies as I pass by.

I'm nauseated by the up-close look at them, but I'm still unable to identify any of them. I slowly approach one that is only a few feet away from where I landed. It's a woman who appears to had been in her mid-forties, face down on the ground just like all the others. I reach down and carefully turn her over, afraid that a faceless head would greet me. I'm relieved to see that she actually does have a face, and even more relieved when I notice that I don't even know the woman. But just like Mr. Lawkins, her eyes are staring straight at the sky behind me, and her face is extremely pale.

Why? Why is the reaction on her face the exact same as Mr. Lawkins's? The more I look at her eyes, the more I have to fight off the urge to check behind me to make sure there's not anything there. I turn her back over and walk to the next body nearby.

This person was an older man, around his sixties. I turn him over and see the exact same expression that I saw just a few moments ago. Blank eyes focused directly ahead.

I repeat the same question again, as if maybe a second time will give me an answer. I pull my journal out and decide to write it down there.

10. Why are faces on dead bodies all the same?

Their faces almost look fake, like a wax dummy. The frozen expressions permanently on their faces look too identical to one another. And their faces are so abnormally white that it reminds me of. . . of the room in my dream last night.

Hard to believe all these people died in one night. Hard to believe this giant wall was built in one night. Actually, the more I think about it, the less it seems that this all actually occurred between Saturday night and Sunday morning. Building a wall this giant in seven hours is impossible. This many people dying, plus the evacuation of a city all happening in seven hours, as well? I don't believe it.

I reach down to touch the man's face. Even though it's been a day, his body should still be a little warm. Once my fingers come in contact with his skin, ice cold runs through my fingertips. This man has been dead for a while. And by a while, I mean way longer than a day.

So what does that mean? Was I asleep for multiple days? It makes sense now, come to think of it. I think back to my first dream. Everybody may have been leaving, and when Dad came in and failed to wake me up, he thought that I was dead. That's why I was left behind. I've already come to that conclusion.

Even think back to that next morning. The milk was spoiled, despite it not being outdated. That means I was out for at least two weeks, but how? I mean, it all adds up, except for the 'how did I sleep for two weeks' part. And that adds even more questions, like 'how did I survive two weeks in a coma without any food or water?' And if I had been asleep for two weeks, wouldn't these dead bodies have started decomposing by now?

What makes things weirder is that I haven't eaten nor drunk anything since I found out everybody left. I'm not even hungry or thirsty, which not only confuses but worries me. I interrupt my thoughts and remind myself that the more I think about this entire situation, the more questions I'm going to add to the list; it would be best if I drop the subject for now. I can get legit answers in Roaksville.

The next body I walk up to is a young black girl, looking about my age. I walk up to her and roll her over.

It's Terra.

I stagger backwards, letting the sudden fact sink in. Terra is dead. *Dead.* It's one thing to assume your friends are dead, but to actually see their body lying motionless on the ground . . .

There she is, staring straight up towards the sky just like the rest of them. She's not going to stand back up. She's not going to talk to me anymore. She's not going to do anything but lie there.

The reality punches me in the gut. If Terra is lying here, then there is little to no doubt that so are Cody, Ryan, and Scarlett. The first few bodies I saw were adults, but now. Now there are people I know, my age, that are affected.

I don't think I can do this anymore. I don't think I can check every single body lying here. This almost guarantees that my friends are out here somewhere, dead. And what am I going to do if I find them?

I can't. I can't do this. I'm just not strong enough for this. I like the small chance of them being alive that I keep in the back of my mind. I can't have assurance. I can't imagine my friends left pale faced and frozen. The thought of finding Scarlett like that. . . I can't. I just simply can't.

And what if it hits home? What if I find Dad out here somewhere? I thought it would be easy to just find him, but it's much more difficult than that. And then what about Grandmother? I can't picture her innocent face being startled like all these around me, I just can't. I've had to live with the loss of a mother and a grandfather, I don't want to have to find the rest of my family dead in the streets.

As I panic, I hear the sound of a wolf howl in the distance. I'm suddenly reminded of my necessary urge to get back inside the wall and find a house to hide in. If those wolves come after me again like they did last night, I'm dead. There's no more running away from them. I need to get back in Westwood while I have the chance.

I slowly and painstakingly approach the green smoke. I study the smoke, wishing there was another way to get in. I still don't know if this is just a straight wall or if it surrounds the city, but either way, that will take way too long and be way too painful. I'll have to go through it and hope I can hold my breath well enough so I won't pass out again.

I walk up to the hole, cautiously standing a few feet away from the green smoke. I place my hand over my mouth and nose and squeeze down on it tightly. I close my eyes and limp as fast as I can through the green smoke, holding my breath for the whole five-second journey.

I reach the other side of the wall and open my eyes. I start to lose my balance, and my vision becomes dizzy. Somehow, someway, the gas got in me. My legs lock up and go numb, and I fall over face first with just enough strength to avoid landing on my burned face. I try my best not to pass back out, in fear of waking up to a pack of wolves or a group of faceless people huddling around me.

I try to keep my eyes open, but to no avail. The wolves will just have to get me . . .

I wake up to the sun stabbing violently at my burned mark. I quickly sit up and look around for any nearby wolves looking to devour me, but none are present. The gas directly behind me taunts me, telling me that since I'm back inside the city, there's no leaving.

I rub my head, which had taken a hard knock when I fell. I have finally decided to stay away from the wall and avoid its mysterious gas as much as I can. No more early-morning heart-to-heart sessions with the exploding, poisonous wall. I limp down the street, needing to find a house so I can get out of the sun and the possibilities of getting mangled by wolves.

As I continue limping down the street, I look around at the houses. They look exactly like the ones on my street just a few yards over: completely trashed and damaged. I can't even walk down the street without tripping over random objects.

The random wooden boxes that appear every two or three houses are beginning to annoy me. Most of them are on the front porches, with an occasional one in the road. I really want to see what is in these boxes, so I begin walking over to one of the boxes on a nearby porch.

This house belongs to our mayor, Mr. Armstrong, and his family. Mr. Armstrong has a son my age named Tyson, but we aren't that close. Really, this family is every bit as perfect as they could get: the husband being the mayor of Westwood, the wife being the principal at the high school, and the son being the star quarterback. The entire family is what people strived to have of their own.

I had been to their house before when I was little, not because Tyson and I were essentially buddies, but because Dad and Mr. Armstrong got along well. Tyson is really quiet and seems like an alright guy. He and Scarlett dated for a few months last year, so I sort of hated him for practically no reason, but I'm over that now. I've talked to him occasionally, but we never really hung out.

I walk up on the porch, relieved to be out of the sun. I'm still surprised at how hot it is in October. I limp over to a box that looks exactly like the ones I had moved earlier. Just like on the other ones, the lid is nailed shut. The only way I'm going to find out what is in this box is to pry it off. Hopefully the Armstrong's will have a hammer or something helpful like that inside.

As I reach my arm out to grab the doorknob, I keep in mind that there is a strong possibility that one of those three are lying in here, dead. With that unsettling fact in the back of my mind, I twist on the door knob.

Something is pushed up against the door from the inside. As I make enough of a crack for me to squeeze through, I see that it's a refrigerator. That's pretty random. As I look up, though, I see that it isn't as random as I first thought.

Tables are flipped over, cabinets have been ripped out of the wall, chairs have been thrown across the room. I don't know what happened here, but it looks absolutely terrible. The other house I was at wasn't this bad, so why is this one?

I walk around the living room, inspecting what happened here all while looking for something that can help me pry open the box outside. My leg continues aching as I walk on it, and I need to find a bathroom to look and see how bad my leg has actually gotten.

After a few minutes, I leave the living room and go to the next door over, which happens to be the garage. If there is a hammer anywhere in this house, it must be here. I search around, finding plenty of other tools, but nothing that can pry open the box. Really strange, though, that they have practically every tool in the book except for a hammer. I come across a screwdriver and decide it will have to work.

I exit the garage and head back in the living room. As I walk past the living room and into their den, however, I notice something a few feet away from me.

I see a hammer leaning up against a wall on the opposite side of the den. Or, at least, that's what it looks like from here. The lights are off, but I have just enough light leaking in from the windows to see the outline of it. I search around the room for a light switch, and find one right next to me.

As soon as I flip the switch on, the same amount of destruction that occurred in the living room is waiting for me in the den. Couches are flipped over. A glass coffee table is shattered on the floor with dried drops of blood on the fragments. I ignore the chaos and walk over to pick up the hammer, but as I'm walking my eye catches on to the wall. I investigate the wall, noticing that someone had beaten indentions it with the hammer. The indentions lead all the way to the hammer, which sits perfectly caddy-cornered in the room.

Looks like someone just walked next to the wall, bashed it in, then carefully placed the hammer in the corner of the den. Weird, but not the weirdest thing I've seen today. This makes me think that whatever thrashed all of these places was doing it intentionally instead of out of some frantic evacuation.

I can't help but grow curious as maybe the explanation is somewhere in the house. The reminder I made earlier echoes through my head, and I begin to prepare myself for finding one of the Armstrongs' bodies. It had sort of slipped my mind, but now I brace myself for whatever, or, in this case, whoever, I may find.

I exit the den with the hammer in my possession and turn to my left down a hallway. I hobble down it and look in each room I pass by. The first one I come across is Tyson's room. I decide to enter it and marvel at his decorations.

Signed football jerseys and posters of athletes embellish his walls. His desks are canopied by multiple awards and action shots of him in football gear. Like I said, Tyson was an athlete, but I never knew how much he loved the sport. It's actually amusing to examine all of his pictures and posters.

I had always wished I was athletic enough for football, but I was fine with watching the games. I had always admired watching Tyson play quarterback so successfully, so I somewhat viewed him as a small-town celebrity. I guess that's another reason why we never became good friends, because I always thought he was too high up on the social totem pole to hang out with us. But then again, Scarlett was high on that pole, as well.

I've spent too much time in here, so I leave his room and continue walking down the hall, where the next room is the bathroom.

I walk in and scan my body in the bathroom's mirror. My face is getting better, but still looks terrible. I take my pants off and look at my left leg. It's scratched up just as bad as it was yesterday, but now has a huge bruise across my shin. Lovely.

I check through the medicine cabinets, looking for something that might help it out, even though I'm not entirely sure what will. I find a long, red tube and, after reading the label, rub it on my leg and face, feeling the chill spread out through my body as it touches the sensitive afflictions.

I study myself in the mirror again. Damn, I'm ugly. That's all the analysis I need.

I exit the bathroom and enter back in the hall. Before I turn to leave the house, however, my eye is caught on a door at the end of the hallway. Since I'm not in any hurry, I decide to go check it out.

Once I reach the end of the hall and pull on the door knob, I discover that the door is locked. Locked. Only the second locked door I've come across so far, with the other being the one at the bowling alley. There must be something important in this room. Something that the Armstrongs didn't want anybody else to find.

I look down at the hammer in my hand and, after giving a sly smile, start clobbering the door, eventually making a hole large enough for me to stick my hand through and unlock the door from the inside.

I pull my hand back out and twist the door knob again. The likelihood of me finding something in this room that I actually want to find is tiny, but I've already began opening the door, so it's too late to turn back.

I find much more than my eyes can catch. I'm left utterly petrified as the hammer falls from my fingers and lands on the ground beside me. There, lying on the floor next to her bed, is Mrs. Armstrong, with a gun in one hand, and a picture frame in the other.

And I can't decide which one terrifies me more: the splattered wall right behind her, or the family picture embraced close to her chest.

8

Sepia

I SLOWLY APPROACH her body. This is terrible. This isn't like everyone else who had fallen over dead on the streets. She killed herself.

And that can only mean one thing: whatever happened here is much, *much* worse than I had thought. It's bad enough for people to be shooting themselves, and that is far more serious than I had anticipated. Falling over dead is one thing, but taking your own life is completely different.

But how bad is bad enough to where people are killing themselves? I can't imagine what Mrs. Armstrong had endured to make her pull the trigger on her own life. Suicide is never an option, and she is the last person I would ever expect to have this happen to.

I stare at the back of her head, wondering whether or not her eyes are like the others. No way I'm going to flip her over and find out. I can't barely look at her as she is, so the thought of seeing her face, frozen or not, isn't going to make a difference.

I look at the wall in front of me. A red mist coats over parts of the originally yellow wall. As terrifying as it is, I can't seem to take my eyes off of it. I can't help but to stand still and investigate the wall, as if it were some admirable painting, despite the fact that it is the exact opposite.

I wonder where Tyson's or Mr. Armstrong's body is. I wonder if they died the same way she did. I can't help but wonder where they are, but I'm aware that the last thing I actually want to do is to find them.

I squat down and look at the gun in her hand. I consider taking it from her, thinking that it would definitely come in handy if the wolves showed up again. But at the same time, I'm uncomfortable with the thought of having it, in fear of what might become of me if I'm left in this isolated state any longer. I decide not to take it. I don't want to have to claw it from her grip, anyways.

I focus my attention to the picture in her opposite hand. Wow. My spine shivers at the sight of the unnerving image. Even in her lowest point, she was thinking about her family. I can't help but wonder what was going through her mind when all this happened. Maybe it was just . . .

My thoughts stop as my eyes begin to fade to black. Am I passing out again? I don't even have time to process what is happening before my entire sight is gone completely. What is . . . are my eyes even open? What . . .

A bright flash explodes out of the darkness. The light hurts my eyes, and I try to raise my hand to shield them, except for I can't even see my arm. As the flash dwindles and I regain my sight, everything seems different. Actually, everything is different.

The first thing I notice is that my sight has somehow educed a golden tint to it, a lot like sepia. But it's not just one specific thing that has taken this color. Every single thing I see is sepia. Have I randomly gone colorblind?

As I check my surroundings, I notice that they have changed, as well. I'm not sitting in the main bedroom anymore, and Mrs. Armstrong is nowhere in sight.

I'm in the den of the Armstrongs' house, which also hasn't been trashed yet. The couch and coffee table are intact, and the walls are perfectly flat and smooth. Whatever trashed the den earlier hasn't touched it yet.

But wait . . . how did I get here? Am I imagining this? Did I some-how go back in time or something? This doesn't make sense. One second I'm looking over a dead body, and the next I'm in a room that is com-pletely different than it was a few moments earlier. What is going on?

As my head fills itself up again with more questions, I hear a scream coming from the living room. Not just a regular scream, though. This one sounds appalling, like someone is being tortured in the kitchen. I begin to walk out of the den whenever I hear another person shouting from the hallway behind me.

"Catherine?" I hear a man call out. "Catherine, what is going on? Are you okay?"

The words I hear have a faint echo to it. I see Mr. Armstrong scamper around the corner in his pajamas with Tyson right behind him. Both of them look as if they had just woken up.

"Roger, it's happening to me!" I hear a lady from the living room cry out. "It's happening! Oh God, you were right! Please, help me!"

Mrs. Armstrong walks down from the living room and into the den, with a hammer held tightly in her hand. The look on her face screams out agony. Something is happening to her, but what?

"Oh, no," Mr. Armstrong utters. The sorrow in his voice is evident. "Tyson, get your mask and get out of here."

"Dad, I can't," Tyson argues back. "Whatever happens here, I'm going to stay. There's no way I'm going to leave Mom here."

"Tyson," Mr. Armstrong calmly says. "I said get out of here. Please listen to me."

"No, Dad." Tyson snaps back.

"TYSON I'M NOT ASKING YOU!" Mr. Armstrong shouts back at him, clearly having lost his patience. "Please, son, get out of here while you still can. Go. Be safe."

Mr. Armstrong's voice cracks as a tear rolls down his face. I don't even know if they can see me standing in the middle of the den, but I can definitely feel the tension. Tyson stares back at his Dad for a few seconds, then heads back to the hallway.

Mrs. Armstrong is pacing back and forth, dismally staring at her feet.

"Roger," Mrs. Armstrong begins. "It's happened. I can't handle this. My head is just . . ."

"Look, Catherine," Mr. Armstrong begins. "Drop the hammer before things get bad."

Mrs. Armstrong looks up from the floor, showing the amount of defeat and weakness in her face. "I can't let go of it," she tells her husband with a somber voice. "It's slowly taking me over, I'm going to go anytime now."

"Catherine, please. Please don't let me lose you."

Mrs. Armstrong looks at him with sadness in her eyes. "Roger, I'm trying my best to fight it. But the pain is just, just too much. AHH!"

Her hands rush to her head, and she buries her fingers in her scalp, hoping to find something that will ease her pain. "I'm about to lose control of myself. I can feel it. I have to do something. . . Roger, is it still in the night stand?"

"No," Mr. Armstrong strongly disapproves of whatever is in the nightstand. "You are not going back in there and you are not . . . doing that. So don't even—"

"Roger . . ." Mrs. Armstrong calmly whispers, "I love you." Before Mr. Armstrong has time to respond, his wife falls forward and lands on the glass coffee table.

"No! Catherine, no!" Mr. Armstrong falls to his knees and crawls over to his wife, who lies motionless on the pile of glass shards. He pulls her head up to his lap and caresses her hair, all while tears fall from his chin onto her forehead.

At first, I think that this is how everyone died, but the lack of that blank expression across Mrs. Armstrong's face tells me that her death may be different. Besides, she didn't die from falling over on a coffee table, she shot herself. So how can she be dead right now?

"Dad, I could only find two of the . . ." Tyson's comes out from the

corner of the hallway, clutching an oxygen mask in his hand while an identical one is placed over his face. "What happened?"

"She's gone! Your mother is gone!" Mr. Armstrong is barely understandable, as his emotions have overcome him. Tyson's eyes wander to his mother, who's arm twitches just slightly.

"Dad, it's about to happen," Tyson tells his dad. His dad looks down at his wife and quickly stands up. As soon as he does, his wife is suddenly jolted back to life. Instead of happily embracing her husband like I expected, she swings the hammer in her hand at him. Mr. Armstrong, however, ducks at the last second, and the hammer is jammed into the wall behind him instead.

"YOU'RE A LIAR!" she yells at her husband as she flips the couch in front of her. She brings the hammer back and swings it at him again. Mr. Armstrong ducks a second time, and pushes his now insane wife to the ground.

"Tyson, we have to go. NOW!" Mr. Armstrong beckons for his son to follow him out the door and to the garage. Tyson, who is clearly entranced by his mother's sudden outburst, hesitates for a moment before making his way across the den.

"GET OUT OF MY HOUSE!" Mrs. Armstrong yells at Tyson as he crosses the room. She hurls the hammer at her son, but the throw misses badly, leaving the hammer to land in the corner of the den.

Tyson pauses for a moment to look at his mother in her current state once more. Absolute hatred has flustered Mrs. Armstrong's face, and she doesn't have the face of a mother anymore. She looks at Tyson with intent on killing him. Tyson, on the other hand, gives a heartbreaking look to his mom, wishing she was back to normal. I can't help but feel empathetic for him.

"Mom," Tyson says as a single tears streams down his jawline, "I love you. Please get better."

"LEAVE!" she responds to her son while angrily pointing at him. She then pounds her head with her fists, all while yelling cries of both anger *and pain.*

"Son, please come on," Mr. Armstrong calmly tells his son. Tyson gives one last sorrowful look to his mom before he buries his face in his hands and follows his dad to the garage. Mrs. Armstrong, however, remains punching her head. After a few minutes of agony, she sprints out of the den and down the hallway. Before I even have time to follow her, I hear the door of the master bedroom slam shut.

The den starts to lose its focus, and everything around me begins to fade away. The same blackness that occurred to me just a few minutes earlier greets me again.

What just happened? What is . . . what . . .

I gain back consciousness, and I'm lying on the ground in the master bedroom again. Everything has gained its original color. Mrs. Armstrong's blonde hair. The red-splattered wall behind me. Everything isn't sepia anymore.

My mind is racing so fast that it starts to ache. What was that? Did what I think just happen actually happen?

Did I just go back in time?

H . . . how? That . . . that isn't even possible. What exactly just happened? I'm starting to get scared as I realize that I may have been wrong all along. I may have already lost my mind.

There's no way. Absolutely no way. Going back in time? Impossible. Even though it did seem exactly like that.

I take a seat right next to Mrs. Armstrong, no longer troubled by her corpse. This is just . . . it still doesn't make sense. Did I really just go back in time?

It didn't seem like I was physically there. Nobody there could see me. Plus, I could walk fine on my leg. Maybe I didn't go back in time. Maybe I just relived exactly what happened to this family.

So what does that mean? Did I relive a memory that didn't even belong to me? That doesn't . . . well, I don't know anymore. I'm to the point where nothing adds up. Still, I guess it was sort of like reading someone's thoughts, but whose? The closest person to me has their brains blasted on a wall behind me. If I did read someone's mind, there isn't even a mind for me to read.

I look down at the lifeless remains of Mrs. Armstrong, thinking about her utterly strange and sudden transition into complete insanity. I don't get it. Why did she change like that? It's confusing and frightening. What if that happens to me . . .

The whole city is trashed. Everything thrown apart. Maybe these people got a hold to whatever it was Mrs. Armstrong had and just completely fell out of control of their actions. It happened to Mrs. Armstrong, so it could've happened to the entire city of Westwood.

And thinking back, Mr. Armstrong seemed like he knew about the whatever-*it*-was his wife succumbed to. He didn't seem that surprised and didn't try to talk to his wife when she went insane, so they must have known whatever it was that caused her to do so. But what is it that caused her to go crazy?

I look back down at the picture grasped in her hand. Mrs. Armstrong, her husband, and Tyson, all smiling happily at the camera. I can't stay in here any longer.

I stand up, pick up the hammer, and head for the door. I need to get this off my mind. I still don't know how to explain what happened a few minutes ago, but sitting next to a dead body and overthinking isn't going to help.

I walk back out the hall, through the den and living room, and out the front door. The sunlight gives me a quick reminder about the abnormal fall heat, and I begin to regret my decision of leaving the house. But I should do what I aimed to do nearly an hour ago, so I pull the hammer out of my pocket and walk to the box.

I slide the claw of the hammer under the top and push down. After a little bit of muscle, the lid pops open, and I pull it off, eager to see what is inside.

I throw the top across the porch and glare inside. Empty.

Seriously? I just went through all this trouble for nothing? I'm outraged by the fact that nothing is in this box, despite all the effort to open it. I want to be angry, but I'm not entirely sure why I should be. As I peer into the empty, worthless wooden crate, I still wonder what purpose it served. It had to have had one. I mean, there are boxes everywhere. They have to have some significance.

Staring into the empty box isn't going to tell me anything, so I turn around to pick the lid back up and nail it shut. I reach down to pick up the lid, but as I do, I hear a noise coming from across the street. I look up from the lid in my hand and see two people run out of the house directly across from me.

9

Safe

I DROP THE lid in shock once I see the people. They're frantically moving over something and, having not noticed me yet, run back inside.

"Hey!" I call out to them, hoping to sidetrack them from their busy task. They don't hear me, though, so I walk as quickly as my leg will let me over to the house, calling out to them as I do so.

Once I make it to the middle of the street, they sprint back out. One of them struggles to carry a wooden crate, the other person . . .

Oh, dear God. No.

The other person doesn't have a face.

And as the person carrying the crate drops it on the porch, I see that he, too, doesn't have a face.

I can't believe this. The couple looked so normal from across the road. One of them has long hair and a yellow blouse, while the one who was carrying the crate has a short sleeve shirt that exposes tattoos that run down his arms. They look so normal, so real. So . . . so terrifying.

I can't decide whether to take another step or not. What if they come at me? What if they start yelling at me again like I'm some kind of villain? I'm fazed, watching them scurry on the porch without knowing I'm here.

The faceless man jabs a screwdriver under the lid of the crate and pops it off. The faceless woman then pretends like she is picking up a pile of something to throw into the crate. They both hurry back into the house, and then, after a few seconds, they come back empty handed.

I have to do something. I can't decide whether I should run away or speak to them. I take a step closer to observe them.

I take step after step as they continue to repeat the same process: go in the house, pretend to put something in the crate, repeat. The faceless man ceases the process every so often to stop and grab his head, but other than that, they continue putting imaginary objects in the crate.

"Excuse me," I hear myself reluctantly ask them. Neither one of the two respond to me; I don't know if it's because they can't hear me or they're just ignoring me.

Suddenly, the faceless man stumbles backwards, holding on to his head as if he were trying to keep it from detaching off his body. The faceless woman rushes over to him, but the man falls over before she gets to him. The faceless woman grabs her husband, looking down on his motionless body in what I can only assume is sadness.

I take a step away from the two, afraid that the man is about to turn insane just as Mrs. Armstrong had. I honestly want to run away from these two, but I can't. I want to see what ends up happening to them.

After a few seconds, the faceless man wakes back up, pushing the woman off of him. The man then jumps up and kicks the woman lying on the ground as she tries her best to protect herself. The sight is truly disgusting, and I feel totally powerless just watching from a distance. Should I intervene? I must sound stupid even considering to help a faceless.

I continue watching, blow after blow, as the woman lies helplessly on the ground, trying to ward off every kick from her husband by weakly blocking them with her forearm. The kicking morphs into stomping, and the sight has grown to be grotesque. I'm surprised that the woman isn't bleeding, but I don't worry about that at the moment. I can't just stand here and let this man do this to her, faceless or not.

"Hey, man, get the hell off of her," I yell from the bottom of the stairs leading to the porch. With the hammer tightly gripped in my hand, I prepare for a fight.

The faceless man quits kicking the lady and swiftly turns his head in my direction. Once I get a full look on where his face should be, the grip on my hammer softens, and I nearly drop it.

My stomach turns at the emptiness. I can feel his eyes cleaving to me, but they don't exist. I can feel the hatred flowing out of him. I can tell he senses my fear, smells it in the air despite not having a nose, tastes it as if it were his wife's invisible blood.

And before I can blink, he charges at me.

I'm too intimidated to react. He's already jumping off the porch at me before I'm able to move. The sudden essential urgency to retreat causes me to simply stumble on my butt and land on the ground as the faceless man prepares to land on me and beat me just like he did his wife.

I watch as the man gets closer to me, knowing that I can't defend myself. Before I can accept my fate, I watch as the man pauses.

In mid air.

His hands made into a fist to punch me, his legs flung behind him, all frozen in time, levitating off the ground. And as his faceless head remains inches from my nose, I don't hesitate.

I spin away from the man and sprint off down the road and towards the city. It's happening again. It won't be long before the houses on both sides of the street fade into a bleach white blur.

My head whips from side to side, expecting a sea of people with no faces to start running towards me. I can feel my heart pound, my breath thump against my throat as the anticipation of the crowd of faceless people coming at me never becomes reality. I cover my ears as I run down the street, hoping to avoid the shouts before they start. Please, not again. I don't want to go through this again.

My leg is wailing in pain with every step. I need to get somewhere safe, but where can I go? There's nowhere safe in this city, but . . .

Grandmother's house. The only place I've ever felt safe. Her house is only a block away. I close my eyes and grit my teeth, trying to ignore the pain the best I can while trying to forget the faceless people even existed.

I fight off the urge to verify whether a mob of faceless people is chasing behind me. With all the strength I have left in my injured leg, I make it to Grandmother's house, sling the door open, and immediately lock it right behind me.

I sink to the floor, struggling to catch my breath. After a few minutes of recovering, I look up from the floor and out into the house that I've grown to love over the years. However, I'm surprised at what I see. Everything is clean. Nothing is broken, tattered, or destroyed like in the other houses. Everything is perfectly intact.

I investigate the living room, still overwhelmed by the condition of the house. I slowly walk past the couch, which is definitely the coziest couch in the world as I've fallen asleep on it at least a thousand times. I make my way to the mantle, which is filled with pictures.

The first picture is one of me, her only grandkid. I was pampered by her and Pawpaw, but one thing was for sure: my grandparents loved me. The picture is of a baby me in a cowboy suit and a huge cowboy hat that covers half of my face, and I'm sort of looking out from underneath it.

I have to admit it. I was a cute little baby.

The next picture is of Grandmother and Pawpaw when they were in their early twenties. The black and white coloring of the picture makes it compelling to look at.

Grandmother never told me much about her and Pawpaw when they were younger, but I heard plenty of stories about my mom when she was little. I don't know if Grandmother didn't want to tell me, or if she just never found the opportunity to, but I would like to have known how her and Pawpaw started it off.

Grandmother is gorgeous in this picture. Pawpaw still has that notched look on his face that he has always carried with him. Both look like two completely different people, on opposite sides of the spectrum, but yet they lasted for over 50 years.

Looking at Pawpaw reminds me of his death just a week before everybody left. He had suddenly gotten sick when in town, and passed away before the ambulance got him to the hospital. It was a shock to us, and the way it happened made things even worse for us.

I really hope I don't find Grandmother's body. If there was any place where she would be found, it would be here. I can't leave, though. I feel safe in here, and that's the only thing that matters at the moment.

I continue down the row of pictures, and the next one grabs at my heart. It's a picture of my Mom and Dad in high school.

Dad has shaggy hair, and the bow tie and tuxedo he's in doesn't really compliment his thin goatee that clearly hasn't grown out as thick as it would have in years to come. But Dad isn't what jumps out at me. It's Mom.

I knew what she looked like back then, but I forgot how stunning she was. Her hair was long, straight and black, the same color it was the last time I saw her. Everything about her looks so. . . so dazzling. Her hair. Her smile. I can clearly tell I have her smile. Everything about her reminds me of how much I miss her.

I pull the picture off the mantle, cradling it to my chest, and fall to my knees. I know it isn't my fault, but I can't help but feel guilty. I just have a feeling that if I did something different eleven years ago, she may still be here. I know I'm not to blame, and I know that there isn't anything I could have done. It was just meant for her to go, and it's still hard for me to understand that.

I don't want to be here anymore. This place holds so many great memories, but now I'm just left surrounded by reminders of the wonderful family that no longer exists anymore. I place the picture back on the mantle and turn around to leave, but as I do so, I hear a sound come from upstairs.

I remain silent for a few seconds to let my brain register what the sound was, but once I determine that it sounded like glass breaking, I try to think of a reasonable explanation. Did a picture frame fall off somewhere upstairs? Or maybe the window in my grandparents' room somehow got broken?

What am I still doing in here? I've already made up my mind that I don't want to be in here anymore, so why am I even worrying about some noise that I probably just made up again? Even though I know that I should leave, for some reason, my feet follow the noise up the staircase. I guess a small part of me thinks that Grandmother could've been the one who made that sound.

As I make my way to the second floor, I notice that the door to my grandparents' bedroom is barely cracked open. I can't help myself. I know that I do not need to go in there because I know what is likely in there. For the sake of my own mentality, I need to stay away. But instead, I watch as my legs make it to the door and my forearm pushes the cracked door the rest of the way open.

There, lying in her bed, in her light-pink gown that barely touches her whitish-gray curls, is my grandmother. Her eyes are closed, but I don't know if she is asleep or . . . I don't want to find out. I just want to pretend she's asleep. I don't want to find out. I don't . . .

I approach her bedside, getting a closer look at Grandmother. As I inch closer to her bed, I notice shards of glass right next to her night stand. It looks like I was right, the sound was of glass breaking, but does that mean she did it? I look over at my Grandmother, hoping that she has noticed that I've come in, but she hasn't. She looks so calm, so at peace. But then again, she always did.

"Grandmother," I whisper to her as I softly nudge her shoulder. After a few seconds, I push just a little harder on her shoulder, hoping that a little more force will wake her up. "Please, wake up. Please." A tear starts to fall as my pushes begin shaking her. "Please, Grandmother. . . Please!" The sound of my own whispering voice does nothing but confirm what I had dreaded.

I take my hand off her shoulder and bury my face in the mattress as my eyes become heavy with tears. She's gone. I know I shouldn't have come in this room. She's dead, just like everybody else left in this city . . .

But despite my remorse and despite the loss of my own grandmother just now settling it, I have the unnerving sense in the back of my mind that I'm being watched. I ignore it at first and try to refocus on consolidating myself, but the feeling continues to press me. My grandmother is dead, yet I can't seem to put all my attention on that. Maybe I shouldn't think too much about her death. The longer I sit in Grandmother's house and look back at her pale face, the more depressing I'll become.

I get one last look at my Grandmother. I try to hold my emotions in as she has done numerous times for me. She wouldn't want me to cry over her death, but to be happy that she isn't bedridden, immobile, and stuck in this dreadful, deserted city just like her grandson is . . .

I get back on my feet and head towards the door to leave, but that's when I notice that something is in my way.

Standing between me and the door is a faceless woman. They are everywhere, I can't avoid these things. The first thing that catches my attention about the woman is how short the figure is, the light pink gown the figure is wearing, and the thin . . . curled braids of . .

. whitish-gray hair.

The faceless figure standing in front of me is my Grandmother.

But how? Grandmother's body is right behind me, dead. I quickly turn around to ensure that her body is still covered up in the bed, and indeed it is. If so, then who, or what, is this in front of me?

I watch as my faceless grandmother brings her hands to the middle of her chin, as she would if she were covering her mouth. I don't know what's going on. I stay motionless. This is pure torture.

I think I can hear the figure in front of me crying, but I'm too terrified to care. I watch as my faceless grandmother takes her left hand off of her nonexistent mouth and slowly extends it to touch me. I'm yet again left in a state of shock, and as each second passes, she's only fingertips away from touching my burned mark on my face.

My voice lets out a yell, one that I haven't even heard myself give. One filled with true terror. One that's been built up with tension and horror for the past ten minutes. As the yell pierces my own ears, I jerk my face away from her hand, all while staring at my grandmother's blank canvas, hoping to see eyes look back at me in return. I make my way around her and out of my grandparents' bedroom. I jump down the stairs on two hops, and sprint out the door without even a slight consideration on looking behind me.

10

Send help

WHAT DID I just see . . . What just happened . . . I continue running down the street, getting further and further away from the house. The sight. The horror. My grandmother, faceless. I never would have expected to see her like that.

What the hell are these faceless things . . . I don't want any part of them. These things are terrible, insidious people. Why do they keep bothering me? Why won't they leave me alone? I just found out about my grandmother's death, and they stand there, mocking me.

As my adrenaline subsides, I become reminded of the terrible pain in my leg all at once, and I instantly fall to the asphalt street. I prop myself up with my elbows and soak in as much of the pain in my body as I can. Everything about me aches. I just want to find somewhere to rest, but I don't think I'll find it in one of these houses, because I honestly don't know what I'll find in them.

I push myself back up and begin limping my way to downtown Westwood. There's a hotel in the city limits that I could stay at. But as I plan for the night, I realize that I haven't eaten for two days. Yet, I'm not even remotely hungry, or thirsty, for that matter. However, I convince myself that it's not healthy if I go without eating or drinking anything, and that I should find somewhere that I can not only rest, but find something to eat and drink. Where could I . . . I could go to the giant super store, Stevenson's. It has everything I would ever need for the night— ranging from food, to clothes, to something to sleep on.

Stevenson's is a little while ahead, but I should get there before it gets dark. I try to keep my mind free of any thoughts as I painstakingly limp into the city limits.

As I silently make my way into downtown Westwood, I become awed by the sight of the stores and buildings that are demolished. Of course, this isn't the first time I've seen them, but me being in a completely different condition brings a completely different perspective.

I look over at Rochester's, the burger joint that marked the beginning of the city limits. Hard to think that my friends and I sat in there just a few days ago. Or was it a few weeks?

I pass by a few more buildings, most of which have shattered windows or items scattered around them. Right now, I'm to the point where I no longer care about what happened here.

I reach in my back pocket and pull the journal out. Along with the thirty numbers is the list of questions I had, counting up to ten.

I chuckle to myself. I find it foolish that at one point I thought that the questions I would have would be able to fit on a piece of paper. I have so many questions that I've stopped caring for half of them.

I pass by Retro's, the motorcycle shop I stopped at yesterday, and can see Stevenson's just around the corner. I speed my pace up a little, and I'm somewhat relieved that my leg is slightly becoming more resilient the more I walk on it. I should be good to go tomorrow. Even if I'm not, I'm just going to have to get over it.

As I enter the parking lot of the humongous superstore, I notice that the same amount of chaos that has run through the city didn't seem to stop here. Cars are parked in different positions across the entire lot. There's actually an upside-down van close to me. To my right, a truck had crashed into a pole, and I can see a body hanging out the windshield.

I remind myself that I'm not here to explore. I'm not here to wonder, either. I'm here to get some rest and food. I ignore the diffused jumble of vehicles and head to the entrance of the building.

I look at the giant letters that formed the word "Stevenson's" directly above the entrance. The letters used to be lit up, but the lights in them had gone out a long time ago. But it's not the blocked words that grab my attention, it's the letters that are added to the end of the word.

The same familiar red letters I've seen before follow after the final "s" in the store name. The red letters combine with the "s" to spell out the words "send help", with the "p" halfway finished.

On the ground below the red letters are a scattered group of eight wooden crates. In the midst of the boxes lies a face-down body, with his hands tucked under his stomach as if he had tried to catch himself while falling.

I flinch at the sight of the body, not wanting anything to do with it, but I can't help but take a quick glimpse as I walk past it.

But as the man floats on top of his dried pool of blood, I decide that I've seen enough.

The doors in front of me are shut, but the glass has long been taken out, so I simply step through.

The first thing I see are the cash registers, which have been ransacked of nearly every dollar bill, with a few bills lying on the floor. My first reaction is to pick up the money, but it no longer has value.

The lights of the store are barely working. Only a few shine brightly. Most of them are very dim or out altogether. However, in the back right corner, I notice that the lights in that section have gone out completely, and there isn't a single light shining in that one specific area. That pretty much means that I am not going in that section, since I absolutely hate the dark.

I make my way to the food aisles, which are a complete mess.

Most of the food has been scavenged, and there are only a few boxes and cans of food on the floor. The shelves have been torn down, and many of the aisles are too trashed to walk down.

I stroll down one that I finally find suitable and begin searching for all kinds of food. I find a case of bottled water, rip the sack open, and pull two bottles out. I yank the lid off of one of the bottles and gulp it down in about five seconds. Wow, I guess I was much thirstier than I had thought.

I continue down the aisle, taking sips of the second water bottle as I do so. I grab a bag of chips from the shelf, quickly tear the bag open, and stuff my mouth. As soon as they hit my tongue, though, I spit them out. They're stale. They've been sitting there for a long time.

I'm really worried about how long I actually have been asleep. Might have been more than a few weeks. And if that's true, it may be harder than I thought to find edible food.

I come across a few cans of pickles. Perfect. I unscrew the lid and chomp down on the baby dills. Finally. The taste of food finally hitting my stomach satisfies a need that hasn't been all that existent.

Finally realizing how hungry I actually am, I sit down on the cold tiles and eat a full can of the pickles. After about ten minutes, I start to get tired of them, but I'm far too exhausted to go looking for any other foods, so I continue chewing on them until I finish a second jar.

After about twenty minutes, I'm full. Either that or just sick of the same taste. Nonetheless, I get up and start to go look for something I can sleep on. The furniture section is in the back, so I'm sure there will be something for me to sleep on back there.

I walk towards the back of the store, my stomach turning from stuffing down too many pickles. I walk past the electronics section, wondering if any of the TVs or DVD players still work.

I reach the furniture section, relieved to see that there are still couches left and that they hadn't been ripped to shreds. The dark corner is just a few yards away, but I try to not get worried about that. I approach one of the leather couches and throw myself down on it. Man, it's been a long day.

I close my eyes and run over the schedule for tomorrow. When I wake up, I'll go back to the wall and hop over it. Then, I'll try to find the nearest car I can and drive to Roaksville. Or maybe I should get a motorcycle from Retro's? I know my first experience wasn't good, but I could just push it through the smoke instead of having to find a car to drive. I might do that.

Roaksville is about forty miles away, so I'm not in any rush to leave. I can easily get there at about or before noon, so I can take my time tomorrow morning. I might even find something to eat for breakfast in the store before I go.

Ew. The thought of food sickens me now. I can't believe I—

I hear a loud thud come from the darkened area. Did . . . did I hear right? What was that? My first thought is that it's another faceless coming to ruin my life again, but this time may be differently. Could it be . . . somebody?

"H-hello?" I call out to the darkness. Not really sure if I want to hear a response or not. After a few moments of silence, I decide that there isn't anyone there. Or, that is, nobody who wants me to know that they are there.

I stand up from the couch and begin tip-toeing that way. I slowly approach the edge of the light, with a clear division between the lighted sections and the darkened one. It's really staggering at how much of a difference just a few overhead lights can make.

I debate whether I want to explore the darkness or not, and figure that if I do go in there, I should at least have a little light with me.

I step back and look around for a flashlight. I walk down multiple aisles and finally find one lying in the middle of the row. As

I unwillingly reach down to pick the flashlight up, I hear another identical thud coming from the same corner of the store. As much as I don't want to admit it, there's only one way to find out what's making that noise, and I'm not totally thrilled with the solution.

I go back to the line between the darkened shadows and the light. I push the button to turn the flashlight on, and shine it into the midst of the shadows.

This area was the Auto area. I know because this was my second home; again, I can't stress enough how much of a piece of crap my truck is. No telling how many times I've visited this part of the store.

Somehow, I find enough courage to take a step into the darkness. As I do, I wave the light around, hoping to find whatever it was causing those thuds before it finds me.

I walk a few steps deeper, spinning around to try to find the source of these noises. As soon as I turn completely, I hear another sound.

Thud.

The sound is extremely close to me, just an aisle over. I become too scared of what it might be, so I turn to leave the dark area. Maybe I can convince myself again that I'm just imagining something–in this case, sounds. But as I walk to the end of the aisle I'm at and turn the corner . . .

I get a glimpse of the object just for a second. Another faceless person. Draped in a tattered, black cloak.

And as he registers in my mind, I drop my flashlight out of fright, leaving me unprotected from my nightmare.

11

Let's go

I FRANTICALLY BEND down to pick the light back up. I grasp the handle and swing it where the person just stood. He's not there. Where . . . where did he . . .?

I spin around, dragging the light across the room as I do so. Where did he go? He was here just a second ago. He couldn't have . . . did he . . .?

I can't take it. I'm too vulnerable right now. I frantically turn back towards the lighted area and break that way. I knock over a tall stack of tires on my way, but I recover quickly and sprint to somewhere that I can actually see.

I dive out from the dark border as if he were chasing me and his boundaries were the darkness. I turn on my backside and slide away from the shadows, facing them as I do. He's going to jump out any minute. I know it. I've got to be prepared.

I make sure the light is planted firmly in my hand, in case I have to use it as a weapon if he jumps out.

I sit there, anxiously waiting for the faceless man to leap at me at any moment. I know he's going to, I know it.

The seconds slowly morph into minutes, strengthening my anticipation that is met only by silence. I'm tired of these damn faceless things popping up every time I turn a corner. I don't even know what their supposed to be or why the hell I keep seeing them.

I suddenly hear the same noise as earlier. A single, loud thud returns, and I begin to internally panic. He's still in there. And I really don't want to go back in and find him.

I shine the light in the dark area, hoping to spot something uncanny, but I don't. I click the flashlight off and slide back a few more feet.

I hear another thud, and this time, it is followed by another noise. The second noise sounds similar to something being slid across the floor, and it sounds like it's heading in my direction.

I grab the flashlight and bring it to a position to swing at a body. As I do so, I see something barely creep out from the shadows. It's a small box, no bigger than a cereal box, being pushed into the light. I shift myself away from the box, not knowing what is going to be on the other end pushing it.

The box makes its way into full view, but I don't see anything pushing it. Maybe the guy just slid it into the light so he can remain hidden?

I stand up and walk towards the box and become surprised to see it start sliding my way again, like it was moving itself.

Before I can even question why this box is moving on its own, I see something poke out from around the corner of the box and focus my attention to it.

I spot long whiskers before I can make out the culprit, and once it comes into full view, I'm left puzzled. It's a rat.

A rat, huh? All by myself, in a deserted town, I am accompanied only by a pack of wolves, a group of faceless people, and a rat? This is the first animal I've seen since the wolves, so I wonder what makes this little guy so special.

So this rat is what I've been afraid of this whole time? I laugh at the thought of the rat being some kind of feared creature, but the fact that the faceless man is still in the dark area still pesters the back of my mind.

I reach out for the rat and beckon for it to come to me. I don't really consider the consequences, since this thing might be infested with all sorts of diseases, but I don't care. I'm just relieved to find something else that is in the same shoes I'm in.

The rat, having noticed me for the first time, quickly hides back behind the box is was pushing. It, too, must be scared to see some-one else in this city. I tip-toe over to the box, looking at the rat from above. It's nervously shaking, and quickly notices my giant presence after only a few seconds.

I give the rat a smile. Yes, because that is what's going to con-vince the rat that I'm an alright guy. I squat back down and hold my hand out again. This time, the rat slowly makes its way to it and sniffs my fingertips. I guess judging me by what my hands smell like is how this rat works, because it decides to slowly make its way into my palm. I delicately lift the rat, as I can tell it is still scared of me.

Thud. No. No way. Another thud from the dark area. I thought the rat was making that thud noise? What could have made that one?

My heart races, and as the rat in my hand starts sniffing my palm, I grab the flashlight with my open hand. Staring into the darkness, I await the faceless man, who, again, doesn't come out.

I hear a very low *squeeeak* and spot another rat running towards me.

Another one? Good lord, how many rats are there? The rat I'm holding starts chirping loudly, excited to see its friend.

I squat down and open my palm for the rat I'm holding to jump from my hand and embrace the other rat, but it doesn't. It sits there and waits for the new rat to come to it. To my surprise, the other rat trots over and happily jumps into my hand, much less considerate than the other rat.

I'm actually ecstatic to have finally found some living creatures that aren't either trying to eat me or scaring the living crap out of me. I'm happy to be able to take my mind off of being so lonely, even if these rats are only going to be here for the night. And they're starting to warm up to me, too. The timid rat is now vigorously scratching at my palm like he was digging in the ground, and its friend observes it like it is the most entertaining thing to ever happen.

I walk back to the couch, holding the two rats in my hands. They're full of energy, perhaps too much energy. They need to chill out before they burrow a hole in my hand.

I lay the rats on the floor and fall on the couch. Once my back hits the soft cushions, the rats jump up on the couch with me and curl up on my chest. The accompanied feeling from their tiny feet hopping on my chest brings a huge smile to my face, and I genuinely feel happy for a brief moment. I guess since these rats are stuck with me, the least I could do is name them.

It's quite difficult to tell the two apart, but as I study them, I notice something very familiar with the two rats' tails. Both of the rats have purple tails. The same tint of purple that's in my eyes, and the same tint of purple that is covered on the wolves.

A part of me wants to be surprised, but I'm not really at all. If the purple color in all of us comes from the green gas in the wall like I'm guessing, then that means these two must have went through the gas somehow. How they made it to the gas and back to Stevenson's in the one day that the gas has been exposed, beats me, but I'm not going to worry about that or the purple tails at all.

I should find some way to differentiate the two rats. I look around for something that could help me out. In the floor, I find a small, red piece of thread that will work.

I reach over and pick the string up. I grab one of the rats and, after checking to see if it's a female, tie the red thread around her neck.

You can be Scar. It's perfect.

Scar gladly accepts the thread, nestling her whiskers against her miniature scarf. Now that I have something to tell the two apart, I just need a name for the other rat, which happens to be male. Hmmm. . . how about. . . Scat. Scat, the rat. Sounds catchy.

I lean my head back and close my eyes. Oh, how eager I am for tomorrow. How ready I am to get out of this hellhole of a city. I guess I should take these rats with me. No sense leaving them behind.

With satisfaction crossing my mind, I drift off . . .

I feel a push on my shoulder, and I open my eyes to the sight of a hooded figure standing above me. I lie completely still for a second, in utter shock. What is going on? Who is this? The hood casts a shadow that hides the face of the person, and I can only assume that this must be the faceless man I saw in the auto area, and now he has come out to get me. I shuffle in my couch in an attempt to get away from the figure, but there's no escape for me this time.

What do I do? I go to speak, but my mouth is too dry to make words. The person raises its arm towards me, but instead of reaching back to hit me like I expect, he stretches out his hand for me to grab. I remain still, inspecting the hand before I grab it. This can't be the faceless man I saw earlier, as this person has pink fingernails. Still a very likely chance that she is still a faceless, but just not the same one I saw earlier. She seems much more welcoming than the others I've seen.

I reach out my hand to grab hers. Why? I don't know, but I do it.

The woman pulls me off the couch and leads me down a hall. What is she about to do? I can't help but wonder if she is going to hurt me or not. I'm too afraid to ask her anything. Even if I weren't, what would I ask her?

As the rush of questions swim through my head, one slips out.

"Who are you?" I ask in a frightened, stale voice. She ignores me and continues facing straight ahead as she escorts me further down the store. Honestly other than her fingernails, she is showing no sign whatsoever that she is a woman. Instead, she resembles more of just a figure. No emotions. No features to looks at. Just a hooded being. If I could see her face, or lack of one, or just hear her voice, that would help me out a lot. Even if she is a faceless, she has to have hair, just let me see that. Something other than those hideous, misleading pink fingernails.

"Please. Please answer me," I insist. I don't really want an answer, I just want her to say something. The longer we walk in silence, the more fear that fills me. "Tell me something."

She stops walking and turns my way. Out of the darkness from under her hood, I see a smile. A beautiful smile, perfectly white teeth glowing from the darkness of her outfit. A pleasant smile. A disturbing smile. All in one.

But a smile nonetheless. That means this woman isn't a faceless. She's a living, normal human, just like me.

She doesn't speak a word and continues leading me down the hall. I don't know where she's taking me, yet I'm still following her. I can't help but feel excited at the fact that she isn't a faceless, but that doesn't mean I should trust her. She's being extremely shady, which leaves me awkwardly ambiguous as I follow her. Suddenly, she takes a sharp left turn and leads me down a random aisle.

At the end of the aisle, she turns again and takes us to a door. She opens it and signals for me to go first. I don't know what convinces me to do it, but I go first, and she is right behind me.

The night air entering my lungs signifies that we are now outside. She takes the front again and leads us to the back of the store. Once there, she points to a ladder. I'm guessing she wants me to climb up the ladder first. Every inch in my body is telling me not to climb the ladder; yet, I still do it.

I step my foot on the top of the roof. Once she reaches the top, she grabs my hand and takes me across the surface.

I still have no clue what she is trying to accomplish. There's nowhere else to go. Is she going to kill me? I try to think positively.

Maybe she is escorting me for a rescue mission. I'm ready for her to flip her hood back and tell me what her intentions are. But even I know that that isn't happening, and I continue following her.

I look across the roof, with dozens of air conditioning units and pipes extending from it, and notice that we are walking straight to the edge of the building. No, I know what she's going to do. She's going to throw me off. There's no way I would survive this drop.

I try to jerk my hand away, but her grip enables me from doing so. Should I try to fight her off? No. There's something telling me to just go with it. Go with her.

With my mind racing with what will happen next, we approach the edge. I look down. We are high up, but the longer I stare down, the ground below us seems to drift further and further away. Absolutely no way I would survive if she pushed me. But as disapproving I am of death right now, I can't prompt myself to back away from the ledge.

I look across the ground beneath me. The parking lot that I walked over just a few hours ago is now looking as if it will be my cemetery.

I've come to the acceptance that she is going to push me off, so I prepare myself for it. I don't run off. I don't try to fight her. I prepare for it, but it doesn't happen. We've been standing here a good minute, but she hasn't done anything yet. I look over to her and see that she, too, is scanning the parking lot just as I was.

She turns her head to me and gives another smile that serves as the only facial feature I can see. I don't think I've ever seen such an admiring smile. But then again, I don't think I've ever seen one frighten me this much.

The smile slowly forms into words, and I hear a soft voice exit her lips.

"Let's go."

That's all she says. She clings tightly to my forearm and takes a very small step forward so her toes are hanging off the side.

I don't know what it was that persuades me. Maybe it is her concealed smile. Maybe it is her allaying voice that conveys me with just two little words. But whatever it is, it leads me to mimic her step, and my toes are also dangling from the roof.

I am literally inches from my death.

Without looking back at me, without saying another word, she takes one more step that plummets her downwards. With me in her grasp, I follow her to our deaths. I look down at the concrete walkway right below me as it progresses towards me faster and faster. Nothing I can do now. I had a chance to save myself; yet, I chose this fate.

And as that final thought enters my brain, I close my eyes and prepare for the impact that I won't even feel.

Except for I feel it. Right on the side of my head.

I open my eyes, and I'm lying on the floor, right next to the couch. I must have just fallen off. It was all a dream. Again.

12

The wolves

I SIT ON the cold, hard floor for a few minutes, taking in the dream I just awoke from. I feel the two rats at my feet, poking their noses at my heels. I know what happened in my dream, but I don't want to say it. I don't want to admit what I dreamt about. But, I mean, it's just a dream, right?

No. Wrong. This is more than just a dream. This is my step into insanity.

I'm losing it. No, I've already lost it. I've got to get out of here.

I can't stay in this store anymore. I can't take the risk of me losing control of myself. I've got to leave, and it's got to be right now.

I stand up, grab the two rats at my feet, and run to the front of the store. Roaksville. Right now, that's my only objective. I'm going to get past this wall. I'm going to find some way to get out of this town. I'm going to find everyone. And it's going to happen now.

I run through the broken door that marks the entrance. The sky is still pitch black. I have no clue what time it is, but I have other priorities right now. I pause for a moment to think, then begin to head towards Retro's. I could take a car, but that means I would have to drive through the hole in the wall, and I don't know if the green gas would knock me out. On a motorcycle, I could just push it through the green gas and then crawl over the wall. That's my best plan, so

I'm going with that.

I don't even acknowledge the pain in my leg anymore. I ignore it. Actually, I don't even know whether or not it is there. I'm not worried about it. I'm only worried about myself at the moment.

But why should I be? It was just a dream. I can't control it. I would never even consider jumping off a building, so why is it bothering me?

Maybe I'm overreacting. I hope I am.

I approach Retro's and grab the closest bike I can get my hands on. Luckily for me, the keys are sitting in the seat. I put the keys in the ignition and crank it up, but before I do, I decide I should find a helmet before I find a way to burn the other side of my face. I walk over to the rack of helmets, find one of my size, and then head back to the cranked up motorcycle, flip the headlight on, and head off. Since my hands are on the handlebars, I put the rats in my pockets.

I drive through the city and down my road. I notice all the obstacles in the street and make sure to avoid them. Last thing I need is another wreck.

After a few minutes driving through the chilly air, I finally reach the wall. I push the motorcycle through the hole and watch as it loses its balance and falls on the outside of the wall.

I walk over to the stairs of boxes I assembled yesterday and climb up them. Once I reach the top, I stand up and turn around to face Westwood. This might be my last look of the city. But surprisingly, I'm not as emotionally affected as I thought, and I hop down from the wall and land safely on the other side, trying to refrain from landing too hard on my injured leg.

Here I go. I walk over to my motorcycle that's lying flat on the ground. I try my best to ignore the bodies that I saw last time here, but I can't help but to glance.

I stand the bike up and jump on it. I know how to get to Roaksville, I'm just not sure what awaits me between here and there.

The further down the road I drive, the less bodies I see. There is still an occasional one here and there, but not as many as there were closer to the city.

My mind is clear with an emptiness that I'm not used to. And it's quite enjoyable, too. Nothing but the sound of the wind passing over my shoulders is present, and for a second, I forgot what wind even sounded like.

However, my moment is short-lived. Ahead of me, just close enough for the edge off the motorcycle's headlight to catch, I see a figure walking across the street.

I'm not even going to worry about it. I need to try my best to ignore those faceless people. As I continue down the road, I hear a noise. A few long, low howls break out from the woods next to me, reminding me of the wolves that I had completely forgotten about. The howls are far off, but they tell me that I shouldn't waste time, especially on anything without a face.

I continue riding down the highway with the wall to my side. Is this wall ever going to end? As I become annoyed by the seemingly never-ending wall, the howls become more frequent. I can't decide if they are getting closer or further away, but I don't want to find out. I just need to worry about getting out of—

There's another one. A person standing on the side of the road close to the wall. This one seemed to have popped up right as I passed by it, barely giving me any time to notice it. Just ignore them, I remind myself out loud, hoping that hearing my own voice will calm me down.

Another. In blue jeans and a green button-up shirt, another faceless man stands, stationery, on the edge of the asphalt road with the trees behind him. My heart drops, but I remind myself to ignore them. But damn, it's like they know I'm trying to ignore them and they just keep getting closer and closer to me.

A faceless woman, standing on the opposite side of the road with her back to the wall, is wearing a wedding dress. I look away from her and try to focus my attention on the road, but I can't. I see her take a step forward, trying to meet me in the road.

I speed up and drive past her, my short, heavy breaths fogging up the visor in the helmet. Two more figures in front of me, one on each side of the road. Except for taking a step, however, they immediately start sprinting towards the center of the road.

No way I'm going to miss them. I swerve off the road to keep from running into them. It takes a few seconds, but I regain control and direct the bike back on the road. I can't stop. I can't let them get me.

Ahead of me, more and more faceless people wait for me, standing on the side of the road at first, then running out at me, trying to crash into me. I veer away from them the best I can, but as I pass by, it seems like another wave of faceless people wait for me, until both sides of the road are entirely filled up.

Once both sides of the road are filled with faceless figures, they stop running out in front of me. It's like they're watching a parade, and I'm the main attraction. Instead, they begin to reach their arms out at me. I keep my eyes fixated on the middle of the road, trying the best I can to not let them touch me.

The lines the faceless people make up gradually funnel inward, making a lane that shrinks the further down I drive. I'm within arm's reach now. As the lane grows narrower, their arms retract, purposely avoiding me. Why aren't they grabbing out for me anymore?

As the lane continues getting smaller, their arms fall back to their side, and they are all uncomfortably close to me, merely inches from my motorcycle as I speed by them. If I swerve just a little bit, I will definitely run over them. As mysteriously calm as they are, I'm still very cautious and anticipate for one of the figures to grab and throw me off the motorcycle.

I speed through, preparing myself for something to happen, but none of them move. The lane eventually ends, and the alley of face-less people subsides into nothing.

I don't see any more figures. No more people. I guess I made it out alive. Although relieved, I try to shake off what just happened, try to throw it out of my mind, but it's now permanently etched there. I return my focus to the middle of the road. I can't even hear the en-gine of the motorcycle anymore, as the rushing adrenaline causes a loud *thumping* to explode in my ears that eventually subsides, leaving the sound of nothing. Dark and silence. My two most hated things.

I'm barely able to catch a glimpse of the blur that lunges at me from the corner of my eye. Out of the darkness, a figure jumps out at me, crashing square into my chest. The force knocks me off the bike and sends me hurling into the ground. I land on the right side of my body, with my arm and ribs taking the impact. The ground jams my elbow into my ribs, knocking the breath clean out of me.

I lay in agony, moaning for help that I know won't come. Luckily, I landed on my right side, and I can feel my two rats squirming around safely in my left pocket. I quickly disregard my injuries and remember the person who I can only assume is faceless that jumped at me and expect it to come at me again. I frantically reach in my pocket to grab my hammer before it comes back.

As I lie on my back in complete darkness, I realize what I just got into. If this faceless person is going to come for me, the whole faceless army will, as well. I'm not going to be able to defend myself. I need to retreat, either find somewhere to hide or get back on the bike.

As I go to stand up, I feel a brute strength vigorously knock me back down. I drop the hammer in the impact but start swinging my fists at whatever this being is.

It wasn't a faceless person. It was a wolf. I feel its damp breath on my neck, and jerk back as it stabs its claws into my shoulder.

Letting out a shriek of pain, I'm able to throw the beast off of me. I feel around for the hammer and find it right as it jumps on me a second time.

The wolf gives a swift swipe across my chest, and my flesh rips as I hear a small snap. Oh god. What did I break? As I hold on to the wolf's paws, I wait for a surge of pain to signify me breaking something, but it never comes.

As the wolf and I are locked in a stalemate, I hear more howls inching nearer. I can't take on more than one of these. I've got to get out.

I build up all my power to throw the beast off of me, and I send it a few feet backwards. As it gathers itself, I swing the hammer at the wolf's skull, and hear a loud *crack* sound to assure that I hit my mark.

I take no time to relax, as I know that I have to find somewhere to hide. I feel my way through the shadows until I find the wolf, pulling the hammer out of its temple. I get back on the road and run down it until I find a house only about a hundred yards away. The howls grow louder and louder as they sound like they are biting at my heels, but I can't look back. I know I can't take another stumble, I'm in enough pain as it is.

As I near closer to the house, I feel as if I'm drifting away from it. A fence surrounds the house, so as soon as I reach it, I jump over it. I land back on my right side, and as the pain restitutes, I grit my teeth and hurry to my feet.

I hear the fence being rattled right behind me, and I know that the wolves have leaped the fence with no problem. I reach the door and pull the handle.

Locked.

Please, no. I look back at the wolves for the first time, and see that there are three of them dangerously close. I don't have time to kick the door in, I just have to find another way in.

Two of the wolves pounce at me, but I dodge them and run towards a window that's a few feet over. The two wolves slam against the door and fall to the ground.

I smash the window with my hammer and throw it in first before I crawl in. Before I get all the way in the window, I feel a tug on my left leg. The third wolf has a hold of my jeans leg.

I pull, but to no avail. I quickly undo my belt, but as soon as the wolf pulls my jeans off, it bites on my ankle.

I feel its teeth break my skin as my blood saturates its nostrils. The hammer is out of my reach, and I can't get my hands on any-thing I can throw at it. I look around in severe need of anything that will help me.

Bingo.

I throw my leg into the side of the windowpane, bringing the wolf into it with me. I can feel my flesh rip as I slam my leg against it, but continue the action again. I crawl back a little, just enough for the wolf to get its head in the room. I kick the windowpane again. As the wolf growls at my struggles, I see the large fragment of glass dangling above it shake. I knock the wolf back into the pane again and again until the giant shard loses its hold and descends into the beast's neck. The wolf gives one last whimper and finally loses its hold on my leg.

I sit up and throw the wolf off my leg. As I do so, I notice a collar around its neck, with a dog bone keychain hanging from the center of it. We're these wolves trained? Is somebody out here domesticat-ing wolves? Or maybe these aren't wolves at all. These could just be deranged dogs that were once pets.

I push the wolf outside and hurry to cover up the window before the other two follow. Right by the window is a bookshelf. I crawl beside the bookshelf and push it in front of the window. As soon as it covers the opening, I feel the two wolves jump, nearly knocking over the shelf. This isn't going to provide much protection, but if they make it in the room, I can at least lock the wolves in this room. I get up and run out of the room, locking the door behind me.

Finally, safety. I take the motorcycle helmet off and look around to see that I'm in a hall. I just need to find a bathroom so I can clean myself up. And some pants. Pants would be nice.

Then it suddenly hits me. The rats were in my pocket, and my pants are in that room. I've got to get those rats out before the wolves get them.

I fidget with the doorknob and swing it open. My pants are lying right at the base of the bookshelf, which is about to fall over. I rush to grab the pants while the bookshelf tips over immediately after.

The two wolves stroll in through the opening, eyeing me up and down. I step back to exit the room, but as I get to the door, the wolves jump on the counter right next to the window. What are they doing? It takes me a moment to realize, but I see the two rats sitting on a medicine cabinet above the counter.

I can't let these wolves get my rats, they are the only company I have. As the wolves are distracted by the rats, I grab the hammer at my feet and run up to them. I land the head of the hammer into the skull of one of the wolves, but the other one immediately leaps at me as soon as I do.

I don't have enough time to swing the hammer at it, so I use the only other thing in my hand to fight it off: my pants. I hold the pants up to shield my face, and the beast latches its jaws into them, pulling them back like a slingshot. I tug at the jeans and the dog tugs back, as if we were playing a game. It's not going to let go of these pants until I give it to him, but that's not what I want. I have this thing right where I want it.

A combination of foam and drool drips from its mouth and lands on my forehead. Its collar is barely visible through it's thick, purple fur, and its nametag flaunts itself above my face. With my arms spread out on both sides of the animal, I rotate my arms in a swift clockwise motion, similar to if I was jerking the wheel of a car. When I do so, I hear a snap, and the beast falls to the ground.

Well, that was brutal, but it worked. I grab the rats and walk out of the room.

I look down at the two rodents in my arms, both of them shaking from fright. I can't lose these rats again, that was too close. I have to protect them.

I walk down the hall until I find a bathroom. I walk in and flip the lights on. I then place the rats on the counter and watch as they curl up together. I immediately wash my face and look at myself in the mirrow. A giant claw mark is imbedded in my left shoulder, my right elbow is scratched up, and my shirt is ripped across. I pull my shirt over my head and discover what the snapping noise I heard earlier was. It wasn't the sound of a breaking bone; it was the sound of my necklace breaking. And sticking out of my chest is the shark tooth. Not sure if I'm lucky or the complete opposite for getting the shark tooth lodged into me, but nonetheless, I'm glad I didn't lose it. I pluck the shark tooth from my chest and place it on the counter. The rats sniff it and start gnawing on it.

I then remember the collars around the necks of the wolves, suggesting that they were either trained or were once tamed dogs. If somebody is out there training wolves and giving them collars, then that at least tells me that there is somebody out there. If they used to be pets, then why have they grown so large, and why are they so savage?

I really need to find some more clothes, so I exit the bathroom and look for some.

I find a pair of jeans and a purple long sleeve shirt in the main bedroom. It seems the owner of the house was some single rich dude. Oh well, I'm not complaining. Maybe he will have a nice car that I can borrow.

I grab the shark tooth and shove it in my pocket. I then pick up my rats and the hammer and search for the garage. I eventually find it, and become amazed at what I see.

A sharp, yellow Corvette sits low to the ground, calling for me to drive it. I run up to it and yank the handle, eager to sit in this beauty. Leather seats, tinted windows, everything about this car is magnificent. The keys lay in the passenger seat, so I throw my belongings in the back and crank it up.

Brmmmm. The entire car shakes as a smile spreads across my face. I press for the garage door to open, put the car in drive, and speed off.

The sound of the engine as I press harder on the pedal nearly distracts me from where I'm going. I remind myself that I don't have time to play around, and that I need to get to Roaksville.

I speed down the main highway as the sun creeps above the horizon, marking the beginning of a new day. Day 3. Three days in solitude, and now that solitude is coming to an end.

I notice that the houses on the side of the road look just as damaged as the ones inside of Westwood. However, the streets are much more clear; less random furniture scattered across it and not a single dead body out here. Oh wait, nevermind, I spoke too soon. One dead body.

It's very strange, though. As I pass by these houses, I notice that the houses that don't have a car outside of them aren't as damaged as the houses that do have one. The only explanation I can think of is that the people who turned crazy, much like Mrs. Armstrong had, didn't get a chance to drive away and instead elected to stay back and destroy their neighborhood. The people who didn't go crazy got out while they could.

I reach down to the radio, which is spitting out loud static. I carefully skim through each channel on FM radio, hoping to find a signal somewhere. Nothing, all static. I turn it to AM radio, but I'm met by the same fate. There are no radio stations anywhere that are working, and that legitimately worries me. What if Roaksville is empty? What if everywhere in Mississippi is empty? I frenziedly turn the radio knob, needing to hear anything but static. Anything.

I give up and turn the radio off. Don't think negatively. There's bound to be a reason why the radio stations aren't picking up. Maybe this guy doesn't have a radio antenna. Maybe the radio just doesn't work, or maybe his speakers are distorted. There's some reason, I just can't think of it right now.

There's people in Roaksville, I know it. Just because the signals from the radio stations in Roaksville aren't picking up doesn't mean that nobody is there. They have much more important things to worry about then radio. I know there is going to be people there.

I let my mind drift about what's to come when I reach Roaksville. How many people I will find, and how they will react to me. I mean, they have to be past the point of finding survivors. Just imagine me pulling up in the city. Dad will run up to me, and I'll cry on his shoulder. All my friends will be relieved to have me back. And Scarlett. The one person I can't get off my mind. I'll have to tell her how I feel. Something I should've done a long time ago.

But then, what will we do? Go looking for more people? I saw the helicopter, and it seemed to had been heading to Roaksville. There's bound to be more people out there, somewhere.

I continue driving for what feels like half an hour. I should have at least seen the Roaksville sign by now, especially with as fast as I'm going. Did I miss it? No, there's no way I could miss it. Am I lost? I might be.

As soon as I begin to worry, I see the sign on top of the massive hill in the distance. I take the turn and drive towards it.

Well, at least there isn't a wall around Roaksville—not one I can see yet, anyway. I drive up the rather large hill that marks the beginning of Roaksville. The city rests in the dip of the hill, so there may be a wall waiting on the other side. As I pass by the city's sign, my heart begins racing. Here it goes. My first step to getting out of this torment starts here. Well, maybe not out of it completely, but at least—

Wait a second. I slam on the brakes and put the car in reverse. I back up enough to read the sign.

Welcome to Roaksville

Where we

AREN'T GOOD ENOUGH TO LIVE

13

Roaksville

BIG, BOLD LETTERS written in red paint mark over the words "Give Our Love to Those Who Give It Back".

My mind switches from anticipation to apprehension as the sign's vague meaning begins to scare me, even though deep down I do know what it means. It's saying that there are dead people in here, but that doesn't mean that there aren't any living people either.

I continue to drive up the hill until I reach the top. I then stop and gaze out over the city, which is mainly made up of houses, as all the buildings await me down the hill and further in the city. I can see a park in the middle of the city, but what catches my attention about it the most is a huge dirt mound that I can see even from here. Interested, I mark that as my destination.

Not a soul to be seen. Yet, anyway. I drive down the hill, slow enough to investigate the place.

The houses catch my attention immediately. Every house looks just like the houses in Westwood: damaged and wrecked. But these houses have something that the others don't. Every house contains a red message written over it, just like the sign did.

I read every message as I drive past it, each more gripping than the other. Some are filled with profanity. Others seem like a desperate cry for help.

NO HOPE
MURDERERS
SAVE US
BURN IN HELL
COWARDS

Something terrible happened here. And I . . . I can't help but to feel like these messages are directed towards me. I feel guilty. Guilty? Why should I? I had nothing to do with what had happened here.

I'm reminded of my first dream, where these exact names were thrown at me for what I thought was no reason. Is this the reason? Is the reason the faceless people are here, yelling at me in that dream and following me, because I did this? No, I know I'm not responsible for anything. Maybe they were mad at me because I survived.

I drive down the hill towards the park and pass by the taller buildings, which also hold messages. At the end of the street I'm driving down is a huge, elegant bank, and written across the three marble columns in front of it, in big red letters, is the same word I saw back in Westwood:

ROT

More similarities. Why is everything repeating itself? I continue to drive and see more red warnings the further I go. I avoid to look at the buildings, but as I turn my attention to the billboards extending high in the air, I find that they aren't any better, as each billboard contains one red word that connects with the next billboard behind it.

WASH
YOUR
BLOOD
STAINED
HANDS

I take my eyes off the billboards and focus on reaching the park. These messages . . . I don't know what they mean, but at the same time, I do. They mean that there isn't anybody here. There isn't a welcoming committee waiting for me. There's nothing here. I haven't even seen a dead body anywhere. It's completely deserted, even more than Westwood.

I reach the park and get out of the car. The park looks quite different than I remember it looking, as all the attractions have been torn apart and the suspicious dirt mound definitely is an addition. The benches are demolished, and the slides and swing sets for the kids had been ripped up from their roots and tossed aside. My attention shifts from the swing sets to the center of the park, where a bulletin post has always stood. Usually, the post had all sorts of papers filled with it, from ads to lost-and-founds to special events. I feel like if there is any information about what happened in this city, it would be at the bulletin board. However, when I approach it, I notice that the board is clean except for two pieces of paper.

One paper is a map of the state of Mississippi, while the other is a regular sheet of paper that hangs above the map, which reads:

"Here it is, a list of people not lucky enough to survive. May God have mercy on the killers' souls because we certainly will not."

The map below is filled with black circles, each surrounding a city. I find Westwood. Circled. I find Roaksville. Circled. Actually, every city on the map is circled. I study the map, trying to find a city that's not circled. But there isn't one. Every. Single. City. Circled. There's nobody left.

But me.

The reality hits me like an uppercut to my chin. I slowly back away from the bulletin post. I turn away and run but realize that I'm running away from my car and towards the mound.

I try to turn back towards the car, but I can't. My curiosity has yet again overcome my fear, and I'm too intrigued to know what this mound is and why it's here. Maybe it has something that will give me hope.

I reach the mound, panting. It's about fifteen-foot-tall, and the base expands about fifteen feet. As I inspect the mound, my heart stops when I see something sticking out of the pile.

An arm. A limp arm dangling out from the dirt.

No. This is... I know what this is, but I can't say it. I swiftly turn and begin to scurry towards my car. As I pass by the bulletin board, I notice red words written on the back of the board that I didn't see earlier:

WE ARE THE ABANDONED.

WE ARE ONE.

The abandoned. One. I stumble away from the sign, not being able to believe reality. I feel myself get lightheaded, and I fall over.

Black. Total darkness. I open my eyes to the familiar sepia scene.

I'm lying in the same place I had just fell, except the red words hadn't been written on the back of the bulletin board yet. I stand up and look around until I hear a conversation coming from the bulletin board.

"That gets rid of Lynchton . . . That's a damn shame, I was hoping someone would be there," I see a young man with slicked back, jet black hair, propping himself up against the wooden post with one hand and using the other to slowly stroke his hair backwards. Around the man's mouth is a small, odd-looking mask, with a tube running from it and to a tank that's hooked to the man's back.

"How many does 'at leave us, ten?", a much older man asks him. This man appears to be at least in his sixties, and he, too, has a tiny, funny looking mask, but has long, gray hair that lays over the tubes hooked to his back.

"Eleven," the younger man who appears no older than thirty corrects the other man as he circles the map stapled to the bulletin board. "Down to eleven cities in Mississippi that we haven't checked to see if people are still alive in them. Besides, were not promised a return crew on those eleven, they're at least one or two hundred miles away a piece, most are more."

"Well, Grant, 'eres only one one way to find out. We gotta go check

those cities out, 'eres bound to be somebody in Optland. Gotta be at least one person."

"Yeah, and what if there's not, Phil?", the younger man snaps back. "What do I tell everybody? That yet another major city is circled? Nearly everyone who has left for major cities has yet to come back, and those that do come back are in much worse conditions than when they left. Who do you think is going to volunteer to go on that mission? Leaving this city is a death sentence."

"Well, itsa death sentence 'ere, too, ya know!", the older man known as Phil reassures Grant. "We can't jus' sit 'ere 'n jus' wait to die. We gotta go find somebody, something, and if we die in the process, well that's fine. But we gotta do something. Sittin' here in Roaksville aint doin' nuthin'."

Grant grows speechless, and after a few seconds of silence, he falls to the ground and pushes the tank on his back against the wooden post of the bulletin board.

"I don't know what to do, Phil," Grant says in a defeated voice. "I shouldn't have been put as leader of this city because I don't know what to do. I've honestly lost hope. I lost hope long ago, and crossing out more and more cities is just adding on to it. What am I supposed to tell everybody else? Am I supposed to put on some ruse and play the hero for them? There is no hero this time. There's no happy ending. It's not happening . . ."

"Well, first off," Phil begins as he joins Grant on the ground. "'Eres only seventeen of us left in this 'ere city, so you don't have too many people to upset."

Grant gives a soft smile, and Phil rubs the young man on the shoulder.

"Ya see, you've been a great leader of this city, ya really have. But so many people have died, and I don't think anyone else 'ere has anymore hope left, either."

"So, what are you saying, we're done?", Grant asks the man.

"I ain't sayin' were done. I'm jus' sayin' that we never had a chance. If were bein' real, me n' you both are gonna die any minute from this damned virus, but as long as we fight our way to the end, it'll be okay. It's

not about the outcome, it's about the fight."

This is the first I've heard of what caused this disaster. A virus, huh? The masks they're wearing tells me that the virus must be airborne, which makes me wonder why I have survived so long without a mask.

As the men sit in silence, a woman comes running up to the men. With tears in her eyes, she tries to hold her composure with a straight face as she talks to Grant.

"Grant. He . . . Jim just egotoned," she says with as much strength as she can. "What, what do I do now?" It doesn't even sound like a question, as it seems like she knows the answer already.

"Just leave him," Grant begins, but is interrupted by the woman.

"No! He said that if he egotoned than to kill him! He wanted to die in the closest thing to a sane state of mind that he could get to. I can't let him go out this way."

"Well, were going to have to let him egotone. We're far too low on bullets." Grant is stern with his response, but as he is getting more frustrated, I'm left clueless as to what they're talking about when they say egotone.

"Please, Grant. He didn't want to be like one of them," the woman pleads, tears streaming down her face and on to the mask that covers her mouth.

As Grant remains silent as he thinks over the situation, a loud thud is heard coming from a house a bit away, and a man charges out from the front door. He grabs a chair next to the porch and tosses it into the street. He punches the window next to him and throws the glass into the house behind him.

This must be Jim. This must be what egotone is. And this must be what happened to everyone in Westwood.

The woman begins to trot after what I assume is her husband, but Phil grabs her by the arm before she gets too far.

"Stay away from 'em, Margaret," Phil reminds the woman. "Don't say anythin' to 'em. He's too dangerous. That's ain't Jim anymore, y'know that."

The woman, with tears drowning out her eyes, lightly nods her head.

The man begins yelling from afar, but his words are barely understandable. I can make out a few words, such as betrayed and unloved, but the rest sounds like gibberish.

The man grabs a shard of the window he punched, puts it in his pocket, and climbs on top of the house. When he reaches the roof, he pulls the shard out and slices it across his hand. The man then begins spelling out something, and I'm suddenly aware that all the red paint that covers the city isn't paint.

After several additional cuts across his arms, the man spells out UNFORGIVEN on the roof of the house. The man then lets out a loud cry and dives off the house head first.

A sharp scream comes from the woman as he hits the ground, and as the man remains motionless, she begins sobbing.

"Well," Phil mumbles to himself where only I can hear, "there's another one to add to the mound."

Phil and Grant walk towards the house where the man had just plummeted to his death. Once Phil and Grant reach the man, they grab his feet and drag him towards the park, where they toss his limp body on the very top of the large pile. As they do so, I start to lose my sight again, and I fall over . . .

I wake up, rubbing my scalp as I lay on the frigid ground. I then stand up, thinking back to the flashback I just had. What about Phil or Grant? They may still be here. I don't know how long ago that flashback was, so maybe they're here, somewhere.

"Help!" I yell out. "Phil! Grant! Anybody!"

I wait for about a minute in complete silence. I give one last yell, as loud as I possibly can. If they're here, they would hear me.

I wait for a minute. Nothing. No one. They're gone, too. Everybody is gone. Everybody is in that pile right behind me.

I quickly turn around and snatch the map off the bulletin board. There's got to be a city Phil and Grant didn't check; there has to be.

I desperately scan the map, looking past over a hundred circles in hope that I will find the smallest unmarked city. Come on, just give me one!

Every possible city on the map is circled. The entire map of Mississippi is covered in black circles, almost filling up the entire paper.

Wait a minute. *Almost.* They almost fill the paper, which means that the cities in the surrounding states aren't circled. Alabama, Arkansas, Louisiana. Have they been searched? Are there any survivors there? I don't know, but it's the only bit of hope I have left to grasp on to.

Alabama is the closest state from Roaksville, but to get there, I'll have to drive back through Westwood. With a new destination in my mind, I run back to the car, crank it up, and drive back up the hill and out of Roaksville. The gas level on the dashboard in front of me tells me that I have just enough gas to make it to the Alabama state line, and since Westwood has a gas station, I could fuel up there when I pass through. I don't let the flashback enter my mind, as I don't have time to let it resonate. I have to focus on getting to Alabama and finding a place with somebody out there.

What am I doing, I ask myself out loud? Am I being realistic here? Am I setting myself up for disappointment? What if Alabama is left in the same condition as Mississippi?

This nervous breakdown I've fallen in causes me to sweat, and I turn the air conditioner on full blast hoping that it would soothe me. As I question myself, I hear my rats giving a faint squeak from the back seat. They bustle their way through the crack next to my seat and nestle themselves in each of the cup holders between the driver's seat and passenger's seat. Even though my rats have been stranded with me here, they seem completely happy with their lives. Maybe if I find one person, just one, then that will be enough for me to be happy. I can't be hesitant because of what is, or *isn't,* waiting for me outside this state. I have to be optimistic. Even the smallest chance of finding somebody is still that, a *chance*.

What if another huge mound of bodies awaits me in Alabama? What if other vicious bloody words are painted on everything in Alabama, just like they are here? As bad as I try to make this sound, I also realize that if I do find this there, its nothing new to me. I've seen the blood, deaths, and bodies, there probably isn't much worse I can find. Even if there is worse, what if I do discover it? I can't convince myself that this is a good idea, but I can't think of any better alternatives. This is all I have to strive for.

I continue cruising down Highway 4 until I pass the house where I got this car. The corner edge of the wall of Westwood enters my sight. I never really found out if this wall wraps all the way around the city, so I don't know if it eventually ends, or if it is just one big square. This is crucial information if I plan on driving through Westwood to get to Alabama, as simply going around Westwood would take much more time. If the wall does, in fact, completely surround the city, how would I leave after crossing through Westwood?

I slow down as the green smoke oozing from the wall's opening becomes visible. The gap is big enough for my car, but I'm more worried about if it is possible for me to drive through the gas. The first day when I went through the gas, it knocked me out. What's to say it won't knock me out again? I place my car into position, pointing it directly into the green gas, so all I will have to do is to slam down on the pedal. But, yet again, I begin second guessing myself. I highly doubt that I will make it through the gas without losing consciousness. Besides, the wall probably encases the city completely, so there won't be a way for me to leave once I get in.

I look down at my rats, hoping they can somehow give me the motivation I need. Scar nibbles on her scarf as Scat replies to my looks at him by twitching his whiskers. Well said, Scat. That's what I needed to hear.

I stomp on the gas pedal, holding my breath as the car zooms through the opening. Once I make it through the wall and through the gas, some of the green gas begins pouring into the car through the air conditioning vents. I slam the vents shut as quickly as I can and begin holding my breath for thirty seconds.

As I get further away from the wall, I roll down the windows to replace the green gas with fresh air. I start to breathe again once the green in the air disappears, and I let out a huge gasp for air.

"That was a close one," I tell my rats. "I can't believe I d-didn't think to, think to close the vents. The vents. The . . ."

My mind bluntly slows almost to a complete stop. I'm barely able to realize that the green gas somehow found a way to creep into my system. I can physically feel my body shutting down, so I need to stop before I pass out.

I need to stop, I repeat to myself. I need to stop. My body isn't reacting to my commands. It's at this moment that I realize that the entire bottom half of my body has already succumbed into numbness. This itself is bad, but it becomes even worse as I realize that my foot is not only immobile, but permanently slamming down on the gas pedal.

I tell my arms to move to my leg, hoping that I can just simply pick my right leg up and off the pedal, but the numbness has spread over my right arm completely. Luckily for me, though, the deadening has spread out over all of my left arm except for three fingers, which are what I use to steer the car.

I have to stay awake, I tell myself as my vision see-saws back and forth. I can't pass out now, not going this fast. My eyes move in slow-motion to the speedometer, and as the needle propels itself over the 100 mph mark, I know that I am in trouble.

My left and right eyes take turns in failing as I try my best to avoid obstacles in the road by using only three fingers. As the green gas makes its way up to my chest, I can tell that I'm going to pass out at any second.

My heart rate drops while the speed of the car continues to increase. I can't help but to question why the gas is taking so long to conquer my system. The first time I encountered the gas, it knocked me out in a matter of one or two seconds. The small exposure I had to it must be what's slowing the process down this time, which makes me wish I hadn't done anything about the gas once it flowed through the air vents.

The control I have over my last three fingers eventually fades. With that, the only thing I have control of is taken away from me: the direction of the car. Now, everything is out of my reach. There's nothing I can do but hope that the unavoidable crash will finish me painlessly. No matter what I hit, I'm going fast enough for a fatal crash. This is it.

The car slightly veers of the straight path when it runs over a wooden bookshelf. Now the car is heading straight to the front wall of Stevenson's. As the car enters the parking lot, I realize that my face is my last body part with sensation, as I feel a tear gently roll down my cheek.

"No! Jaden, stop! Please don't!"

What? What was that? Like an alarm clock, my body instantly wakes up, and I slam the brakes before the gas in my system takes my feelings away again. I hear the brakes screech, but they are used a little too late. I do manage to slow myself down considerably, but I still crash into the wall. The air bags thrust into my face, nagging my head against the headrest. The car alarm goes off, smoke immediately rises from the engine, and blood runs down my temple. I open the driver's door and plunge myself onto the asphalt.

"D-Dad?"

14

Tiffany

I WAKE UP with the sun directly in front of me, telling me that I've been out for a few hours. I fight the stiffness in my neck and raise my head up to look around. The car is still smoking, and I can barely hear the car alarm sounding. My ears are ringing very loudly. My head hurts. I reach up to feel it. Blood has dried on my hair and left a small puddle on the ground. I let out a call for my Dad, but I can't even hear myself speak. Dad. He's around here somewhere. I heard him . . .

I go to stand up. My legs are very feeble, so I put my hand on the car for support. Nice car, too bad it's ruined.

I reach for my rats through the open driver's door. I bend down to pick them up, almost falling in the process. I put them in my pockets, where they immediately poke their heads out to see what I'm doing. Luckily, they're completely unharmed. I see the hammer in the floorboard of the backseat and grab it, as it could come in handy later.

Oh wait, Dad. Where is he? I heard him earlier, but where did he go?

I yell out for my dad, but it sounds more like a whisper to me. Did I whisper it? I make sure I scream out my dad's name this time, but all it does is make my head hurt even more. I need to quit yelling.

I need to quit standing. I need to rest somewhere.

But Dad. He's somewhere. Maybe he's inside Stevenson's? No, there's no reason he would be inside. Maybe he's. . . I don't know where else he would be.

I look out from the parking lot and into the city. I see buildings nearby and consider which one he might be at. I see a convenient store. Maybe he needs to get some gas? No, he wouldn't be there. Next to it is an auto repair shop. Maybe he's getting my truck fixed. I'm sure it needs it. The next building I see is a liquor store. He might be there, but he promised me that he would never go back there. But where else would he be?

I walk towards the liquor store, repeating the phrase to myself.

He promised he would never go back. But where else is he?

He promised he would never go back. But where else is he?

He promised he would never go back. But where else is he?

Wait, I know where he is. What day is it? I'm pretty sure it's still October. Mom died in October. He might be at her grave. It might be the 17th. Is it? I don't know, but it might be. I pull the journal out of my pocket to see how many days it's been, but the words in the journal somehow appear blurry. They also appear upside down. Oh well, I'm just going to say that it's the 17th.

I can see the church, which is in a secluded part of town, from where I'm at. I begin walking that way, repeating a different phrase this time as my head rocks back and forth.

Mom died this month. I should check up on her.

Mom died this month. I should check up on her.

Wait, now. I'm not looking for Mom. I'm looking for Dad. Dad. I heard him. Where is he?

I trip over a cash register in the street and fall down. Ow. What's a cash register doing out in the street? Weird.

I get closer to the church and examine it as I walk. It's been a while since I was here. Eleven years ago to be exact. The last time I was here was for Mom's funeral, and ever since then, just looking at the church has made me sad.

I pull the front door open. The inside is really beautiful. The carpet is red, it's always reminded me of red velvet cake. Really pretty. But wait. I'm not going to find Mom in here. She's in the cemetery. I should go there.

I walk through the church's back door and look at the hill that's filled with headstones. Really scary. But Mom is in here somewhere, so I'm safe. Dad might be visiting her, so he might be in here somewhere, too.

I walk up and down the rows of graves, calling for my dad while looking for my last name. Farmer. Fisher. Fordham. There she is. Foxx.

Dad is nowhere to be found, but I'm too overwhelmed by seeing my Mom to care about him anymore. I read the epitaph on the stone:

Here lies
Tiffany Ann White Foxx
A loving wife, mother, daughter, and friend.
Gone, but will never be forgotten.
Born: August 28, 1970 – Died: October 17, 2003
"Fly away, feel free to depart. But a safe place you will stay in our
heart."

I haven't read this saying in so long. It's been forever since I visited Mom. I really feel bad for not having visited her. I'm a terrible son. I really am. I should make it up to her somehow. What could I do? What could I do?

Oh, I know! As I look around the cemetery, a thought comes to mind. I begin to walk around, softly humming to help ease my headache as I grab every single batch of flowers I find. I pick up every bouquet, every basket, every single blossom lying on the surrounding graves and bring it back to Mom. I make sure to ask every grave if I can borrow their flowers, though. I don't want to be rude.

It takes me a while, but I eventually gather all the flowers and place them around Mom. The red flowers I make special, placing them on top of her grave since she loved the color red so much.

I sit down on the ground and place my fingers on Mom's grave, which is so cold. I'm such a bad son. I should have visited her more often.

I pull the rats out of my pockets and place them next to me.

"Scar, Scat. This is my mom."

As if they could understand me, they run up to her headstone and rub their heads on it. I take that as a greeting.

I continue sitting there and strike a conversation with my Mom. I really enjoy my time with my Mom. I haven't talked to her in forever, so I sit and tell her about everything. About school. About my friends. About my crush on Scarlett. About my teachers. About Dad and my grandparents. About her. About life.

And she listens to me until the sun starts setting. The sun sinks lower after every sentence I say. I'm so happy right now, laying down in the bed of flowers, talking to my mom about everything that pops in my head as my rats nibble on my fingertips beside me. I would like to hear my mother respond, but she's tired. It's okay for her to be quiet.

Hours pass. I think I even dozed off for a few minutes. By the time I've shared with her everything I could think of, the sun has faded away completely and left me, my rats, and my mother in the cold darkness. I've always been scared of the dark, but Mom is here to protect me. She's here, she always will be.

"I remember when I was little," I tell Mom, "when I would have nightmares, you would run into my room and sing to me. Sometimes I wouldn't even have nightmares, I would just be scared of the dark, but you would still come in my room and turn the light on and sing to me. Do you remember what you used to sing to me?" I wait for her to reply, but she must not want to talk right now. "I remember. Even today, when I get really scared, I think back to those nights where you held me in your arms and sang to me." As I look into the vast darkness above me, I wish for just one more night like that.

I lay on the bed of flowers next to her until I hear howls in the distance. I then decide to head back to Stevenson's, so I grab my rats and kiss my mom goodbye.

As I get closer to Stevenson's, I can hear the car's alarm slightly better. The ringing in my ears is still there, I had just forgotten about it. I walk right through the parking lot, ignoring the muffled alarm, and walk into the store.

It's been a long day. It seems like it's been rough, but I can't really remember what specifically happened to make it so bad. My memory is a blur.

I let my rats run around free, since they are happy to be back home. I walk to the back of the store. The rats go about sniffing everything they can find: crumbs of food, money, clothes. They seem to be having fun.

I make it to the furniture section at the back of the store next to the familiar dark area. I stretch out on the couch and relax as my rats jump on my chest.

I release my thoughts and fall asleep . . .

I open my eyes. Where am I? I feel like I'm lying down in a dark room, but at the same time, I feel like I'm moving. What's going on?

A light from above shines down on me, blinding and catching me by surprise. As I turn my head away from the light, I notice another light, but this one shines down to a spot in front of me. I see someone sitting in the little circle of light facing the opposite direction. Who is it? It looks like . . . No, no way. But it does look like her, so I call out anyway.

"Mom?" I hear a cracked voice escape me. Is it her? It looks like her. The person continues looking away from me. I begin to call out again, but the person quickly turns around to face me. I see her ruby earrings swing from her ears before I even recognize her face.

"Jaden?" Mom responds, as if I was the last person on Earth that she was expecting.

Her voice. I haven't heard it in so long. I forgot how it sounded. Her voice sounds shaken, sounds frightened. Did I scare her? I didn't mean to. I hope she will forgive me.

"Mom! I'm so happy to see you!" I excitedly tell her. "Mom, I have a lot to tell—"

"Jaden? Where are you?" She asks me.

What? How can she not see me? She is looking me straight in the face as she says it. She has to see me. She has to. She . . .

Why can't she see me?

"Jaden? Where are you?" She repeats in the exact same tone as the question she asked before. She continues looking at me as the words exit her lips. She repeats the question again, in an identical tone. She then repeats it again. And again.

Why is she doing this? My heart sinks. All my excitement has vanished, and I feel I'm being frowned upon. The emotion in her face slowly falls, and after a minute, she is left with a scared look. I feel like she can see me, she just doesn't want to see me.

She continues repeating the same question. Same tone. Same expression.

"Stop," I beg her. "Please, stop. Please. You're scaring me. Please, Mom. Just talk to me."

She ignores me and continues her repetitive question as if I didn't say anything.

"Mom. . ."

"Jaden?"

"Please answer. . ."

"Where are you?"

"Mom. Please."

"Jaden?"

"I'm . . . I'm sorry. Whatever I . . ."

"Where are you?"

"If I did something wrong, I didn't mean to."

"Jaden?"

It's no use. What did I do wrong? What did I . . .

"Is this because I swung at Dad?" I call out to her, referring to night before everybody left. "Is this why you seem upset with me?"

"Jaden?"

"I didn't mean to! I swear I didn't mean to!" Tears fall from my eyes as I drop to my knees. But as I begin crying, she finally quits her repetitive questions. Instead, she tilts her head to the side while staring intently into my eyes, and musters out and even more crushing question.

"Who are you?"

Who am . . . Who am I . . . She doesn't even know who I am anymore . . . This is a nightmare. This is hell.

I sit up on the couch, breathing heavily. I knew it. Another dream. I immediately place my hands to my head and cry.

15

Company

WHAT HAVE I done?

My own mother doesn't even recognize me anymore. I'm a monster.

No, no it's just a nightmare. They have no significance. They're just random. I have to quit applying a reason for these nightmares. The nightmares I had when I was little had no meaning, and neither do these.

I stand up and go to the bathroom with my rats falling close behind. My head is aching. My whole body hurts, truthfully.

I walk into the men's bathroom, the lights barely shining. In the handicapped stall, I see a pair of legs sticking out from under the door. Unfortunate for that person that their deathbed is a bathroom.

I look in the mirror. The first thing my eye catches is my cheek. My eyes then run up to my hair, which is almost entirely maroon from my own dried blood. I must have lost a lot of blood. If Dad was here, he could take care of me.

I didn't find Dad yesterday. Was he actually even there? I know I heard his voice yesterday. He must have been hiding from me, but why would he be hiding? I thought he would be excited to see me.

As I continue wondering about the whereabouts of my dad, I turn on the sink and wash the blood out of my hair. It's hard to get out at first, but I eventually succeed.

I dry my hair with the paper towels and leave the bathroom. A part of me wants to continue driving to Alabama in order to find other people, but another part of me doesn't want to go anywhere. I don't want to leave Westwood, I don't want to leave Stevenson's, and I definitely don't want to get in another car and have to worry about getting around the wall.

The way I look at it, that wall finally has me trapped. I'm not going anywhere, even if I wanted to.

My attention switches to the rats licking my shoes. I bend over and pick them up. My friends. My pets. So happy not to be in this city completely alone.

I look at the red string that resembles a scarf around Scar's neck, which reminds me of my past life, of a person I once loved. Just thinking of the word "love" makes me blush.

The color red jostles my memory, and the events from yesterday run through my mind for the first time.

Roaksville. The houses. The map. The dirt mound. The car crash. Yesterday was absolutely terrible. I don't want the slimmest chance of experiencing what I did yesterday again. And for right now, there's only one place that I'm certain is safe for me, and that's here in Westwood.

I look back at the red string. It gives me a sudden idea. Red. Red. The color my mom loved. The color of the words in Roaksville. The color of blood.

I have an idea. A pretty good one, come to think of it.

I walk around in the store, looking for certain things. I first head to the Outdoors section, then search around for other materials. I feel so sneaky about this, but this should be fun.

I head out the same back door that I went through in my second dream and walk towards the back of the building.

It's still relatively dark outside, but the sky has just a little bit of blue creeping from it. Plus, the tall poles in the parking lot have large, shining lights that are illuminated enough for me to see where I walk.

I approach the ladder at the back of the building and climb up it. I've never even visited the back of the store, yet it exactly matches what I saw in my dream.

I reach the roof and walk to the front of the building and look over the edge. Directly below me is the car I wrecked, with the alarm still roaring. To the left of it and closer to the entrance are the dispersed boxes with the man lying in their center.

I place the four objects I gathered in the store on the roof: a harness, a rope, a large paint brush, and a bucket of red paint. I securely tie the rope to a pipe that extends vertically from the ceiling, making sure there's not too much slack. I then strap the harness over my torso and hook myself to the rope.

I carefully descend from the roof. The amount of slack I gave myself drops me about ten feet down the side of the building. Perfect. I begin painting on the large concrete blocks with the rope and handle from the paint can in one hand and the brush in the other. As soon as my rope runs out of length and I can't reach any further, I climb back up the building, untie the rope and tie it around another pipe close by. I continue the process across the side until I complete my first sentence. I then repeat the process again, but this time, giving myself more slack in order to write another sentence underneath the first one.

When I finish my project, the sun has already peeked out. I'm exhausted, dripping with sweat. This is the last thing somebody in my shape should be doing, but I'm not worried. This is something I want to do, and something I felt needed to be done as soon as the thought came to me.

I climb down from the roof and walk to the front of the store. The car alarm is still blaring loudly, but I disregard it. I would've thought it would stop by now, but I'm too eager to see my finished work to care.

As I reach the front parking lot, I look back at what I wrote. I read the words aloud, feeling accomplished to hear me say the words.

I AM THE ABANDONED.

I AM ONE.

If there just so happens to be survivors somewhere out there, and they eventually make their way to this city, this will be my lasting legacy. And if those faceless people are following me, mad at me because I survived, then this is the proof that I resorted back to what the people who egotoned did: brandishing their minds in red letters. Maybe this will satisfy them enough to stay away from me and finally give me peace.

My rats find me and come clawing at my toes as if they're trying to tell me that something is bothering them. And if I had to guess it, I would bet that it's the car alarm. I've actually grown to ignore it, but if it irritates them then it irritates me as well.

I approach the car, hoping that pulling the keys out from the ignition will turn it off. I cover my ears and inch closer to the vehicle. The car alarm sound attacks my ears, so I quickly open the door, reach for the keys, and yank them out. Nothing. The car is still honking loudly. I begin pressing buttons on the key, hoping that maybe the unlock button is the shut off switch, but no. None of the buttons do anything. They don't do it. The key doesn't do it. What else is there to do?

After waiting a few minutes, I run to the store and come back with a five-gallon jug and a large box of matches. This car isn't going anywhere anymore, so I might as well have some fun getting rid of it.

I walk over to the gas station which sits outside the parking lot. There's a gas pump with the hose limply dangling beside a truck, and below the hanging nozzle is someone who must have died while pumping gas. I pick up the nozzle and, to my surprise, the gas still pumps through, and I fill my five-gallon jug full.

I walk back to the car, which is rammed into the front wall of Stevenson's, with the jug in my hand and pour the gas all over the interior and exterior. After I emptied the jug, I strike a match and throw it on the driver's seat. As the leather on the seats curl back from the increasing flames, I slowly back up to avoid the heat.

I watch from a distance as the fire completely consumes the inside of the car and starts to spread to the outside. As it gains intensity over the entire car, I back up a few more feet before the fireworks commence.

I sit down on the asphalt, admiring the sight. The flames really do look nice. They really do. I let my mind run free as I become lost in the fire. I think about how everything was before this happened, about how I would have never guessed for things to go like they had. I think about my Dad, my friends, and how happy I was to have finally made plans for just me and Scarlett to go somewhere far away. But all that is irrelevant now.

I look at the rats sitting in my lap. They look so peaceful. They don't have a clue what's going on, and that's a good thing for them. As I pat their little heads, I hear what sounds like footsteps coming from behind me. Of course, I know that they aren't, so I don't even bother with looking up. But the footsteps grow closer and closer until I hear the sound of someone shuffling their feet to sit down next to me.

I look to my left to make sure I'm not just hearing things. A faceless woman sits down cross-legged right next to me, looking towards the fire as her long, blonde hair covers her empty skull.

The faceless looks quite beautiful; you know, except for the whole faceless look. For the first time, I don't become frightened at her. I stay seated. She hasn't acknowledged that I'm even here yet. She seems totally harmless at the moment.

I continue looking at her, waiting for her to do something. But she just continues staring at the burning car. Of course, I don't know how she can see the car without eyes, but I don't ask.

I shift my attention back to the car and try to pretend she's just some regular human. It's good to have company. A bonfire is always more fun when somebody else is with you.

The crackling of the fire has replaced the blaring of the horn. I look down to my rats to see their reaction to the faceless woman, but they haven't even turned in her direction yet. I don't know if they haven't noticed her yet or are just simply ignoring her. Am I the only one who can see her? I look back over at the faceless next to me, who's still focused on the car. Should I say something? I feel awkward just sitting here silently.

"Nice fire, huh?" I ineptly ask her. Oh good Lord, why did I ask her that? Now I made things even more awkward.

As I sit and criticize my choice of question, I see the faceless woman turn to me. Nervous, I turn back toward the fire, stuttering for something different to say.

"Uh, did you see what I wrote on the wall?" I ask her, pointing to the red letters. "I feel like ya'll, uhm . . . you faceless people sort of, well . . . is that what ya'll wanted from me? You know, for me to end up just as desperate as those that had egotoned?"

The woman turns to the wall and after studying it for a few seconds, gives me a light shrug. She must think I'm stupid. Maybe I am a little stupid for overthinking why these faceless people have been following me. They might not hate me; this lady seems at least neutral around me. I didn't purposely give them a reason to hate me. I don't know what to think, so I look down to my rats to distract myself from overanalyzing.

I grab Scat's arms and playfully move them up and down, making him my own little marionette. Out of the corner of my eye, I see the faceless woman turn her head towards me, and I look back over to her in return. From this close up, I can tell that this woman would be gorgeous if only she had a face. The lack of any identity disturbs me. Why are these people faceless? This lady would be so beautiful. Why is her beauty revoked from her like this? Is this what I will eventually end up looking like?

The features that should be on her face don't even show a sign of ever being there. No indentions where her eyes should be, no sign of a mouth ever being present. Just a smooth, convex, tan face without qualities. I feel the unexplainable desire to reach out and rub my fingers over her slick surface, to feel the mystery with my own fingers.

Before I have time to stop myself, I see my arm rising involuntarily. I don't even remember deciding that I should reach out and touch her, but I don't stop.

The woman remains still, accepting my movement as if it were a kiss. My fingers are inches away from her. Just before I come in contact with her, she then shakes her head and backs away from me, seeming to regret letting me get this close. We both pause and look at one another for a brief moment, trying to understand the reasoning behind the other person's actions. The faceless woman then stands up and runs away from me and towards the fire. Actually, she heads into the fire until she hits the car, submerging herself in the thick, dense smoke.

BOOM. The car blows up, throwing glass and other debris across the parking lot. I become both upset that the fire has ceased and unnerved at what I just saw this faceless woman do.

I continue watching the vehicle smolder for an hour. Once the fire slows down, I approach the charred heap. The wall directly touching the car is completely torched from the flames, but they're still stable. Hopefully it won't cause the whole wall to cave in because I would hate for my writings to fall through with it.

Once the fire has completely ceased, I look around the scorched remains of the car for a body. I check inside and outside the car, but my search is limited since everything is still hot. I don't find anything. No sign of the woman whatsoever.

The sun is still bright and the day is still young, but I head inside to call it a day. I need to rest anyway. Maybe the TVs inside the store still work. I couldn't get any TV channels at home, but maybe I can pick some up here. I desperately need to find a news station that can tell me something. Maybe I will just unwind and find something to eat. All I know is that I will enjoy the relaxation, and I will mentally get myself out of this city.

Once I enter the store, I drag one of the couches over to a TV.

After spending an hour failing to pick up a signal from the satellite, I find a few movies and put one of them in. I then throw my assortment of snacks that I've collected on the ground and curl up on the couch with my rats. No better way to spend life in isolation . . .

After about five hours of watching movies on the couch, the act begins to bore me, and I begin to drift off to sleep. I'm really scared to fall asleep because I don't want another nightmare like the ones I've been having. Actually, I don't want to dream at all anymore. Even the good dreams will do nothing but make me face the disappointments of reality. I should fight to stay awake. The windows above me that are dispersed evenly across the top of the store indicate that there's still daylight outside, so –

The TV cuts off, and the lights above me turn off, followed by the rest of the lights in the store. I can hear the electricity in the store all leave at once as I'm left in a dim darkness with the only light source coming from the windows.

Now I'm left defenseless and scared in my new home. But I'm surprised that the electricity went out this early, I expected it to last much longer. I feel like something – or someone – caused it to go out. And I can't help but to take this outage as an answer to the light shrug I got earlier. Maybe that writing wasn't enough for them. Maybe they want more.

16

Focus

WHAT DO THEY want from me? Do they want me to go insane? Do they want me dead? Do they just want me to stay in fear the rest of my life? As I look around in the shadows of the store, the aching in my head returns, and I begin to panic. I don't like the dark. I can still see, but the dim atmosphere bothers me.

I can't stand staying in here much longer. I should go find the fuse box, but I don't know where to even start looking for it. I sit in total silence, thinking of what I should do. It just takes me a few seconds to realize that I'm not sitting in silence after all.

I hear a muffled sound coming from the roof. I can't make out what it is, but it's loud enough for me to lightly feel the vibrations coming from it. What the hell is on the roof? There's only one way to find out.

As I stand up, I realize that lying down for such a long time had made my legs weak. They're both hurting, but I have to fight it off. I have to find what's making this sound.

I begin walking to the back door with my rats nipping at my heels close behind. I see the shape of a human in the distance, but I blow it off as another faceless. I'm starting to feel paranoid, not knowing what the faceless people are going to do with me now that they have me in the dark.

As I reach the door, I hear a voice calling back from the middle of the store. "Hello?"

Did I just hear correctly? Did the faceless just talk? They haven't done that yet. I turn around and begin walking back quietly towards the voice, waiting for the person to speak again.

The person calls out again, and this time he's closer to me. The voice isn't like a regular voice, though. It sounds somewhat concealed; he must be talking into something instead of directly to me. I tiptoe through each aisle, trying to run up on the faceless before he discovers me.

As I turn down an aisle, that's when I see him. We both lock eyes at the same time. This isn't a faceless. Much more terrifying. A person, covered head to toe in a white suit. But my eyes can't seem to leave the mask that he's wearing.

Two eye spots go at an angle that makes the person seem to be glaring angrily at me. Across the lower half of the mask is a single meshed oval that curves into a smile. The combination of the two on the mask resembles something similar to a demented clown.

"We found you," the person calls out to me in a smothered voice. He sticks a hand out for me to grab.

No. I can't do it. I won't do it. The last thing I need to do is go with this person. I don't know what he wants to do with me or where he wants to take me. I can't ignore the possibility that he might lead me to the edge of the roof and persuade me into doing something I don't want to. And his appearance isn't suggesting that he wants to help me.

I grab the hammer out of my pocket and swing it at his extended hand, hitting him right on the forearm. I hear a *crack*, and the man gives out a shriek of pain that is greatly suppressed by his mask as he grasps his arm and falls to his knees.

I could finish him off, and I consider it, but instead I run from him. I need to find somewhere to hide from him. It'll be much harder to find me in the darkness, especially in a store that he doesn't know anything about. Maybe if he can't find me, he will eventually leave.

I hear him mumble to himself as I run off, my mind racing with this sudden change of events. As I make my way across the store, I scamper down a food aisle and throw myself underneath one of the fallen metal stands.

I'm breathing too heavily. He will hear me. I try to calm down, and once I do, I tune my ears to the no longer empty store. My ears turn to the unknown object on the roof, which I'm now assuming has something to do with the masked man, since they both appeared out of nowhere at the same time. I want to find out what that sound is, but the masked man is still here, looking for me, I just don't know where.

I remain lying down for ten minutes. Twenty. Thirty. The sound on the roof is still lightly humming, so he must still be here. It feels like an hour has passed now. I'm getting tired of lying here, so I convince myself that he has left.

As I slide out from the metal stand filled with shelves of food, I think back to this guy's suit. Horrifying. Why would someone make a mask look so frightening? This person wants to hurt me, I know it. I turn the corner of the aisle and head towards the front of the store. If I could just find out what's making the noise on the roof I'll be able to know something about this masked man, and maybe even what his intensions are.

The broken glass entrance door is in sight. It's a much safer route to go out the entrance and walk around to the back instead of walking through the store and risk running back into the man. As I'm walking, I suddenly spot the masked man out from the corner of my eye, and before I have time to react, I feel his strong hand clamp down on my arm from one of the aisles to my side.

"Jaden," he says to me in a much angrier tone than before as he tugs me to the back of the store, "you're coming with me."

I try to pull away, but his grip is too strong. "No!" I repeatedly yell at the man until the words fall into a whisper only I can hear. I need to break free. I need to hurt him before he hurts me. But that's the thing, I already have, so why isn't he letting go? I look down to see that the arm I hit earlier is hanging limply to his side. I could hit it again with the hammer. Or, better yet . . .

Since I keep trying to pull away from the man, I can see his back, and notice the reason he has this suit. There's a tank hooked up to his back, very much alike to the ones that Phil and Grant had on. That has to be his main source of oxygen, and if I take it out, he will have to go with it.

"You're lucky we found you, kid. We almost gave up on you," the man scolds me as I contemplate my plan. He gives a snicker before he begins talking again. "You're just as insane as I thought you would be. Must be something about this city."

What? Rage builds inside of me as the man's last sentence registers in my brain. My anger rushes to my shoulder as I strike both the man's injured arm and his tank. As the hammer bashes against the tank, air shoots out and flutters into my face. The man let's go of me and grabs his arm again as I hear loud screams of pain coming from under his sinister smile.

The man quickly turns to me as he discovers what I did.

"What the hell, kid?" He yells at me. "I'm trying to help you."

"Don't you insult me," I growl at the man as I glare through his mask, "and don't you ever insult my city."

I pull the hammer back for another blow, but the man kicks me before I can swing at him. As I grapple my stomach, the man takes off sprinting through the store.

The urge to kill this man suddenly overwhelms me. How dare this man come into my city and insult *my* city to my face! I want this man to learn his lesson. You don't come into Westwood and insult not only it but its ruler. And who does he think he is, trying to take me away with him? He said he's trying to help me? Did he not read my warnings?

I am the abandoned. I am one. I don't need anybody else.

There's no reason to run after him. If he leaves then he does exactly what I want. If he stays, then I kill him. As simple as that.

The man takes a sharp turn to the right and out of my vision. I ignore my earlier remarks as my walk transforms into a jog, and I begin yelling throughout the store to the man.

"Where are you going? I thought you wanted me? Well come and get me! I'm right here for the taking!" A menacing smile of satisfaction comes to my face. I knock over racks standing in the middle of the hall, trying to make as much noise as possible. As I turn to my right to follow the man, I swing my arm across a shelf, knocking over an entire row of paper towels. Whatever I see still standing, I push over.

The anger inside me begins to boil the longer I fail to find the man. Everything I see I knock over. Clothes racks. Food stands. TVs and other electronics that are set up. I want this guy, and I want him now.

"Come out and play, big boy! Can't fight without your tank, can you? Or maybe it's just this crazy city?"

As I continue to get no response, I start picking up random items on the floor and throwing them far in front of me. I swing my hammer at whatever I can break it with. As entertaining as this is, I'm still furious I haven't found the man yet. Where did he go?

He's here somewhere. I know it. He hasn't left the building yet. Or, has he? I pause my rant for a second to try to hear him.

Along with the sound from the roof, I hear the squeal of the compressed air a few aisles over. He's closer than I thought. I pick my jog back up and head down that aisle.

"I heard you! Where'd you go? Why don't you take me with you now?" He hears me, he has to.

The aisle I'm in is empty, so he has to be down the next one. As I reach the end of the aisle, I turn to my right, and am met by a strong force to the face . . .

Black . . .

No, white . . .

No, nothing. I can't see anything. Wait, yes I can. It's coming to me in a blur. A bright blur. A dull blur. Which one?

Am I in a flashback? As the blur slowly forms into shapes, I notice that the coloring is normal. I try to regain my focus. Focus. Focus . . . I need to focus. Where am I? My eyes tell me that I'm on the floor. My lips are wet, my burned cheek is cold, and my head is throbbing again. Not only my head, but my nose is in more pain than anything.

I can hear my pulse. It's really slow. Slower than usual, it seems. I see my rats come running up to me. They sniff my face, and when they back off of me, I see blood on the tips of their noses from where they touched me.

Where am I again? Stevenson's, right? What happened? My eyes look around some more for an answer. I see a laptop directly in front of me with a dent in it. I can even see a few drops of blood on it. That must be what I was hit with. How? How did it hit me?

My eyes lose focus again. Focus. I need to focus. I need to find that man. He might get away. He might be heading to the roof right now to make his escape. Helicopter. That's what it is. It's a helicopter on the roof. That's how he got here.

He's getting away. No, I can't let him. I have to catch him.

I push up on the ground and stagger to get up. My head feels like it's losing its balance and may detach at any moment. My eyes go back into a blur. Focus. I need to focus. I need to find him.

I look at the small drops of blood on the floor. I put my hand at my nose and swiftly jerk it back. It's sensitive. And it's still spewing. I can't worry about that now. I have to focus on getting to the roof. Focus.

I walk down the aisle towards the side door, yet I can't maintain my balance. My head hurts too much. I can't make it. He's going to get away. No. I can't let him. I have to find him. He's on the roof, I know it. And that's where I'm going.

I make my way to the side door, open it, and go outside. Dusk. I can hear the helicopter blades loudly now. I was right.

I limp to the back of the building where the ladder is. As my legs struggle to make it to the back, I reach up and grab my head to stop its swiveling. The aching is becoming unbearable. My nose continues trembling in pain. My face and my head have been battered enough. I can't think without a sharp bolt tearing through me. But I have to. I have to stay focused. Focus.

I turn the corner and spot the ladder. As I begin climbing up, the thumping from the blades starts pushing against me. I have to fight it. I have to find this man.

I reach the top of the ladder, but don't fully get on top of the roof, in fear of being seen. There he is. About thirty yards away is the masked man stepping into the helicopter. There's another man with his back to me standing outside the helicopter, motioning for the masked man to go inside the helicopter. He's wearing an oxygen mask with a hose running in it through the bottom, just like the men in Roaksville had.

The man follows the masked man in the back seat of the helicopter. Before he gets in, he turns my way, and I completely recognize him.

That slicked back, jet black hair. That's Grant.

Grant survived. He was in the same situation as I am, yet he survived. That means that wherever they're going, there is safety. And others. Other people. Just like me.

I just now realized, the masked man was trying to help me this whole time.

I begin sprinting towards the helicopter, calling out Grant's name. I've got to get his attention. I've got to go where they're going. I need to be taken with them in that helicopter. They may not come back for me. They might take my act of violence as a sign of insanity and leave me to die. No, I can't let them. I've got to stop them.

As I run towards the helicopter, the force of the air from the blades send me on my butt, throwing dust in my eyes and face. I try to recover, but by the time I successfully get all the dust out of my eyes and gather the strength to stand up, the helicopter has begun to rise off. No. They're getting away. They can't leave me. I've got to get their attention.

I stop running and jump up and down, waving my arms frantically. Please notice me! Please don't ignore me! I'm tired of being ignored. Save me! Please!

They're rising higher and further away. They don't see me. Either that or they're ignoring me. No, I can't let them. I've got to get their attention.

The hammer. My only weapon. I've got to use it somehow. I throw it at the helicopter and watch as it soars through the air. It makes contact with the side window of the chopper. Great. That's what I needed. They had to have heard that. They know something is up. They know that I'm here.

So I stand in my spot and watch the helicopter as it flies away. I tell myself that it will turn back any second. Any minute. They know I'm here. I know they know. But as the sun falls, and dusk becomes night, I know that they have chosen to ignore me.

They're not coming back. They're never going to come back.

17

Drinks

STUPID. I'VE CALLED myself this for the last hour since they left, but it's true. I'm so stupid. They were trying to help me *the whole time*; yet, I was too stubborn to see it. I had my opportunity. The rescue mission I had hoped for had finally come, and I blew my opportunity. They're not coming back; they know I'm too far gone. They think I've lost it. They probably think I've egotoned.

How did I not see that connection? The masked man knew my name, even said that he thought I would be crazy. He knew I was going to be here, so why didn't I know that he was there to help me? I was too busy being paranoid that I couldn't put two and two together.

This is my fault. I'm still in this city because I chose to be. I saw them as a threat, and they saw me as one, so they left me. They left me. They . . .

Tears squeak through my clenched eyes. They left me because of me. Not that I was accidentally left here or that they forgot about me, but because they chose to leave me here.

I look in front of me and see the harness, rope, and paint still sitting right where I left it when I was done writing the warnings on the wall.

I hook the rope and harness up and slide down to paint an

addition to my writing. Not that much, just a few letters. After I finish adding on to the writing, I lift myself back up the roof and sit down on the edge. As my feet dangle off the side of the building, I look out into the dark city. This is now my city because I chose not to leave it. I didn't want any intruders. I own this city of nothing.

I lick my lips and become reminded of my bloodied face. My nose has stiffened solid. There's no doubt it's broken, but what am I to do about it? I can't heal it, and there's no reason to complain about it. I've just got to come to accept pain.

Pain. I'm tired of pain, of feeling it constantly. I want to get away from it. I want to escape the pain without causing even more pain. But how?

The answer to my question comes immediately, and I regret the reply I come up with. My eye catches a hold to the liquor store just outside the parking lot. That's where Dad went to escape his pain. I can do that here, can't I? Why not? Nobody is here to stop me.

But I can't help but to think of the horrible effect that his drinking has had on me. How many times I had been hit or yelled at. Dealt with some sort of pain, whether it was psychological or physical. But for Dad, drinking seemed to had worked. It hid him from his problems, which is exactly what I need here.

I climb down the ladder, walk across the parking lot, and turn around at the building to look at my addition to the wall.

I AM THE ABANDONED.

I AM ONE.

THIS IS MY CITY

AND I AM SORRY.

As I admire my statement, my foot stumbles across the hammer that I had thrown, and I pick it back up. I turn back and walk to the liquor store while I stuff the hammer back into my pocket. With every step I take towards the liquor store, I wonder why I'm heading there. I've never touched alcohol, never wanted to, but now it appears that it is my only solution. I feel the same way Dad did. He had no-where else to turn. But why am I following in his footsteps? Why?

As I open the doors to the store, the sight of shelves upon shelves of drinks intimidates me. Different shapes of bottles, different col-ored drinks, all with names that were once very familiar to me but I haven't seen in years. I don't know where to start, and honestly, I don't know if I even want to go through them. I know the trouble that these bottles bring, but I can't help but fall in their trap.

I snatch off a bottle on the shelf and read the label. *Old Fashioned Whiskey*. I stare at the bottle in my hands. My eyes hate what they see as the familiar label brings back terrible memories. Memories of when Dad would punish me simply for being around him.

I slowly lift my hand to pull the top off of the bottle, but once my hand reaches it, I can't seem to make myself open the bottle. I can't do it. I cannot go through with this. I don't know if it's my pride that's stopping me or if it's seven-year-old Jaden that's stopping me, but I can't make myself drink.

The bottle slips from my hands, making a loud crashing sound and sending the brown liquid splashing on to my shoes. I have to find another way to ease my pain, drinking isn't it. But how? I'm be-ginning to think that maybe it's impossible for me to ease it. There's nothing else, I'll just have to suffer through it until . . . I don't know. I don't know how long or until what. That's perhaps the scariest part.

I hear bottles shuffle against each other from across the store. I shoot my head up towards the sound and see a faceless man leaning lazily against the shelf directly across from me. The faceless is wear-ing a pair of dark grey suit pants and an untucked, halfway unbut-toned white-collared suit with a green tie hanging loosely around his neck. The look is all too familiar with me. Way too familiar.

In one hand, the faceless is holding a bottle by the neck and throwing it up to his nonexistent mouth. However, instead of spill-ing on to the ground as I would expect the liquor to, it disappears just as it would if the faceless was actually drinking it. Whatever, with or without a mouth, I don't care where the alcohol is going. All I know is that this faceless sports a look that brings back unpleasant nostalgia.

I would usually already be home from school when Dad would come home from work, but he wouldn't actually stomp in the house for hours later, as he would sit in his parked car in the garage and get drunk there. The overly-casual, almost sloppy business look that he wore every night was what I saw him in more than his scrubs. And I hated that about him. I don't know why, but I hated the fact that he would dress for work as if he were some lawyer, then immediately change into his scrubs when he got to the hospital. Thanks to him, I can't go my entire life untucking a button-up shirt or throwing an undone tie around my neck because when I was little, I knew what that outfit meant.

And this faceless matches that outfit perfectly. So perfect, in fact, that I want to run away before he starts yelling at me.

Is this my dad? This faceless doesn't have his hair and looks a lot taller than Dad is, but the appearance is just too . . . I can't come to grips with it. The faceless moves, pointing his finger at me with the hand that's holding the bottle. He stumbles over his feet when he tries to stand up straight, but regroups and continues vigorously jabbing his finger at me. The faceless takes a step towards me and points to the wall that he just came from. I feel like he is yelling at me for something, but this time, his lack of a mouth prohibits him from shouting.

Apparently the yelling gets more heated because he spikes the bottle he's holding hard into the floor, then looks at me as if I were the one who caused him to do so. This is too familiar. And I'm left just like I was back then, confused and unknowing of what I did wrong.

The faceless turns around to a stand of shelves full of bottles in the middle of the store and slams the entire stand on the ground, smashing numerous bottles and sending the liquid bursting out across the floor. The faceless then turns back to me and jabs his finger in my direction, throwing what I assume is insult after insult that I can't hear. The lack of sound, the lack of expressed anger. . . A part of me wishes I would hear my dad's voice yelling at me, just so I could yell back at him.

"Okay, that's enough," I finally find myself shouting at the faceless. I can't help it. He's acting just like my dad used to. I'm not just going to sit here and let the same thing that happened to me eleven years ago happen now. "I've had about enough of whatever it is you think you're doing to me."

The faceless doesn't pause in his rampage, and only walks closer to me to throw even more inaudible insults that I can't even see being formed.

"I said THAT'S ENOUGH!" An anger that's been hidden for a decade finally surfaces, and I yell at the faceless man as if he were my dad. "I didn't deserve for you to beat me those years ago, and I don't deserve for you to be angry at me now! So shut up! I'm not your damn rag doll, I'm your son!"

And the faceless ignores my cries, just like my dad did back then. Finally, for the first time in my life, I get that monkey off my chest, only to have it cling back to me. The faceless man reaches down to his waist, unbuckles his belt, and pulls his belt out from his pants. He then folds it up and holds it, ready to strike at me, just like my dad did to me oh so many times. The faceless paces at me until he's within arm's reach, then pulls his arm back to hit me. I don't even wince. I've flinched so many times at this moment, yet now I'm embracing it. Do it.

But the faceless stays in that position, with his arm cocked back, ready to strike. I continue waiting for the swing that would prove to me that my dad is still the man that I hated back then, but the faceless doesn't move.

"Do it," I tell the faceless. He doesn't respond to my command, remaining completely motionless. "I said do it." Nothing.

I stare into his barren head that holds no features. How dare he push me to the ledge only to leave me dangling.

"DO IT." My commands are still not affecting the faceless, leaving me in the ignored state I've been in all week. "DO IT ALREADY."

But this is where the faceless doesn't match my dad's characteristics anymore. He remains stationary. Paused in the moment, like a statue.

I reach behind me and grab a bottle off of the shelf my back is against. I stare at the motionless man for a few more seconds, then swing the bottle in my hand at him, doing what he cannot find the courage to do. This finally snaps the faceless out of his trance, and he dodges my attack. Before I can regroup for another swing, the faceless bolts out across the store and towards the door.

I run to chase after him, but slip in the pool of booze. He is too far for me to catch by the time I stand back up, so I throw the bottle still in my hand at him. I then watch the bottle soar at, then through, the back of the faceless man and crash on the floor directly in front of him as he then pushes the door open and runs out.

I can't believe what just happened. The bottle just passed right through him, like he didn't even exist. I chase after the faceless, but once I push the door open and make my way outside, I notice that it has just begun pouring rain. The rain falls heavily on my head as I search desperately for the direction the faceless went.

I give up, falling to my knees and letting the storm soak my body. I can't have even one moment of peace anymore. Either my thoughts are haunting me or a faceless is around to taunt me even more. The only thing even close to peace that I have felt is actually right now, as the cold rain drenches my skin and cools me off. Making me forget about that faceless, my dad, and my life. This rain relaxes me to a point that I finally realize just how exhausted I really am. I could pass out right now, but I want to enjoy this moment of forgetfulness as long as I can. I'm soothed by the sounds of the rain pounding into the puddles around me and of the thunder dangerously crackling above me.

But, of course, this moment is lived shortly and is soon interrupted. Not by a faceless, however, but even stranger.

An eagle hovers from above and lands right in front of me, staring me directly in the eyes.

An . . . An eagle? What the . . . why is an eagle here? Are they the next surviving species? Before I have enough time to question the bird's appearance, I notice something about this eagle that catches my eye.

Its body isn't covered in feathers, only half of it is. The other half is made up of a metallic gold structure. Like . . . like a robot. Its head is the same way, too. Its head is separated between the eyes: half of it's head is like a regular eagle's head, while the other half is robotic, with a green, twitching eye glaring at me. The eagle scans me up and down, and I can hear its neck make a tiny mechanical noise as it moves.

I throw my hand out to touch the marvelous creature, but I'm afraid that my hand might fall straight through it. My hand softly lands on the eagle's head, and the eagle buries its half feathered, half-metal scalp into my palm, like a cat would if I were petting it.

What is . . . I don't even . . .

I fall over in a puddle and pass out.

18

Grim

I PRY MY crust-filled eyes open. The sun blares down at me as I try to regroup from my uncomfortable night of sleep. I roll over and reach into my back pocket, pulling the journal out from my pants and taking the pen out from it's spine. I open the journal and flip to the only page I have written on. I then draw a line through the six, signifying my sixth day in isolation.

My arms fall to my side and land hard on the rugged roof of Stevenson's. My eyes focus on the sky above me, anticipating the sight of the eagle I spotted two days ago. Instead of hearing the caw of an eagle, however, I'm left with the oh-so-comforting sound of silence to painstakingly remind me of just how lonely I am. I've remained in this exact position for two days and now two nights, vulnerable in the intense sun the entire time, waiting for the robotic eagle to swoop down and prove to me that it wasn't just another mirage of my unstable mind. Too unmotivated to find a source of shade, my skin glows a bright red as a result of being exposed to the scorching sun for two days.

My face is incredibly sensitive, but I've tried to reside on my charred cheek, keeping it out of the sun as much as possible, even though it is being forced down into the super-soft roof at the same time. I took off my shirt long ago, but it is now used as my only source of warmth in the cool nights. Even though the left side of my body has retained a majority of the sun's impact, my entire body has received an incredible blister, leaving myself too delicate to move.

Honestly, I don't even feel the heat anymore. Pain altogether has become an unnoticed sense, a factor that has no longer played a role in my decisions. And that's just pathetic on my part. My mind is too dead set on a particular task, but I can't decide if that task is to locate the eagle or to cook myself to death.

The only fount of happiness I even moderately obtain anymore comes from my pet rats, which are now sheltering themselves in the shadow of the pipes that extend vertically from the building. They're still here with me, but that may just be because they might not be able to get down from this height without my assistance.

I love those rats. Even though I've been wallowing in my own self-pity for the last two days due to my lack of ability to make friends, they have always been there with me. I don't want to lose them. They're the only reason I haven't forgotten how to smile yet.

The only other possessions I brought up here are a case of water bottles, an open can of baked beans, and a block of cheese. Although I am still yet to suffer from hunger, I remain eating the beans for the sole reason that I know it can't be healthy to go so long without food. They taste like crap, but I've tasted worse, honestly. The block of cheese has given off a putrid smell from being exposed to the sun for this elapsed time, but my rats remain nibbling on it. They're just as nasty as I am, and I like that. They own much more of an appetite than I do, but that may just be because they're more daring than I am.

I dwell on the sapphire sky that contains patches of misshapen puffs of clouds. Not a single indication of any bird gliding through it. Not a single hint of any life existing within or beyond it. I should have expected the eagle to be a figment of my imagination this entire time. Besides, what was I going to do if I ever detected it?

Who am I fooling? I'm not sitting up here to look for a friggin' eagle, I'm here because I'm still holding on to the possibility that Grant and his costumed friend will come back to save me. And we all know that's not happening.

I sit up, feeling my tightened, scalded skin sting in tenderness from its lack of movement. I look out into the parking lot and the accompanying buildings outside of it. I frequently remind myself of the empty city that I am now ruler over, but I can't find any significance with the title. I don't suppose one is necessary, but I would like to feel relevant.

My rats, seeing that I have sat up from my continuous reclined state, skip over to my side and playfully jump onto my lap. Scar rubs her nose against my belly button as Scat gently tickles his whiskers against my abdomen. I scratch the heads of both the rodents to show my affection.

As I look into the vacant parking lot, a sudden figure appears in the midst of the area. The figure appears rather quickly, as if it exposed itself during the darkness of a blink.

Oh great, another faceless. I was just thinking that I hadn't had my daily dose of random, uninvited, walking mannequins. Even though a large part of me hates the vagueness that these figures strut, I feel a connection between us. We share this city, at least. They can understand and comprehend what I've been through this week. And I guess that they are humans, although that description is still pending.

Don't get me wrong though, I still don't know where they came from or where their faces went, but I'm not about to ask them.

But this faceless seems peculiar. This one just seemed to appear out of thin air. I lock my eyes to the figure to watch and see if it disappears just as easily, but it never moves. It just remains turned in my direction without a face to actually face me with. Wearing a blue ball cap and a red t-shirt, the faceless and I are locked in a stare down that I'm quite certain I'll lose. It's completely still. My eyes grow dry from staring at the figure for so long, but as my eyes blink and re-gain its vision, the faceless has company. Now, about twenty faceless people are facing me from the parking lot, all evenly dispersed.

I can't help but feel astonished by this abrupt happening, but fear is nowhere close to what I am feeling. Intrigued, yes. But frightful? Not so much. Just curious as to where they are coming from and how they are making themselves shown so fast.

I blink again, and again the population increases. This time from twenty to around fifty. I blink again, and just like before, the amount of faceless people grows, landing somewhere around one hundred. All of them stand in the parking lot in front of me and faced in my direction. I become a little disoriented by this increase, but I try to refrain from becoming scared

I continue blinking for the sole purpose to add to the number of these people. Two hundred. Five hundred. Soon enough, the entire lot is completely filled with faceless people. As I continue blinking, they expand to the outskirts of the lot and further into the city. After a full minute of blinking, nothing but faceless people occupies my view from the roof. Stretching for what seems like dozens of miles without a single space between any of them. The amount of these faceless people seems to never end, and as the infinite crowd all look at me without eyes to look with, the relevance I wanted overwhelms me.

All these beings, face me as if I were their ruler. Their king. They all view me as the highest person in their vicinity. Do they respect me? I'm not sure anymore. Do they want me to say something? Maybe so, but I can't really determine. Are they just admiring me? Or are they evaluating me, waiting for my next action to see if I'm capable of being their leader?

"What are you?" I softly whisper to myself, asking the question that's been pricking at my tongue since my first dream.

But just as they came, with my next blink, they all disappear. Every single one of them, vanished, literally in a blink of an eye. Thousands of the figures, having dissipated like dust in the wind, all without leaving a trace behind.

And I'm honestly left in a disconcerted state, but a voice coming from my left interrupts that feeling.

"It's quite rude to make them come and go like that," I hear the voice of a younger man slice through the silent breeze. "You know, you're not that good around other people."

And as I turn to discern this unknown man's face, I realize that he doesn't have one.

There, hovering above me, wearing a tattered, dirty-blue button-up shirt and a smudged, orange bowtie, is a faceless.

"Did you just . . . did you just talk to me?" I ask, paralyzed by shock. This faceless man just communicated with me. He . . . he doesn't even have a mouth.

"They have other things to do and places to be," he ignores my first reaction and continues on with his initial statement. "The world doesn't revolve around you, you know."

I'm left not only bewildered at what it is this faceless is talking about, but also greatly disturbed by the fact that he is, indeed, talking to me. I'm staggered, unaware of what to say to the faceless, or even if I need to say anything to him at all. Is my mind playing tricks on me again? Who's to say I'm not just imagining this faceless? And if I'm not, how do I respond? I don't know how he's going to react towards me. What if he decided to attack me? I'm vulnerable and weak, I wouldn't stand a chance.

My facial expressions must emit my thoughts, as the faceless begins talking to me with a much softer tone this time. "Lighten up, I was just joking. I'm not going to hurt you. No need to be so frightened."

But I can't help but to feel completely frightened. I don't know how he will respond if I start asking him questions. I don't want to go into another screaming nightmare, where all the faceless people I just saw reappear and start charging at me. I . . . I don't know what to ask, but I know I should ask him something.

"What . . . what are . . . what exactly are . . ." I timidly begin, but I'm too uptight to finish my sentence.

"What am I?" He finishes my sentence for me. With my mouth perplexed enough to hang open, I give a sluggish nod. "Ha, good question, I was hoping you could answer that for me."

What is that supposed to mean? Is he joking with me? As my mind freezes as I think of a response, the faceless walks behind me and out of my sight. "Good Lord," he tells to me with distaste. "I got a question for you: what exactly you been doing up here?"

I slowly turn around to see the faceless picking up my shirt and wiping his forehead with it. What is he doing? Making himself comfortable? The fear I have towards him is slowly being mixed with enmity, as his complacent approach towards me annoys me. I wish he would just tell me what he's doing here and leave already. After a few pats, he throws the shirt down, pauses, and gives a few loud sniffs.

"Damn, kid, you smell like straight failure. You know what a shower is, right?"

Of course his comments offend me, and I want to say something to him, to get him to go away, but what do I say? I'm still recovering from the fact that a faceless is finally talking to me, and to add to that, he's talking to me like nothing happened. As if I haven't spent the last week alone, or as if he doesn't have a face. He's acting like we've known each other, like we're friends.

As I'm lost in thought, the faceless makes his way over to the block of cheese a few feet from my shirt. "No, wait, I found the source," he verifies to me, as if I care. "Wow, this is disgusting. This is super nasty. I mean, a part of me is disappointed in you as a human to have this just sit here and marinate so close to you." He picks up the block of cheese and pulls his arm back like he's going to throw it off the roof.

"No!" I blare out to the faceless, surprised at my own sudden outburst. "That's for the rats."

He turns his head to me, and despite not having a face, I can tell he's giving me a weird look. "Of course it is." He drops the block of cheese and returns to where he initially stood when I first saw him. I wait for him to say something to me, but after a few seconds, it's clear that he's too focused on staring out over the parking lot.

"What are you?" I finally convince myself to ask the faceless. "What are you faceless people exactly?"

"We're actually not as complicated as you would think," he replies as he looks out towards the parking lot where the army of faceless figures once stood. The man's voice is hardy and dignified but relaxed at the same time, suggesting that he may have been a businessman or perhaps an actor. "We all exist, but at the same time, we don't. You know what I mean?" He pauses and waits for my reply, but my mind has drawn blank, and I simply stare at him with addled eyes. "Okay, maybe we are just a *little* bit more complicated as you have assumed."

I feel like a smile would follow that statement, but without a mouth to form one, I am left uncomfortable at his combination of sarcastic tone and lack of visible emotion.

"What is that supposed to mean?" I finally snap out of it and impetuously question the man.

"What I mean is that we exist only to a certain few. We are all a part of your mind, but at the same time, we exist in the real world. Well, let me rephrase that. *Your* world." he briefly responds, sounding intent with finally telling me this information. "Ooh, mysterious, yes, I know."

"And, just tell me, what is *that* supposed to mean?" I mockingly jab back at the man, clearly unimpressed with his dim responses.

"Okay, I know that can be a bit confusing, but instead of telling you, let me first give you a little history lesson," he proclaims to me as he straightens up his bowtie. The man may try to sound amusing, but his roguish attitude irks me. "You know about this whole virus situation, right?"

I don't respond, but instead glare at the top of the man's head. I've finally decided that this faceless is perhaps too comfortable around me, perhaps too friendly, and I hate it. I am insulted by his assumption that I lack knowledge about the situation, but the truth is, his assumption is somewhat correct. However, I'm still not happy with his mellow tone. Once the man realizes I haven't answered yet, he stops messing with his tie and looks up to make sure I'm still paying attention to him. As he catches my intolerant scowl, he turns back towards his tie and continues.

"It's a bizarre situation we are all put in, it is. An airborne disease with something like a 100% fatality rate to everyone that contracts it. The virus causes incredible emotional instability and induces large amounts of pain. Pretty gruesome stuff. But, I'm sure you know by now that before the victims very aggressively kick the bucket that they go through this process known as egotoning."

"I've heard it mentioned once before," I respond, referring back to my flashback in Roaksville, "but I'm not sure if I really know anything about it."

"Ah, yes, fun story time with Mr. Foxx," the faceless man says, earnestly rubbing his palms together. I guess I'm just going to have to get used to his attitude. "Alright: egotone. First, let me start off with the basis of the word. Let's think back to fourth grade science class, shall we?"

I warily nod, having no clue where he's going with this.

Once he catches my response, he reaches his hand behind his back, pulls a large book in front of him and begins flipping through the pages. While he does so, I'm left totally clueless as to why or how he could be caring this huge book in his much smaller back pocket.

Before I have time to suggest to myself that he somehow pulled it out of his ass, he begins reading.

"Here we go: Ecotone. With a 'c'. Noun. The transition zone between two different plant communities." He slams the dictionary shut, tosses it over his shoulder, and carries on. "However, there's a plot twist: we're not talking about plant communities. Sounds simple enough, right?" The word is fuzzy to me, and as my mind intensively muses with what he's trying to get at, he takes my silence as a response.

"Good Lord, kid, how'd you make it to your senior year of high school?" he remarks. "Alright, an ecotone is like . . . It's sort of like the edge of the roof of this building." He walks to the edge and looks below as he softly glides half his foot on the roof and the other half off the building. "This side, what me and you are currently on, is one environment. We're all safe and dandy, minus a few sunburns and puke stains from yourself. But the edge of the building separates this safe zone with another zone, but that other zone is not so safe. Let me give you a demonstration."

Without a pause, he jumps off the roof and towards the ground. My stomach drops with the man, and I swiftly crawl over to the edge. What did he just do? Why did he jump? My heart pounds inside my eardrums as I look over the edge to find the faceless man, but cannot find him anywhere.

"Ow, oh no. Pain. The agony." I hastily turn around to find the faceless man making sarcastic and nonchalant moans of pain behind me. How did he . . . What the hell did this guy just do?

"Don't ponder too hard on that stunt, Foxxman," he ensures me as he returns to the edge of the building as if nothing happened. My heart continues beating from the thought of him killing himself right in front of me, but it races even more from the uncertainty of the nature and capabilities of this faceless.

"Like I said, this isn't Bill Nye speaking, so we're not talking about any plant communities. Let's look at the word again. Egotone. It's like the combination of the words 'ego' and 'ecotone'. Wow, mind blown. It's literally one giant, deadly, and human-race-eradicating pun."

"So what you're saying . . .," I begin as my mind finally hurdles the whole jump-off-a-building-but-land-right-behind-me ordeal, ". . . is that it's people's egos, their personalities, that cross some line?"

"There we go. Look at you using your noggin," he tells me in the overbearingly sarcastic tone he's used in the majority of our conversation. He stomps his foot on the roof and continues. "Here everybody is in their stable, safe personality. But oh no! What's this? A random virus swoops in and pushes us towards the edge until we eventually fall off." He, rather believably, pretends that somebody pushes him. "There's a struggle between the person and the virus that lasts about a minute, but eventually . . ." Just like before, he falls off the edge of the roof. A part of me jumps at this sight again, but I know better than to be fooled twice by him.

"When the people who are egotoning land on the other side," he continues right behind me, like I had expected, "they become insane, violent, and inhumane. They show absolutely no traces of the individuals that they were once before. They become these deranged, rabid maniacs who can no longer even be called people. And that's when things get bad. As fun as I made egotoning sound, there's nothing fun about it. It's absolutely terrible."

He pauses with his lecture and brings his right hand to the top of his head, sliding it from his forehead across his spiked brown hair and to the back of his neck. He then digs his knuckles into the top of his spine.

"Right there," he signifies as he knocks on the back of his head as he would a door. "That's how I died. Got shot in the back of the head after I egotoned." He turns around to me to see if I'm still following along with him. Although I am a bit disoriented, I show that

I try to understand him.

He tilts his head a little to the side to have a better view at me and to continue his story. "My wife did it. I had already egotoned, so I was running at her like a mad man, mainly because, you know, I was one. She kicked me to the ground and took me out the executor's way. Even though I had no control over my actions, I could still tell what I was doing. It's hard to explain the feeling . . . You know those dreams where you run from somebody, but your feet don't move as fast as you want them to? Well, that's what egotoning feels like. There's nothing you can do about your situation, except for sit back and wait for the nightmare to end. You can't control your actions, and you can't control what you say. You are overpowered by some anonymous force. It's a really horrifying experience."

The man pauses for a second, and I can hear him give off a soft sigh. "If she wouldn't have shot me I would've killed her . . ." He finds a small pebble close to his feet and kicks it. "She's dead now. I don't know, there's a small chance that she survived, but it's obvious. Am I realistic for holding on to that small chance?"

"So, wait," I begin, ignoring his last question and addressing his story, "let me get this straight. You vividly remember not only egotoning and going after your wife, but you also remember getting shot in the head? So, what, what are you then, some kind of ghost?"

"Exactly! Look at you catching up with things!" He actually sounds thrilled that I guessed correctly. "We're all ghosts. That's what everybody without a face is. I mean look at us!" He puts his index finger to where his eyebrow would be and briskly swipes it across his forehead, and just as they had disappeared a few minutes earlier, thousands of faceless people refill the parking lot and its surrounding areas. An infinite ocean of faceless people, all looking in my direction.

The faceless man takes a step back and squats down to the ground where our shoulders are nearly touching. "Look at all these people," the man passionately directs his finger in front of me as his voice can't hold back his eagerness to tell me whatever it is he has to say. "Every single person you see out there is a victim. Every single one of them has egotoned, and whether they eventually died from the virus or from somebody else, they are one of us. Now, this is our afterlife. Millions upon millions upon billions of us – yes, with a B – with no facial features to distinguish ourselves from one another, which you should really look into because your face looks like it's seen its better days.

"Every person who has ever egotoned and been killed from this virus becomes one of us. A Grim, as we like to call ourselves."

"Grims, huh?" I hear myself recite aloud. "I didn't know ya'll have a name." I replay the word over in my head. "Why Grims, though?"

"Good question, kid," the Grim says as he takes a seat next to me. He swipes his fingers across his forehead again, and this time, all of the Grims standing on the ground disappear. "Like I said, the infected people gradually make their way to the edge of a safe zone, and once they have fully egotoned, they have five minutes to either kill themselves or get killed by somebody else. After their five minutes are up, and they somehow managed to survive both of these circumstances, a Grim is sent to kill them. In metaphor terms, if you fell off the edge of this building with a gun in your hand, you could either wait five minutes to hit the ground or take the shortcut."

"What? You Grims keep a time on how long until people die? Like it's some kind of game? What kind of sick monsters are you?"

"Hold up now, Foxxman, don't go throwing labels on us." I hear him give a soft chuckle. "It's not as heinous as it sounds. Let me give you a quick example. There was a woman by the name of Dolores Griffin. She was the owner and head chef of Rochester's Burger Joint. You may or may not have known her. When she contracted the virus, the public was already aware of what egotoning was and what it did, but she tried to outsmart it. Minutes before she began to egotone, she went to her office at her restaurant, took every object out of it, and locked herself in it until she had fully egotoned and had lost control of her own actions. She thought that maybe she could survive from egotoning if there's nothing in the room to kill her. Besides, she had drywalls. Are you following me so far?"

I hastily nod.

"For five full minutes, she ran into her walls and banged her head over and over on the floors. Gave herself a pretty good headache, but none of it killed her. So, one of the Grims was sent to Delight her. Delight is another term we Grims came up with." He stands up and starts pacing in a circle, looking at his feet the entire time as he tries to gather and verbalize his thoughts. "We're called Grims because we kill people who have egotoned by touching them. The simplest touch is enough to kill anything or anybody. Once we come in contact with somebody, their soul immediately leaves the body and joins the coveted fraternity of Grims. Our presence is death-inducing, just like the good ole' Grim Reaper – hint to where we got our names."

This makes sense, but at the same time, it doesn't. The concept of Grims having a dangerous touch doesn't surprise me, but now that I think about it, every Grim that I have seen has avoided touching me. Why? Why did all of these Grims refrain from touching me when they had multiple opportunities to do so?

Before I can ask the Grim about this, he continues on. "The tiniest nip from any of us is enough to end anyone instantly. That's what Delighting is about. It gives the person who looks for an escape from life the essential help."

The Grim quickly swipes his finger again and points out to the parking lot. I turn my attention to the location his finger is pointing. Perfectly in the middle of the lot is a faceless woman wearing a maroon apron with her hair put in a bun. "That lady right there is Mrs. Griffin. She's a lovely lady, she truly is." He then gives her a friendly wave, and she returns the favor. The talking Grim then repeats the odd finger swipe once more, and Mrs. Griffin is gone. "I've had to Delight quite a few people. I mean, it's not as bad as it seems. It's actually quite amusing to greet a new Grim as their body is left permanently in a state of shock."

I perk up at his last words. "What did you just say?"

My sudden gain of interest surprises the Grim. "Their faces are left totally frozen in shock. Now, I forgot to mention this earlier, but we Grims are invisible to the regular, healthy human. Invisible to anyone who has not egotoned. And it just so happens that when people egotone, they become both irregular and unhealthy. After somebody has completely egotoned, that's the only time we become visible. Don't ask me why, I have no clue. And when they do, you know, they don't expect some faceless guy to come running at them out of nowhere, so when they see us, they're practically paralyzed until we Delight them. When they're Delighted, their bodies remain in that exact state: completely frozen from shock. They're bodies don't even decompose, which is good because if they did, the smell would be pretty bad around here."

I want to continue on, but I'm far too astounded to talk. That means that every single body I've found is now a Grim. Mr. Lawkins, Terra, Grandmother . . . "What about that faceless I saw in the liquor store? Was that my dad? Does that mean he's dead?"

"That wasn't your dad," he assures me. "That was Timothy Greaves, a Grim who played a very convincing role as your dad."

"So you Grims are acting out people in my life, huh? What is this, some version of The Truman Show that you creeps have set up to toy with me?"

"Hostile," he says with a short breath. "You're so hostile. No, we're not toying with you, but we are here to tell you things without actually speaking to you. Well, except for right now. But Timothy was trying to tell you not to drink anything in that store. We've been giving you guidance, and you didn't even realize it."

"Why, though?" I ask, but a better question then pops up in my head. "Better yet, if only people who have egotoned can see these Grims, then why can I?"

"A little impatient, are we?" he insists as he shows me his palms, telling me to slow down. "You're begging for the main entrée before you even finish the appetizer." He slides his feet back over to me and sits down beside me, but I maintain my personal space by shifting away from the Grim just to be safe. "Okay, you remember that time you ran your motorcycle into that huge wall filled with random green gas, causing a huge explosion and burning your cheek off?"

"Yeah," I condescendingly respond, clearly not amused at the reference that I would definitely remember and wondering as to what that has anything to do with this situation. "But how did you know that? Have you been watching me since then?"

"Ever wondered what that green gas was?" the Grim ignores my question and asks me as he reaches to scratch the top of his scalp. Of course, I have wondered about the gas, but I'm also wondering why he ignored my question that is beginning to bother me.

"That green gas was the virus. Not all of the virus from across the globe, of course, just from Westwood. The same virus that has killed like, I don't know, billions of people had had just the amount in this area trapped within the actual wall that surrounds Westwood. The virus that once filled the air of this desiccated city had been captivated in that metal structure, building up pressure, waiting for something to set it free. And when you and your motorcycle came along, you did just that. Not only did you release that small amount of the poisonous virus back into the air, but you also ignited a spark that set off a huge explosion when it came in contact with the not only dangerous, but inflammable gas.

"And all of that leads to your face being burned," the Grim concludes as he points to my charred cheek. Most of this is information I already know, and, yet again, he had veered off from answering the original question.

"Okay, yeah, thanks. But that still doesn't tell me why I can see—"

"Hold up," he abides on. "I'm just going to wrap things up. Your face is burned by the virus, right? And in order to be able to see us Grims, you have to be exposed to the virus and succumb to it, correct?"

"Yes, but I didn't succumb to it," I answer him.

"Indeed, but you were still exposed to a compressed amount of the virus. That's why you can see us, Jaden. Because you came in contact with so much of the virus, you can see us Grims. The thing is, you came in contact with a significant amount of the virus that nobody could have survived. Except, you did. You survived the over exposure to the virus, you have survived from us Grims, and you have yet to egotone."

"But why?" I loudly plea to him. I saw Grims even before I ran into the wall, so that explanation doesn't add up. "And why have I survived all these things that should have killed me?"

The Grim drops his head and fervently begins to laugh. "You can't know everything, Jaden."

"Yes, I can. And I need to." I stand myself up and look down at the Grim in total frustration. "Why do all of you choose not to kill me? Thousands of Grims all had the chance to reach out and grab me and take my life, and I even almost touched a few, but they all chose not to touch me. They acted more like a guardian instead of an assassin." My voice has steadily grown in intensity, and I'm now angrily yelling at the Grim. "Why? Why didn't they touch me?"

"You can't know everything, Jaden," he repeats, trying his best not to spill.

"Yes, I can! I've been secluded for a week now; I deserve an answer!" My emotions have overcome me, and my shouts echo across the city.

"You can't know everything, Jaden."

"Tell me or. . . or I'll make you touch me."

The talking Grim turns to me to see if I'm serious, but as I try to maintain a somber look, he gives off a loud chuckle through his nose. "Yeah, I'd like to see you try to do that. Try to touch me, I wish you would. Besides, it's not like that's how you die anyway."

My mind pauses at his last statement. "What did you just say?"

The Grim obviously doesn't realize what he just said, but once the statement registers, he regrets saying it. "What? I didn't, er, I didn't say anything."

"You said that's not how I will die . . . Do you know how I will die?"

"I don't know what you're talking about, kid," the Grim unpersuasively tries to deny what he said.

"You know how I'll die." As the words exit my mouth and hit my ears, I'm thrown back even further. "You know how I'll die."

"Okay, I do," the Grim releases his built-up tension and bolts up to meet me at eye-level. "I know how you die. We all know how you die. All of us Grims know exactly how everybody dies."

I'm left speechless as his words settle. He does know how I will die. How everyone dies. "But how? How do Grims know?"

"Look at us, Jaden," the Grim tells me with anguish in his voice. "We don't have a face. You said it yourself, we're all ghosts. We're dead, for Christ's sake, which means were definitely not human. And since we're not humans, we can do things that humans can't, which includes seeing how everybody dies." He pauses for a moment to let me digest what he just said, but I will wait until he's fully done to do that.

"We know what happens. We're able to look at any person, whether they're living or they're a Grim, and see the moment they die, whether it's already passed or won't happen for another thirty years. We know everybody's fate. It's a curse, it's a punishment, but it's an ability we have." He shakes his head furiously, and his voice sounds like he's ashamed of himself. "And our job is to make sure you don't diverge from that death. That's why we've been around you this week, trying to prevent you from drifting away from your already assigned death . . . If you would have stayed watching that burning car, you would have grown curious and approached it right when it exploded. If you would have gotten drunk you would have ended up throwing yourself off this building. The same for when you found your Grandmother's body."

I hate to admit it, but those are very reasonable. "What about, about the ones with the crate, the ones on Highway 4, the one in Stevenson's . . ."

"We try to keep you from doing things we don't want you to. We didn't want you searching through all the crates, and we didn't want you driving to Roaksville. As for the one that snuck up on you in the Auto section in Stevenson's, that was just for giggles. That was Vernon, he's hilarious. You would like –"

"You know what happens?" I interrupt him as if the reality just now hit me and pause as I glare into his expressionless but yet disgusting face. This man can basically see the future. "I don't believe you."

"Fine then, don't believe me. But can you say that to Dr. Williams?" The Grim has grown brisk and uneasy as he drags his finger over his nonexistent eyebrows and points to a new visitor in the parking lot. A tall man wearing a white lab coat is standing in the center.

"Dr. Williams spent seven years at a university to become a pharmacist, only to be one of the first people to die from this virus due to all his clients being already infected with it. He left his loving wife, two children, and seven grandkids when he fell over dead while he was vomiting in a bathroom stall. Lucky him, him puking his guts out was his way of egotoning. But that's not good enough for you? Still don't believe me? How about somebody you've heard of, Mr. Lawkins."

The Grim, again, swipes his finger, and Dr. Williams is immediately replaced by Mr. Lawkins, the former town barber who was the first dead body I discovered. Perhaps the strangest thing about him is that he wears the same khakis and orange flannel that he wore when I found him.

"He watched his family die. Locked them in a room once they had egotoned and purposely cried loudly just so it would drown out the sound of his family killing each other. It didn't do him any good in the end, because he got the virus and turned psychotic just like his wife and their three kids. Is that still not proof enough for you?"

"No, I get it," I softly whisper, ashamed that I caused this lesson.

"Are you sure about that? Because I might have some people you care about that may convince you otherwise?" He gets close to my ear where his voice rings through my head and I can feel his warm breath blanketing my charred cheek, which makes me fear that he's going to touch me by accident. "Huh? Do you want to see how they died? You don't even know who I'm talking about."

"No! Do not bring anybody I love into this," I snap at the Grim and back away from him. I feel like he is beginning to disrespect me. "Do not tell me about them. Just tell me about myself."

The Grim laughs again, but this one sounds more malicious than playful. "I can't do that, Jaden."

His inability to tell me only spikes my interest, and I know that at this moment, I have never desired anything more in my life. "Tell me. Now."

"You can't know everything." He repeats again.

"Tell me! Tell me what happens. I'm tired of not knowing anything! I want answers!"

"You can't know everything."

I drop my hand and remain stationary, staring at the Grim.

"Fine," I calmly reply. Neither one of us dares say anything to the other. I begin to question whether anything this guy is telling me is even true. What if Delighting doesn't even exist? I wait in silence for about fifteen seconds, then dive at the Grim.

The Grim reads my move and steps away from me before I land hard on the unwelcoming roof. I regain my composure and get back to my feet quickly, but I'm left to watch as the Grim leaps off the roof and falls to the ground.

I anticipate a loud thud, but it never comes. Before I have time to even approach the edge and look down to see if the Grim had even hit the ground, I spot him sprinting across the parking lot towards the wooden liquor store.

And the only sound filling this barren town is four simple words:

"You can't know everything!"

19

Cocktails

I RUN ACROSS the roof and climb down the building to chase after the Grim. He has to tell me what will happen to me. Right at the peak of all this information is the link that will bring all of this together; yet, the Grim will not tell me...

I watch as the Grim turns the corner of the liquor store. As I make my way through the Stevenson's parking lot and to the front of the liquor store, I lose the Grim's trail. I spin around in circles, shouting for it to come out as I begin to make myself dizzy.

"Where are you? Show yourself!" My throat is scratchy from yelling so loud, and I quit spinning around in order to prevent from falling over.

As I've done far too often, I grow silent waiting to hear a response to my outcries. I don't expect to hear anything in return, but a sound coming from the liquor store behind me startles me.

I quickly turn around. There, standing inside the building and looking at me through the front window, is the blue-shirted Grim, lightly knocking on the glass window between us.

I scamper to the front door, but once I grab and tug at the handle, I discover that the store is locked. He locked himself in the store so I can't get to him. He really doesn't want to tell me what I want to know.

I back away and look around on the ground for something to throw at the windows. I find a decent sized clod of asphalt, more than enough to shatter the, what seems to be fragile, glass. I pick up the heap and chunk it at the glass, but right before it comes in contact with the glass, I see the Grim swipe his brow, and just like that, the clod vanishes.

It's no use. Anything I throw he's just going to make it disappear. I step back from the building while thinking of a way into it. But what's to stop him from just disappearing once I get to him?

"So what?" I bellow at the Grim, with sweat pouring down my neck. "What, you're going to stay in this store until I find a way in it, and then disappear when I do?"

"No, sir, Mr. Foxx. I promise not to take the coward's approach to this situation," he yells at me from inside the shop, leaving his voice muffled. "This is actually pretty fun. It's like we're playing the most epic game of tag ever. But you can try your little heart out, kid, there's no way you're going to touch me."

"Oh, so you lock yourself in a building, but you're not a coward?" I scorn at the Grim.

"Touché, Jaden," he responds to me as he takes a seat on the floor. "I guess we are locked in a stalemate then."

As my mind runs through with suggestions on how to get inside, an idea crosses my mind. Without paying any attention to the Grim, I dash off hoping that the Grim doesn't follow me to see what my next move is. Luckily, he doesn't, as I hear a muted "Good luck!" taunt me from the building to my back as I run out of the Grim's sight across Stevenson's parking lot. I know how I will get in that liquor store. He may not be human, but he isn't invincible.

Distraction. That's all I need. I need to be holding something big, preferably the biggest object I can find while hiding my actual weapon. What I will do is carry this object, maybe something like a huge rock, and make the Grim think I'm using this to break the glass with, perhaps questioning his dissipation skills. I'll throw the giant rock at the window, but as he focuses on getting rid of it, I'll pull the intended weapon out of its hiding place and throw it at the glass. He won't have time to react to it, maybe he won't even see it, and it will break the glass before he even knew what was coming.

But what if he just replaces the glass window? Then I'm back off to square one. Even worse, what if he does take the coward's approach and just disappears from the entire scenario? Besides, what am I going to use that can crash through the window but is also small enough to hide from him? I think about all the options I could use as I search Stevenson's parking lot for a large object I can carry back to the store.

The perfect gadget I can think of for this situation is a grenade, but I'm pretty sure Westwood is clean out of those. I could get a pistol, but I'm still afraid of resorting to a gun. Besides, my inexperience with one may even cause me to accidentally shoot myself. Okay, I know I'm not that clumsy, but I don't like the idea of using a gun. I could just find another medium-sized rock that might fit in my pocket, or maybe even a brick. A baseball could work, or I could stick a metal pipe down my pants and hide it behind my back. If all else fails, I could simply just charge at the window and try to ram through it. There's no way he could simply swipe his eyebrow and make me disappear.

But as all these options cross my mind, I always boomerang back to my earlier questions. What if he just replaces the glass? What if he just makes himself disappear? And as the uncertainty of how he will react flutters through my mind and overrules nearly every suggestion I make up, I come across a set of large recycling containers that prop against the side of Stevenson's. The bins stand as tall as I am, and are encased by a dark green metal with a small hole for people to throw whatever it is they want recycled in to. One is meant for paper, another for plastic, and one for . . .

I take a few steps backwards and dip my head around the corner, catching my eyes on the charred heap of the once-luxurious car I drove into the wall a few days ago. And a few yards away from the coals and cinders are a box of matches and a gasoline jug.

And I now know how I'm going to get him: by smoking him out. Molotov cocktails.

I run up to the recycling bin that is meant for glass and stick my arm in it. I feel around for any large bottles, knowing that there should be at least one in here, especially this close to a liquor store. There's plenty of broken glass in here, though, and I have to be really careful not to cut myself while I'm blindly searching. I finally pull a bottle out that still has a little bit of warm beer swishing at the bottom and fight off the urge to chug the delicious drink. This bottle isn't large, but it should work.

I turn the corner and run over to the car's remains, grab the box of matches, and head up to the roof of Stevenson's. I walk over to where I rested for the last two days, with the only proof of my residing being my shirt, the untouched foods, and my two rats. As my rats squeak in happiness at the sight of me and tug on my shoelaces, I kick them to the side, perhaps more forceful than I had intended. The rats are thrown onto their backs, and I feel remorse for them, but I don't have time to apologize. Instead, I rip a sleeve off of my shirt, toss it back to the ground, and make my way back to the parking lot.

I then dash to the gas station that dwells on the outskirts of the parking lot. Luckily, the gas station is just far enough out of sight from the Grim's view, so he won't see me in the midst of my plan. I fill the bottle up with gas from one of the pumps, soak my sleeve with the gas, and force half of the sleeve down the throat of the bottle. I then put the bottle behind my back and stuff half of it down my pants where the waistband on my jeans keeps the cocktail from falling.

As I carefully walk back to the corner of the liquor store, I find the cash register I tripped on earlier this week and decide that it will be used as my diversion. I struggle to pick it up, then wobble across the street with it until I reach the liquor store where the Grim remains.

I quietly set the register on the ground and reach for the matches. I strike a match and place it against the soaked sleeve that extends from the bottle in my pants. As the sleeve catches fire, I can instantly feel the flame singe my lower back, and I know that I don't have any time to lose before this bottle either sets my pants on fire or explodes.

I pick up the cash register and slowly tread out from behind the building and into the sight of the Grim.

Sitting cross-legged in the floor, holding a magazine in front of his face, the Grim recognizes my presence without even moving the magazine. "Oh I'm sorry, sir," the Grim begins, trying to change his voice, "I'm afraid the person you were looking for has left." He drops the magazine from in front of him to show two black dots and a poorly drawn smiley face that he obviously put on himself with a black marker. "Just kidding, it's me! Ya see I drew a face on myself, trying to fool you into thinking I'm someone else. You and I sort of look the same now!" I don't respond or even look at the Grim, and my lack of acknowledgement to his very, very hilarious jokes upset him. "Actually," he continues, "if I wanted to look like you, I should've just drawn half a smiley face than just scribbled all over the other half of my face and then complained about how ugly I am for the next, what is it, six days?"

The Grim remains conversing to me, but I disregard him. Keeping my back out of eyeshot from the Grim, I skirmish to raise the register above my head, ready to toss it at the window. The Grim finally realizes that I'm not taking any of his crap and wipes the drawings off his face.

"Damn, how did you find out my weakness of cash registers?" he teases me. "Now, you know good and well what I'm going to do to that thing once you throw it. You sort of just wasted your time and effort with that." However, I solidly ignore him, far too concerned with both the weight of the register and the flame stabbing through my kidneys.

"Say, kid, while you were register shopping, you didn't happen to find a lighter did you?" I pause for a second, thinking he somehow found out about my Molotov plan. "I found a pack of cigarettes in here but I left my lighter at home. After I poof that bitch your carrying goodbye, can you be a sweetheart and fetch me a lighter?" I heave the register at the body of the Grim. As soon as the weight leaves my hands, I reach for the burning bottle and throw it towards the glass door to my right.

As expected, the Grim drags his finger across his lower forehead like he has multiple times already, and the cash register disappears. As soon as the register vanishes, however, the Molotov cocktail plunges through the door and makes its way into the building. The Grim's head suddenly turns in disbelief to the flaming bottle, clearly not noticing that I threw it. We both watch as the bottle travels to the middle of the store and lands right in the remaining puddle of liquid that the earlier faceless had caused when he knocked the shelves over just days before. Before either one of us have time to react, a flash of fire pervades the room, and the entire store slowly becomes incased in a hot, riveting flame.

I step back from the store as the fire spreads across it and towards me. As I back away, I watch the Grim wag his finger at me, in what I guess is admiration. "Smart move, kid," he says through the crackling of the flames. He pulls a cigarette out of the pack in his pocket and sticks the tip of it in the flames of the store. "Appreciate the light." He gives one puff, then swipes his forehead. Just like I had anticipated, he vanishes, avoiding the blazing fire that surrounded him.

I continue stepping away from the now burning building and

plump down on the ground. Even though I failed at capturing and interrogating the Grim, the sight of the liquor store burning is a marvelous exhibit. The place that had caused me so much pain in my childhood is now consumed in flames. I only wish this was done over a decade ago.

The sight of the fire increasing in severity is peaceful. For a moment, I forget about the talking Grim. I forget about wanting to know how this all ends, about how I was abandoned, and what I was so worried about for a week. All I know is that this fire is marvelous. As the warmth from it grazes my face, I reach into my back pocket and pull my journal out. I feel I won't need this anymore. I toss the journal into the flames as a sort of sacrifice, watching as it immediately becomes engulfed.

After half an hour, the flames begin to dwindle. I decide that I want to see more burning buildings. I genuinely enjoyed watching that building burn, and I don't want that to be the last one I see. I jog back to the recycling bins next to Stevenson's and dig my arm in the glass container until I pull out eight bottles: three wine bottles and five beer bottles.

I make my way back to the roof to get my shirt. I look for my rats while I'm up here, but I don't see them anywhere. I feel bad for kicking them earlier, and I want to take them with me. However, since I can't find them, I'll just come get them later. I throw the shirt over my shoulder and make my way to the gas station, where I find a shopping cart to drop the bottles in to.

I fill all eight bottles up with gasoline, then rip my shirt into eight equally shredded lengths and place them in each bottle. Pleased with my assortment of objects lying in front of me, I push the cart out of the gas station and pass the smoldering liquor store.

I pass by multiple stores as I make my way down the street, but come up with an excuse on why I shouldn't burn each one down. I walk by the school which would be perfect to burn down, but it is made of brick. I then pass by the pharmacy, but decide that I might need something from it. I walk by the town dentist, Dr. Miller, but I don't really want to waste a bottle on *that* building, as he never hurt anybody. There's something different for each building. As I begin to exit the city limits, I turn back to look in the city. I have eight bottles and only one smoke cloud in the sky.

I could go back in the city and try to find eight buildings I could use them on. Or… or I could just turn around and burn some houses. All the houses are made of wood, and practically none of them serve a purpose anymore. It sounds good. The idea excites me, and I push the cart down the street with the city to my back.

I reach the first houses a few yards down, one on each side. As I push the cart down the line of houses, I pick a bottle up and light the rag sticking out of it. I chuck it through the windows of one of the houses to my right. As smoke spews from the windows, I stand and watch as the fire slowly takes over the house. Not really sure who used to live there, but I don't really care.

As the crackling of the fire becomes audible, a smile spreads across my cheeks. Here I am, bloodied up, burned, and broken, and yet I'm having the most fun I've had in the past week by burning random people's houses down. Never thought it would be so amusing.

The immensity of the fire eventually causes the house to collapse, and I go back to pushing my cart down the street. The ride is bumpy, as I'm running over the same picture frames and clothes that I did a few days ago on the motorcycle. Out of curiosity, I reach down and pick up one of the frames lying in one of the yards to my left.

The picture is of a married couple at their wedding – the man wearing a white suit and his wife wearing a beautiful white dress. At first glance, they almost look like they don't have a face, but after a second look I see that they do. They're both holding the other's hands, staring deeply into the eyes of their new spouse. It's hard to believe that people actually lived happy lives here. At some point, these two were a loving family, may have even had children. But nobody is happy in Westwood anymore.

I toss the picture frame in the house of the yard where I found it, then throw a bomb in after it. As the fire spreads over the house, I question what I just did. I don't know the reason for choosing this house that sheltered this loving couple. But really, it doesn't matter anymore because they're dead, just like everyone else.

I have six bottles left, and I continue down the street until reaching the house of someone I knew – Terra. I forgot all about her. The only one of my friends that I actually found. The image of her dead body runs through my mind, and I try to suppress it from my mind. Finding her body really woke me up to my situation. And imagining her as a Grim for the first time greatly disturbs me.

I look at the bombs in my cart and then back to her house. Do I want to burn it? I mean, we weren't the best of friends, but we were still friends. This was actually somebody I knew, somebody I conversed with nearly every day. Would it be bad of me to do it?

Before I can even react, I've already picked up a bottle. I feel like I should burn it down. Besides, who do I have to offend anyway? The Grims? I couldn't care less about what they think. I wish they would come Delight me, to be honest.

But still, do I want to do this to Terra? Wait . . .Why am I even asking myself this? Terra's dead. All these people are now just bodies on the streets. If they're not that, then they are irrelevant, faceless people. The memories I had of her belong only to me, so why should I even care what she *would* think. She's gone. They're all gone. Nothing I can do about it but burn it down. And that's exactly what I do.

After Terra's house creates a huge smoke cloud, I continue on down the street. Whose house am I to get next? Beats me. Heck, why don't I just burn all these houses down? I'm sure there are some more empty glass bottles in that bin. Actually, I like that whole idea.

Burn down the whole neighborhood. If I'm going to rule a city of nothing, might as well make it *nothing*.

I pick up a bottle, light the cloth, and throw it in the closest house to me. The gradual increase of fire is so amusing. I could stare at this all day, really.

I'm down to four bottles, for now. I pass by the house of one of my old teachers whom I never really liked. Now, three bottles left. I continue down the street until I see a house with a body lying on the porch. I'm now left with only two bottles and stroll on looking for a specific reason for each house.

Then I come across the body of Mr. Lawkins, and I know exactly where I am. I turn around to see the front door of my house. I pick up one of the bottles and hold it in my hand, looking back from it to my house, considering whether I should toss it through the window. I . . . I can't do it. My home was too special to me.

Wait. It *was* too special to me. Now it's just a house. It holds no meaning to me. As I reach for the matches in my back pocket, I'm still indecisive on whether or not I should burn it down, as I don't even know if I'm strong enough to do so.

Of course I'm strong enough. I'm Jaden Foxx. I'm not the same kid who wore that name a week ago. I've matured. Call me insane, or call me cold, I like to call myself different. I don't need this house. I don't.

However, if I am going to burn it down, I at least want one more look at it from the inside.

I leave the cart and bottles on the street and walk up to the front porch. I haven't been in this house since I woke up and found the city left in the way it is.

I pull the door knob and walk in. As soon as my foot lands on the inside carpet . . .

Black.

Then light.

Then sepia. As my eyes gain focus, I see that I am exactly where I was a few seconds ago. And I mean exactly. My foot had just touched the carpet, and the door is still swinging open.

As I enter the house, I notice the cheap birthday streamers hanging from the ceiling. I see Grandmother and Pawpaw sitting on the main couch, eating cake on little paper plates. Dad is sitting on the chair next to them, conversing with his in-laws. In the kitchen, I see young Jaden talking to young Cody, and placed on my shoulders, I see the hands of my mother.

I swallow hard and try to hold in my emotions. The only thing I can think of is her saying "Jaden? Where are you?" over and over again like she did a few nights ago. I slowly walk to her, listening in on the conversation between her and Cody's parents. Both Mom and Cody's parents hold cocktails in their hands, sipping on them while laughing at whatever-it-is they're talking about. Dad, however, isn't holding one, as he's been sober for a few months at this point in time. I can hear me ask Cody what he got me for my birthday. He doesn't tell me, but insists that I will like it. And I did. It was the remote control monster truck that I played with all the time. That is, until Dad went into one of his alcoholic rages and smashed it against the wall about six months later.

The whole atmosphere is so friendly, and the thing is, I didn't really need to have a lot of friends to feel happy. Cody was my only friend at this age, so all the people I knew were his family and mine. And I was totally fine with that. I mean, I had just turned seven. Not much you have to do to please a seven-year-old.

I watch as young Cody and young Jaden run to a table with three gifts: one of them is from my grandparents, one of them is from Cody, and the other is from Cody's parents. I remember Mom and Dad gave me their present after everybody left, but I don't remember what it was.

I watch young Jaden randomly pick up one of the presents which happens to be the one from Cody. Everybody then gathers around the table. "Hold up, bucko," Dad tells me as he pulls a camera out of his pocket. "Let me get this camera working before you start tearing things apart." He fiddles with it a little bit, then gives in and hands it to Mom. She gets it working and hands it back to him in exchange for a kiss.

I can't even look at my parents. I can't bare look at Dad in a happy state, unknowing that he will lose it in four months. I can't look at Mom, the person who loved life, yet doesn't even know she's going to have it taken from her soon. And me. I'm ecstatic, carefree, not worrying about a thing. The only time that I was truly happy in my life was when I had nothing to be sad about, when I wasn't missing a void that only she could fill.

As I turn away, I can hear young Jaden opening a present, then becoming excited that the monster truck he just unwrapped is exactly what he wanted, even though he didn't even know he wanted it. I wish I could go back and enjoy every moment of my innocent life before things went bad.

A tear flows down my cheek. I crave the happiness I had at such a young age, yet I feel bad that I was only able to experience it for a few months. My parents had just quit fighting at this point, and everything looked like it was going to be okay. And then . . .

I can't look. I can't stand to remain in here. I have to leave.

And just like that, my vision swirls to black, and a brightness slowly spreads.

I feel a sharp pain on my nose before I even open my eyes. When I do open them, I see that I'm face down on the floor. My nose has started bleeding again, and it's hurting so bad that I can't even feel it anymore.

That flashback did nothing but confirm that I want to burn this place down. The only way I'm going to get away from these memories are by letting them burn. It's terrible to think, but it's true. Nothing about my family or this house is going to help me from here on. I push my arms on the ground to get up, but my sight starts going in and out. Is it happening again?

Before I even have time to answer, I fall back down on the carpet and black out again.

I'm met by the same sepia color, but find it even stranger that I'm at the exact spot I was when the other flashback started. The door still swinging open, and my foot stepping onto the carpet. Everything seems the same, but I can quickly tell that it's not.

In the living room, my Grandparents sit in the same couch they were at earlier, both nowhere near as talkative as they were before. I see Cody's parents talking to them in a somewhat low voice. Not exactly sure why, but I can guess.

In the kitchen I see Dad cutting a cake and handing Cody and me a slice. Both of us aren't as energetic as we were before, and Cody grabs his cake and hurries back to his parents.

I watch as young Jaden drops his head and buries it in Dad's ribs. He pats my head and bends down to tell me something. I inch closer to try to hear what he says.

"Jaden, I'm sorry, son. I love you so much," he whispers to the younger me. "I wish you would cheer up. It's your birthday. That's something to be happy about."

"Yeah, but . . ." I begin in a defeated voice. "Mom's not here."

"Yes she is, Jaden. She's watching us right now, you just don't know it!" He's trying his best to cheer me up, but to no avail. "You wanna know how I know she is watching us?"

My young head rises up to meet his eyes as young Jaden is suddenly interested on how he knows. I know what he's going to say, I just can't believe I forgot he said it. Oh man, I can't believe I forgot.

He looks around then grabs a picture off the fridge and shows it to me.

"You see your mother right here?" He points to a picture of all three of us at a nearby theme park. "A picture of your mother is proof that she is watching you." He looks down at it and admires it. "It tells us that she will always be here, even when she's not. She will . . . uhmm . . . she will always be watching." He gives a strong smile.

The words cheered me up for the longest time. I carried a picture of Mom with me wherever I went after he said that. I'm not sure when I quit doing it, but I regret stopping. I'm just so disappointed that I had forgotten that he told me that. It helped let me know that he felt just as devastated as I was over her death. Prior to that, the only emotion I saw him respond with was anger.

It's weird, though. Even after eight months, my mom's death still affected us as if it were the day before. I watch as Dad and I walk to the table, which this year is filled with sympathy gifts from people who I didn't even know. I enjoyed the presents, but nothing really helped me that day more than what Dad said. It's really a sweet thought he shared with me. Showed me that he cared.

As I watch myself open a present, everything swirls into blackness again.

I hear my own sobs before I even open my eyes. As a trail of blood and tears meet on my burned right cheek, I realize how much I miss everyone, especially my family. I feel bad for wanting to burn my own home down. I feel bad for forgetting what Dad told me. I feel bad for swinging at Dad the very first night before everybody left. I feel bad for all that I've done.

And right in the midst of my self-pity, I hear my name being called from the streets behind me. The voice that emits the sound is one that I've longed to hear, one that immediately causes my head to perk up and turn around to confirm the voice is, in fact, coming from whom I hope it is.

And standing in the middle of the road, with a golden scarf around her neck, is the stunning Scarlett Avalon.

20

Friends

"JADEN! FOLLOW ME!" A gleaming smile escapes her luscious, crimson lips as she beckons for me to accompany her.

Scarlett? Is she alive? How did she survive? How have I not seen her this last week? The questions fill my head, but I don't concentrate on them and instead focus on getting up and meeting her in the street.

I exit the front door and step down off the porch, adoring how ravishing she looks. I can't believe how gorgeous she is. She hasn't even changed a bit from the last time I saw her when we went out for her birthday. I'm just overwhelmingly happy that her beautiful face is still there. The apocalypse hasn't affected her appearance, and I can't help but to match her smile in intensity.

But then I realize how much of a wreck I must be in her eyes. Cheek scarred, nose broken, and tears streaming down my eyes with blood trickling from my nostrils. I look like a disaster, but I don't care. I only care about this magnificent woman who I have craved to tell how I feel, yet never thought the opportunity would come to me again.

"Scarlett . . ." I remain aghast as no other words travel through to my tongue.

Before I even reach her, she takes off running down the road towards the wall. As she yells for me to catch up, I turn and begin sprinting after her, grinning from ear to ear the whole way.

I try my best to catch up to her, and once I eventually do, I see that she is overflowing with joy, giggling after every footstep she takes. I, too, can't help but laugh along with her. I don't know where we're going, but I don't think she does, either. That's the beauty of this situation. Here we are, running down these empty streets, laughing our heads off without a destination in our mind other than away from here. I have always wanted this time with Scarlett, just me and her. And right now, that's literally all that's left. The last two people in this city.

"Where are we going?" I yell at her as I excitedly gasp for air, physically not prepared for this full-out sprint.

"Here, take my hand," she turns her head and stretches her hand out for me to grab as we're now running side by side.

Without even thinking it through, my arm begins to extend to meet hers. The last time I tried to come in contact with somebody, he refused to be near me, so I jump at the opportunity to hold a welcoming hand, especially Scarlett's.

But it doesn't happen.

My hand passes straight through her hand and falls back down to my side.

I stop in my tracks and gawk at my hand, which I now view as unwanted. I didn't even consider it. I didn't even think that she may be my imagination going wild. She's not here. I'm running around the streets by myself. Laughing uncontrollably, by myself. Falling in love with nobody.

I glide my hands through my hair and tug on the strands as sweat runs down my ribs. This doesn't make sense. I saw her face, I know it was there! I imagined her this whole time. I'm crazy. I'm insane. I, I've lost it. I drop to my knees, pulling at the hairs in my head, trying to rip them out. I begin to hyperventilate, my chest trembling from the tension put on it by this reality. I mumble to myself to try to keep myself calm, but I don't even know what I'm mumbling.

As they have done far too often, tears exit the corners of my eyes and roll off my chin. I was so happy. I had waited *years* for that exact moment . . .

I clamp my eyes shut and wish to go back into unconsciousness. Wish to somehow be taken aback in one of my flashbacks, to be taken out of this dreaded world that seems to be void of any happiness. But as my inability to control these flashbacks still burrows through the back of my mind, I'm left with my knees plowed into the stiff street, with the only thing for my ears to catch being my soft sobs and a low growl.

Wait. A low growl?

I hastily lift my head to check whether that sound is existent or not. Having replaced Scarlett's presence is a lavender-colored, rabid dog, with his head tilted down at me and his vicious eyes locked onto mine. As the foam from its mouth drips with every nearing step it takes, I notice he isn't alone. Behind him, I count five more of the canines, all eyeing me down, all eager to rip me apart.

I slowly crawl backwards away from the dogs, all while making sure my eye contact with the leader of the pack doesn't break. I forage in my pockets and slowly pull out the hammer, which will act as what seems like my only weapon.

There's no way I can stand here and fight off six of these deranged dogs with just a hammer. I have to think of some way to get away from them, but how? I can't outrun them, so I cannot escape them. I can find a way to elude two or three, at the most, but there's absolutely no way I can evade six. They outnumber me, so I can only fight them, but with what? The hammer isn't going to do the trick. I may have to resort to throwing these random objects scattered across the street at them and hope that . . .

An idea on how to fight them off emerges. I'm going to have to use a gun. Even though I don't want to use one, I'm going to have to if I want to survive. It's my only choice. I can't keep running away from these dogs. I'll need a gun to defend myself, eventually.

And the only place I can think of where a gun might be is in between the fingers of Mrs. Armstrong.

I swallow hard at the resolution, but I have to get that gun. There's no other option. The Armstrongs' house isn't that far away from where I'm at, so if I can slow these animals down just for a little bit, I can make it there.

I quickly turn my head around to look for the nearest object I can distract the beasts with. I locate a small jewelry box and pick it up. As I turn back around to pelt the dogs with the box in my hand, the leader has already reacted to the interruption of our locked eyes and lunged at me.

As it knocks me down and opens its mouth to feast on me, I quickly jab the jewelry box into the dog's jaws. The box barely even hinders the dog, though, as it briskly rips the box to shreds. However, the dog's attention swaying from me to the box in those fractions of a second gives me enough time to pull my other arm out and drive the hammer into it's skull.

The crushing blow takes care of the first canine, and I hurriedly throw its lifeless body off and take off towards the Armstrongs' house before the other five have time to react. However, as soon as I begin running away from the scene, I can feel the group nipping at my heels, as they haven't skipped a beat.

I notice a lamp a few feet in front of me, so as I pass by it, I scoop it up and heave it towards the pack behind me. It hits one of the beasts square in the head and knocks it down. Unfortunately, the other four don't flinch, and they gain even more ground on me than before.

My eyes constantly switch from in front of me to the pack behind me. They seem so much faster than they were before.

As my attention was focused on the group behind me, my leg catches on a suitcase in the road, and I trip face first on the ground. I quickly flip over on my butt and weld the hammer in my right hand. No sense getting up, I don't have enough time. As the dogs get closer, one of them pounces in the air at me. This is it. Do or die.

I pull my arm back, ready to sling the hammer into its skull. But as I prepare myself for the attack, I hear a gunshot go off.

A gunshot?

The sound leaves me completely still as my right ear begins ringing. Before I can even respond, the midair dog lands on my stomach, motionless, a single gunshot wound to the head.

I hear another gunshot soar through the air. Then another. As I lay in complete confusion, I still keep in mind that three shots do not kill five dogs. As soon as that thought processes, I look to my left and see the remaining two dogs run away from the perpetrator, looking profoundly threatened.

I throw the animal off of me and look across from where I'm sitting. Two dogs, plus the one right next to me, lie on the street, dead. What if this person was aiming at me, instead? I snap my head to my right to see who shot the dogs to make sure I'm not the next target.

In a full white bodysuit, I see the sinister looking mask that met me earlier this week in Stevenson's and tried to take me on their helicopter. With a rifle in his hand, he runs over and helps me up. This time, I accept his assistance, as I am more than ecstatic to see a real person. No more scaring them off. This is my last chance, so I better take it.

As I get to my feet, I hear a grunted voice coming from the mask.

"Follow me," I hear the man command me. I don't think twice about it, I don't question him, I just do as he says.

He grabs my hand and takes off running toward the wall. My rescue plan that I had dreamed of for so long is finally happening. I don't want to scare the man, so I don't ask him questions. I remain silent, staring at the long road ahead of us that leads to the wall.

As we approach the wall, he hectically turns to me.

"Kid, do you know how to get out of here without going through that gas?" he asks me in the deep, muffled voice that comes with the mask.

"Uh, yeah," I begin in a shy voice. "There are a stack of boxes close to the opening down there." I point to my right, where the stairs of crates remain standing a few houses over.

He pulls me that way and I follow. If he doesn't know how to get out, that means he had to have climbed in somehow. I imagine a fire truck with a ladder waiting on the other side. Not exactly what I expected to get rescued in, but it doesn't matter. I couldn't care less about that. I'm just excited that I'm finally being saved. Finally. I can't mess this up again.

As we reach the boxes, the man hurries for me to go first. I climb up the three boxes and make it to the top. I look on the other side to see that my escape vehicle is actually an ambulance that is nearly scraping the wall. As the man begins to climb up, however, I notice a dog running towards him in the distance.

I yell for the man to turn around, and as he does, the canine collides with the stack of boxes and knocks the man down with them. As the boxes hit the ground, they fall apart and burst open, covering both the man and the dog with wooden fragments.

The dog observes the man, who is grappling his knee on the ground, recovering from a sustained injury. As the beast gets closer, I see the other one trailing from far behind.

"Hey!" I call to the man. "There's still another one coming! Get up, quick!"

I can't let this dog rip the man to shreds, but I feel helpless sitting where I am. I want to go help, but what exactly can I do? Besides, if I get down, that's just one more person to have to worry about getting to the other side, and since the boxes have broken, that task is going to be much more challenging than expected.

The man finally looks up and sees the animal creeping his way. He grabs the rifle on his back and points it at the creature. As soon as he does, the dog leaps towards him, as if it recognized the weapon.

Another loud gunshot fills the air, and the canine falls to its side. As the man gets to his feet, I remind him about the last dog that's approaching.

He looks up at me from the ground. "I'm out of bullets. What should I do?"

I'm totally shocked at his question. He's asking *me* for help? What do I know? I've been isolated for at least a week, probably more.

But despite me questioning his reason on asking me, I know the answer.

"That suit you have on is supposed to protect you from the air, right?"

"Uhh, yeah, it is," he replies in a bewildered tone.

"Well run through the opening right there," I then point to the source of the green cloud to my left. The man looks at the hole for awhile, obviously debating on whether he should run though it or not, and definitely regretting asking an eighteen-year-old for advice.

"But what about the last one?" he asks me, pointing to the dog that is now slowly gaining ground toward him.

"I recommend you hold your breath as you go through the gas, just in case," I ignore his question, hoping that it gives him an answer.

The man gets the memo and dashes for the opening. Once the dog spots its prey running, it furiously chases after him. The man throws the rifle on his back and runs through the green gas that occupies the hole.

The man makes his way through the opening, and the canine follows shortly after him. Once it is on the outside of the wall, it pauses, staring at the man. Here's my chance.

With the hammer held high above my head, I jump down from the fifteen foot wall and land on top of the creature, driving the claw of the hammer down into its head while using its body as a cushion to break my fall.

I pull the hammer from the dog and wipe its blood on my exposed chest, then put it back in my pocket. I look back to the man, who is looking straight ahead into the woods.

"Alright, great job. Now please, take me out of here," I plea to the man.

No response. The man reaches up and grabs his head, and I can hear him breathing loudly through the filtered mask.

I walk up to the man and become face to face with the horrifying mask.

"Are you okay?" I ask him.

He doesn't answer me in words. Instead, he falls to his knees and pulls the helmet off.

I see the face of my hero, a middle-aged black man with a goatee. But the face itself holds a feature that causes my heart to drop.

His eyes are focused straight ahead, telling me that the gas has already began to make him egotone. I don't bother about to turn around to see what he's looking at. I hear the man whisper "my head" to himself as he drills his fingers deeper into his temple.

I grab the man's shoulders and shake him. "No! You can't go! I need you to help me!" All the excitement I had, all the enthusiasm that consumed me a minute ago, now vanishes.

I continue shaking the man. "Please respond, please, you have to stay alive, you *will* stay alive. I know it. Just, please, I need you to give me a response."

The weight of the man exits at once, and he falls limply through my hands and onto the ground. He's gone. I can't believe it. I could've helped him up the wall. I could've helped him get more boxes. But no, I had to tell him to go through the wall. His death is on me.

My second rescue plan has failed once more all because of me.

Looking down at the man, I grit my teeth and clench my fist. Stupid of me to tell him to go through the gas. I knew how dangerous it was. That mask and suit wasn't going to save him, no matter how thick it was. I . . . I caused this. I ruined everything.

I continue looking down at the man and notice his eyes blink. Is he alive? I squat down and see him blink again.

I see the man's lips crease open, and I listen to him.

"Ki. . .kill. . ."

Yes! He's alive! With a smile on my face, I pull at the guy's arm to help him up.

The man turns his head to me and slaps my hand away.

"Killer! You're a killer!" the man shouts at me. He kicks my legs out from underneath me, causing me to fall.

The man grabs the rifle on his back and points it to me. He pulls the trigger, only to be greeted by an empty *click*. The man, surprised at the gun not going off, grabs the stock of the rifle and swings it down at me.

I roll out of the way as the gun breaks in half as soon as it hits the ground. I can't believe I forgot that he would egotone. Once I get to my feet, the man tackles me.

The man and I skid across the ground, stopping just a few inches away from the edge of the green gas. With the man on top of me, I grab his head and push it above mine. I push his head further and further up, until his face is submerged in the green gas. I struggle to keep his face in the gas as he squirms to try to break away from me. He then punches me in the chin, sending my own face to reach the edge of the gas. The man then falls over, and his eyes remain permanently centered on the sky above us.

I pull my head away from the gas as quickly as possible. I can't let the gas get to me. I can't let it knock me out. But as I stand up, I begin to lose my posture. I fight to stay awake and regain my balance for a second, but the dizziness permeates through me shortly after.

My eyes lose focus, but I have to stay on my feet. I have to stay awake. More people might come to save me, I can't let them think that I'm dead.

Blackness fills my eyes but quickly leaves. I stumble to the ambulance and lean up against it. My hand grips the handle, and I fall on my face. Black.

Nothing but black. No white, no sepia, just black. Am I dead?

I see a small light emerge through the darkness from far away. What is that? The light grows bigger as it gets closer to me and fills my sight completely. What is this light?

My eyes bolt open, and I feel a tug on my arm.

"Who's there? Back away! Get away from me!" I reach for my hammer and swing it around, hoping to hit whatever grabbed me. "Get away! Leave me alone! I didn't do anything to deserve this!"

"Were going to have to stabilize him. Rick, get the needle," I hear a distorted voice say. Is it another man in a suit? Is he here to help me?

"Please! Please help me! Don't leave me! I need help! I'm here by myself, please take me with you! I need . . ." a needle enters my backside, and I become sedated. "I need . . . friends . . ."

Black.

21

Crowds

SEPIA.

I'm in the midst of an enormous crowd. There's a low roar beyond them, and the overall mood feels worried. Worried about what? Where am I, anyway?

I'm in Westwood in what feels like the middle of the main intersection in the middle of the city. There's seems to be tens of thousands of people here, so apparently the whole population of the city is gathered here for whatever reason. Everybody in the crowd is wearing some kind of mask, whether it be an oxygen mask or a surgical mask. Apparently, at this point in time, the disease has already spread. However, the agitation swarming throughout the crowd leaves me worried with what exactly is about to happen.

The crowd slowly begins to hush, and as I turn my attention to the stage that stands in front of the crowd, I realize where I am. The Mayor of Westwood, Mr. Armstrong, walks across the stage, silencing the ocean of people, and the only sound is the steps of Mr. Armstrong's shoes on the wooden platform.

Mr. Armstrong approaches the microphone, clears his throat, and after two soft thumps to check the microphone, he begins.

"Okay. I know ya'll want to know what's going on, and I'll try my best to fill you guys in on as much as I know so far, so I'm going to start

from the very beginning. A few days ago, the first victim, Steven White, fainted on the streets of Westwood. As a group of bystanders circled around him to check him, Mr. White suddenly arose and became a very dangerous threat, which we later discover is the egotoning process.

"Doctors tried to find the cause of Mr. White's death, but more and more citizens were falling to the exact same fate, and as we all know, it's spreading throughout the country right now. Doctors from over the United States have finally found that it is, in fact, an airborne disease, but that it alters the brain activity once the victim contracts it. At this point, when a person's behavior is dramatically changed, there is no recovering from it. Once somebody egotones, it is fatal."

The crowd begins to chatter, and I feel that many of them already knew this.

"However," Mr. Armstrong loudly declares, grabbing the attention back to him, "this disease is nothing to be worried about, if it is treated correctly. There isn't a known cure for this disease yet, but doctors are working very hard to find one. In the mean time, there is an idea that the people here in Westwood have come up with as a way to try to hold off the virus from being so dangerous in our city. If the disease is obtainable through the air, then filtering it out is the only reasonable resolution that results in a happy, normal life for our citizens. Some of the most intelligent men around our area, including doctors, architects, scientists, politicians, and myself, have developed the blueprints of a wall to surround our city."

A low grumbling spreads throughout the crowd, mixed with questions about the project and on whether they had heard correctly. Mr. Armstrong clears his voice to quiet the crowd. As the crowd quietens and Mr. Armstrong prepares to continue, a man's voice extends from the silence. "I hope you're kidding about this wall." The crowd grows anxious, but Mr. Armstrong calms them down and tells the man to continue. "We're not in pre-K playing with Legos anymore, this is the lives of our families we're talking about. We need to do something that's going to work." The crowd erupts in a mixture of agreeing and disagreeing yells to the man's comments.

"Look," Mr. Armstrong retaliates, "it's just an idea, but right now, it is a very reasonable solution and the best option for us there is. And if it doesn't work, then so be it, we're back where we are now. We have to try this out if we want any chance of getting through this. Now, this fifteen-foot tall, metal wall will filter the air and trap the virus inside its empty shell. Simultaneously, it will let out safe, breathable air for us to use. It will act like a lung, to an extent. If this plan carries through, though, there will be a few minor consequences.

"First, the wall will surround the entire city and the attached suburbs with it, but cannot reach the houses outside of Highway 4. Highway 4 is a very important route, and we will need it to transfer the supplies needed to build the wall."

The crowd meets this declaration with mixed reception. Some feel un-affected mainly because they live in the suburbs, but those who live outside Highway 4 protest, asking where they will live.

Mr. Armstrong points down to a citizen not far from where I'm standing who has her arm raised. "Well then, where exactly are we sup-posed to go?" the woman angrily barks. "You just going to kick us out because we live on the wrong side of a road?!"

"Ma'am, please," Mr. Armstrong requests politely. "to the people who live outside Highway 4, you'll have to find housing within the wall. But, to all citizens, the building of this wall is not an easy project. We are currently trying to get all the metal that is required to build this metal wall that will surround the city five miles across and ten miles long, and we have half of the metal so far. With that said, assistance for this project is mandatory for all those who are capable of doing so. To those outside the wall, once the wall is built, we will create your own houses within our boundaries. With everybody's help, we can get the wall up in two days, and we should be back to our normal lives all safe and sound after it's up."

The mood of the crowd seems a little more encouraged, but there is still a lot of doubt flowing through the minds of these people.

"*We need to start on this wall now, even with only half of the materi . . .*"

Mr. Armstrong's voice fades away along with my vision. Before I even have time to take in what Mr. Armstrong just said, my sight comes back again. I expect to open my eyes to the real world, but another flashback introduces me to new surroundings. I realize that I'm still in the sepia world. I am standing in a similar scenario as the one I was in, except for this time, there are only about thirty or forty people forming a circle in the park of Roaksville.

"We're getting out of here," I hear my dad's voice direct to the group. My dad. He's . . . He's still alive. Well, at this point anyway. But he survived this far. He . . . he still has to be alive now.

"And how well did that work for us last time?" An unknown woman replies with sass that irritates me. "I suppose we're just going to run around in circles for the rest of our pathetic lives?"

"Staying here is not going to solve anything," I look over to see Ryan for the first time in what seems like centuries. Ryan made it, too. Even though I can feel the animosity flowing in this flashback, I can't help but smile as I look around the circle and see familiar faces. Cody is still alive, too. And Scarlett stands right next to him. However, she, along with everybody else in the circle, has an oxygen mask over her face, hiding her beauty that I wanted to see. That doesn't matter though, both of them made it. "If we go to the refuge in Illinois . . ."

"We dun' said this before, we don' know if 'eres a city still ther' 'er not!" Phil yells at Ryan from across the circle.

"Well, there's only one way to find out!" My head diligently follows the voice to the woman of my dreams, Scarlett. "People are dying way too fast here, and this city in Illinois has a wall just like . . ."

"Wait a second," I turn to see Grant step out into the circle, eyeing down the man who's directly in front of him, which happens to be my dad. "Have you already brainwashed these kids into thinking that your 'wall' idea may still work?"

Dad doesn't break eye contact with Grant, and he, too, takes a step into the ring. "You can't brainwash them with facts. The wall worked, we just didn't have enough time to filter all of the disease out of Westwood."

"Oh, forgive me," Grant sarcastically says with a frown. "I forgot about the facts. Maybe it was just the 30,000 PEOPLE WHO WERE KILLED IN WESTWOOD that made me forget about how great the wall was!" The sudden outburst of rage startles me, but Dad doesn't move. Behind him, I see Mr. Armstrong take a step forward and stand next to Dad.

"The wall was a great idea that Anthony contributed heavily too," Mr. Armstrong states, "and without his idea then this city in Illinois wouldn't even be alive."

"WE DON'T KNOW THAT IT IS!" A man that I don't know on Grant's side yells at Mr. Armstrong.

"If you don't want to go, then DON'T GO!" Mr. Armstrong shouts back, and as tensions stir, I see a tear surprisingly fall from Mr. Armstrong's eye. "I don't have anything to lose. My wife is gone, and I just lost my son, too. I'm going to Illinois to find this city, and I don't give a damn if any of you come with me or not!"

Mr. Armstrong slowly makes his way out of the circle, and I can hear him sobbing as he walks. I didn't know Tyson died from this. I feel saddened, not so much at the death of Tyson, but because of how broken Mr. Armstrong seems right now. He feels that this city in Illinois is his last hope.

"We're not going, Anthony," Grant tells my dad. "If you want to take your son's friends with you to Illinois then be my guest. But the rest of us are staying behind. It's far too risky."

"You say that as if there is no risk in staying here!" Dad argues back to him.

"If wer' gunna die 'en I wan' it to be 'ere and not in som' car in the middle of the road," Phil replies, firm on his choice. I feel that everybody else that is on Grant's side are just as firm as Phil is. But I can see why they would be suspicious. Driving three states over is practically a suicide mission. Dad accepts Phil's decision, then turns to tell Cody, Ryan, and Scarlett to follow him. Everybody who has chosen to stay has a tint of disgrace in their eyes, but I don't know if it's at my Dad and my friends for having chosen to leave on practically a death wish, or if it's at themselves because they don't have the courage to try it.

"If the city is there and thriving," Ryan speaks up as he walks away, and every eye in the circle dramatically shifts to him. "We will come back to get you guys." Cody, my Dad, and Scarlett throw Ryan harsh looks, but he continues. "This isn't a competition to see who die's first and then point fingers. This is a group effort. The human race is on the brink of extinction; we can't hold grudges because our actions don't follow those of others. If ya'll don't want to go with us, fine, but arguments like this is what got people in Westwood killed in the first place."

"No, kid," Grant says with a grimace. "Anthony's beloved wall is what killed those people."

Once the words exit his mouth, Dad strides over to Grant and swings at him, hitting him in the cheek and knocking him to the ground. I can't keep myself from wincing at my dad's violent move. I'm glad he did it because somebody needed to shut him up, but I'm also disappointed in him. What Ryan said was right, and Dad punching Grant just confirmed that this civilization is going to stay in it's dog-eat-dog attitude.

Grant sits on the ground with a bloody lip, still eyeing my dad as he spits two of his teeth out into his hand. "Don't worry about us, Avalon," Grants calls out to Ryan in a voice that sounds much more battered than it was earlier. He then turns to dad to eye him with bitter hatred. "Just leave us to fucking die."

My vision spirals and falls back to black.

My eyes shoot open. I'm staring into an overhead light that is beaming at my face, and I'm more than glad to see that it's not sepia. Wait, why is there an overhead light here? I hear voices surround me, all talking in a hurried manner.

"Did you check his lung capacity?"

"He's lost too much blood; we're going to need to find someone with O negative."

"We need to put stitches on his leg right here."

"Hey, guys! He's awake!"

The voices stop. I lift my head up to see about six doctors, all surrounding me and looking me dead in the eyes.

"He's . . . awake. How did he—"

"What's going on?" I interrupt the woman. All these people, all concentrating on my health.

I go to stand up, but I'm quickly held down by the group of doctors, all telling me to calm down. Calm down? I've been in a city by myself for a week and they want me to calm down? "What do ya'll want from me? Let me go!"

I bite the hand of one of the doctors, and hear a shriek of pain come from him. I struggle to get out of their grip, not knowing what exactly I will do if I escape from them.

As I'm skirmishing with the doctors, I hear a door slam shut behind them. As two of the doctors continue holding me down, the others move out of the way for me to see who is coming.

And there, in teal scrubs, is my dad.

He did survive this far. I knew he would. He slowly makes his way to the table I'm held down to. Once he comes within arm's reach, I hold my hand out to touch him. Once my hand touches his skin, a sudden relief spreads throughout me, and I know that I'm finally safe. I then look up to his face and see features that I guess I ignored when he first walked in.

His face is cleanly shaven, no facial hair whatsoever, which is an appearance he hasn't ever taken since I've been alive. Not only that, but his hair has thinned, and he has become much skinnier. His neck is now pervaded by wrinkles, and he looks as if he has aged years. And, for all I know, it may have been that long.

He wipes away a tear from the corner of his eye as his mouth stays trembling. I'm so glad to see him, and he's so glad to know I'm alive. I watch as his lips form words, and I become lax at his voice that I can now hear come from him and not my imagination.

"Jaden . . . You made it. I'm so glad you made it."

A smile stretches across his face. A familiar smile that I have yearned to see. His hand moves to my cheek, and he gently rubs my burned mark.

"What happened here?" he says with a concerned smile. I begin to answer him, but as I do, I feel a needle enter my backside, and I pass out again.

22

The outlier

"I WAS FROM Canada," I hear a faded voice coming from a woman as I gain my consciousness. I hear the voice, but don't see anybody, as I can't open my eyes just yet. "Lower part of Toronto."

"Cool. That's pretty far off, right?" Excitement overcomes me when I hear this person's voice, but my eyes are too heavy to open, and I can't react.

"About as far as Mississippi is," the woman replies. She sounds like she's going to add something to what she said, but she pauses for a moment. "His heart rate just increased." The woman's voice grows anxious, and I feel her grab my wrist with two fingers in response to this.

Of course my pulse went up. As the woman holds my wrist, I try my best to open my eyes, to move in any way, but my body is numb.

"How long until he wakes up?" the familiar voice asks the woman. With every word he says, I try to fight off the rust, to let him know I'm awake, and to finally see him alive for the first time.

"I have no clue. It might be another –"

I finally force my eyes open. At first, it seems that only one eye is open, but I quickly realize that there is some kind of gauze over the right side of my face, bandaging up my burn mark and covering up half of my face, including my nose.

I'm in a hospital bed, covered in sheets and blankets. The room is marvelous. Hardwood floors sparkle cleanly below me, and the walls look like they were just recently built. Hovering above me, I see a skinny, frizzy-haired woman in white scrubs, holding a clipboard. And in a chair at the foot of my bed is my best friend, the guy I didn't think I would ever see again. With his flat top still the same way it was the last time I saw him, I try to speak to him.

"Cody," I hear myself whisper to him.

"Oh my god." He instantly jumps out of his chair and practically tackles me as he gives me a huge hug. The rest of my body is too numb to move, and he actually begins hurting me a little. "Jaden. Man, you . . . You don't know how glad I am to see you." His voice cracks, and he begins to cry.

This moment takes me by surprise, but I try to hold back my tears for the first time in a while. "I'm happy you're here, Cody. I really am."

"I missed ya, buddy," I can feel tears dripping from Cody onto my shoulder, and as the feeling in my arms returns, I put mine around him, as well.

He finally backs off of me and pulls his chair closer to me. "Man, I don't know where to begin . . . This is crazy. I'm so glad you're alive."

"I'm glad you're alive, too. But what about everybody else? Did I actually see my dad here or did I just dream it?"

"Nah, you actually saw him," Cody informs me. "He's the main doctor here, I think they call him the chief physician. He was here with me and Nurse Amanda about ten minutes ago, but he had to help a patient. You know, doctors' stuff."

I'm actually surprised that Dad progressed from being a nurse in Westwood to becoming the chief physician, but I couldn't care less. He's here. That's all I wanted to hear. He's here with me, and we are both okay.

"What about everyone else?" I pester him. "Scarlett, Ryan, Terra.

Did they make it?" I pause before I say Terra's name, as Cody doesn't know I found her body back in Westwood.

"I don't know what ever happened to Terra. But Scarlett and Ryan. They're umm . . . They're gone."

My heart drops. No . . . Not them. They were in that flashback; how did they not make it? Cody made it, Dad made it, why didn't they? Ryan is dead. Scarlett is . . . dead. And I never even told her how I felt. I never got to do what I promised her.

I sink in my bed as my heart begins to break. The one girl that I had always liked, no, loved, I'll never see again. I never told her my feelings for her because I was too scared. Now it doesn't even matter. There's nothing I can do to tell her how I feel. Losing her and Ryan just adds on to the list of people I care about leaving my life.

It takes every inch in me to keep from crying, but I can't hold back a single tear as it runs down my face.

"A part of me knew they were gone," I somberly admit to Cody. "But, then again, another part of me thought you were gone, too. I just . . . I never got to tell Scarlett how I felt about her . . ."

"I know how you feel," Cody assures me as he pats my leg. "Terra never made the first trip to Roaksville. She got really sick that night we all went out for Scarlett's and Ryan's birthday, remember? I think her parents took her to the hospital that night, but I never saw or heard from her after that night. It just . . . It ripped me apart for the longest time. I'm just now getting over her." Cody wipes his eyes with his sleeves as he looks up and gives me a comforting smile. "We will be alright. We've made it this far."

He's right. This breaks my heart, but I'll have to get over this. It'll be hard, but I've gotten over Mom and Grandmother, so I can get over them. But still . . . there will always be that part of me that screams 'what could've been' with me and Scarlett.

I look over at the night stand next to my bed to see my hammer and the shark tooth necklace. I pick up the shark tooth and roll the object in between my fingertips, studying the smooth surface of the gift. This will be what I remember her by. As I gently place it back on the table, the nurse interrupts the silence.

"I'm terribly sorry, sir, but I'm going to have to ask you a few questions. Is that okay?" I look at Cody, and Cody gives me an impressed grin in response to this probably thirty-year-old woman calling me 'sir'.

"Yes, Ma'am, that's totally fine with me." I have a ton of questions to ask her myself but those will have to wait.

"Ok. I'm going to start off with some basic questions. What is your name?" the nurse asks me, as she gets her pen ready to write.

"Jaden Foxx." I tell her without hesitation.

"When is your birthday?" She continues.

"June 18, 1996."

"Okay good. What is your father and your mother's name?"

"Anthony Foxx and Tiffany Foxx." I wonder why she asks me for my mother's name, at first, but I just assume that it doesn't have any actual meaning behind it.

"Okay. So far you're three for three." She congratulates me. "Now I'm going to have to ask you questions that you may not know. Where are we located at right now?"

I pause for a moment to think it over. They don't know that I know that we're in Illinois, so I feel that if I answer correctly, then they're going to ask how I know. And I can't exactly tell them 'oh, I passed out and had this weird-colored dream that told me'. "Alabama?" I pretend to be clueless.

They both snicker at my guess. "That's okay, we expected for you not to know," the nurse notifies me. "You are currently in Tryton, Illinois."

"Illinois?" I ask, trying to act surprised by that not-so-surprising news. I'm a really good actor. "How did we end up way up here?"

"To make a long story short," Cody begins to fill me in, "at first, everybody in Westwood relocated to Roaksville. Once we got there, things just seemed to get worse. The disease began spreading even faster once we got outside the walls in Westwood. As people started to get the disease, everybody that had survived was sort of lost as to what to do. Your dad somehow found this place, and me, him, Ryan, Scarlett, and Mr. Armstrong we're the only ones who left Roaksville to make the drive all the way up here."

"If that's the case, then how did Ryan and Scarlett not make it?" I finally ask a question that I don't already know and hope that there is some way for them to still be alive.

"I-I don't know," he tells me, ashamed to not have an answer. "It was us five: your dad and I in one car; Ryan, Scarlett, and Mr. Armstrong in another. They were following behind us and somehow we lost them. One minute they were there, the next minute we checked, they were gone. There was literally nobody else on the roads, so they couldn't have had an accident. They just disappeared. Your dad and I waited a little while for them. We didn't have time to go back and look for them. Honestly, if we did, your dad and I may not have made it to Tryton."

I sit in silence, wondering what he meant by 'not have made it to Tryton'. What, was there some kind of time limit? Before I have time to ask him, the nurse continues.

"Ok, another question for you, Mr. Foxx. Do you know what day it is?"

I'm sort of thrown aback as I try to transition from 'how Scarlett, Ryan, and Mr. Armstrong got left behind' to 'what day is it'. "I'm just completely guessing that it's a Tuesday."

The nurse and Cody trade surprised looks. "Wow, you're actually right," the nurse tells me. I puff my chest out sarcastically and give a huge smile as my random lucky guess makes me look way more informed than I actually am. "Okay then, do you know what today's date is?"

Crap. I should've guessed the wrong day. Honestly, I have no clue what today is, and I hadn't known since I was left in Westwood. I feel like my guess here is going to be way off. "Uhm, I'm gonna guess that it's sometime in October."

The nurse, as if expecting Cody to correct me, throws her hand in front of him as a way to stop him before he starts. "October of what year?" she compels me, as if this question is the most important question in the universe.

"Well, I'm going to guess 2014. I know I haven't been out there for a year." I'm shocked at why she would ask me the year. It obviously isn't October of 2015. Right?

The nurse scribbles furiously on the notepad in her lap, which worries me. "How long have I been out there?"

"Well," the nurse begins as she looks over the paper on her clipboard. However, to me, it looks like she's just avoiding eye contact with me. "The virus began spreading in October of 2014. Today's date is April 29th, 2015. You've been in Westwood for . . ."

"Six months . . ." I finish her sentence for her. I can't believe what I'm hearing. Six months. But . . . but that doesn't even make sense. Six months? There's no way. No possible way I could have been in Westwood for six months. "How?" As I hear myself ask them, I realize just how completely lost I am.

"We don't know," the nurse tells me. "The last known survivor to come to our city was four months ago, and even at that time, he was an outlier."

I turn to Cody, hoping he knows how six months passed without me knowing, but he looks just as confused as I am. "It was definitely a surprise to hear that somebody from Westwood had made it this long."

"What, has it been six months since you guys brought me here? Have I been asleep in this hospital bed for six months?" I can tell these claims sound rather silly to them, but I honestly don't know if

I had or not.

"No, everybody in Tryton found out that you were still alive about a week ago," Cody informs me. Does that mean that I was asleep in my bed in Westwood for six months? There's no way I could have survived a coma for half a year . . . I look to the nurse for assistance, but she is too busy writing down what I say and what I don't know.

"How did they find me then?" I question them.

"Okay, that much I do sort of know. Well," Cody commences what seems like will be a long story, "so there are supply helicopters in Tryton that travel to all the ghost towns across the nation and take all the abandoned items they think we might need. You know, food, water, nudie magazines, things like that. One of the choppers was flying close to Westwood when they spotted a huge green smoke cloud coming from the city."

That must have been when I crashed into the wall.

"The helicopter pilot stopped to see what had happened and saw you lying on the ground, so they thought you were dead. Once they saw the wall had exploded, they came back and told the mayor what they saw. Mr. Jenkins then addressed the city and told us what had happened. The discovery really helped with how everyone acted around the Tryton wall since everyone just learned that the gas, the virus itself, in heavy doses is flammable, but learning that there had been someone alive to cause an explosion was a big surprise to everyone. So, at one point, an exploding wall was more important than your dead body, incase you're feeling special."

"I'm so honored," I say with a smile.

"They didn't say that the body was yours, but once they said it was somebody from Westwood, your dad began freaking out, thinking it was you that had died in the explosion. I mean, it was a possibility, but I thought you had died when the virus spread through Westwood."

Thinking of the explosion brings back painful memories, and I lift my hand to my charred cheek as a reaction to the thought. The feeling of a fuzzy bandage over my face replaces the feeling of a rough, skinless region, and it makes it seem like the burn never even happened.

"So," Cody continues on, "your dad insisted on telling the men to go back to Westwood. Your dad gave the pilot flying the helicopter a picture of you, and the pilot agreed to go back to Westwood to see if it was you or not. When the man arrived at Westwood again, he found a totally new smoke cloud that wasn't there the first time. He then searched for your body, but you weren't lying where you were supposed to be."

The new smoke cloud must have come from the car crash into the wall of Stevenson's.

"The pilot came back and told what he saw. Everybody was like 'there has to be somebody causing all these smoke clouds, they don't just pop up', and we thought we should send a squad in to look for this person. Your dad and I volunteered to go in case it was you, but Mr. Jenkins wouldn't let us. When one of the guys in the group that was chosen to go came back with a broken arm and a slashed air tank, we knew something was up."

"Yeah, I didn't know what was going on," I defend myself. "We know, it's not your fault," Cody tells me. "We were all just afraid that you had egotoned. So, everybody in Tryton spent the next two days voting on whether or not we should risk a rescue mission for you, preparing a plan on successfully recovering you, and creating a ground group to drive in and get you in case you did egotone. That way, there was no real chance of you throwing someone out at a few thousand feet in the air or accidentally killing the only person capable of flying the helicopter." He gives a short chuckle and I echo it.

I can't help but feel guilty. I know I must have been a nuisance to them. I'm so glad they didn't give up on me.

"Once the men came back to Tryton with you in the truck, the whole city went crazy. Everybody had followed you since you were discovered. I mean, we even got a camera to follow you around. You were the only thing that put meaning in some of these people's lives. You were the only happy story any of them had heard of in half a year."

I find myself too attached to what he just said. "A camera?" The word itself fuels a suddenly present anger. "You guys had a camera? You guys were spying on me? Watching me like I was some kind of entertainment?"

My voice gradually rises with each question I jab at them. "Mr. Foxx, please calm down," the nurse places her hand on my arm to try to soothe me, but it doesn't help. Cody looks stunned at my sudden outburst, and even though I'm not angry at him, in particular, I'm not sure he knows that.

"What the hell is wrong with you people!? I was stuck in that city for six months. And you guys just watched me. Ya'll just ignored how terrified I was. How hopeless I was. How . . . how desperate I was for somebody, anybody, to help me. And no. You guys just . . ."

Black.

Sepia.

Oh my god. Not now. As mad as I was a second ago, I find that I'm somehow surprisingly calm right now, despite how frustrated I want to be. And I have every right to be frustrated.

I stand on the roof of a building. At first, I think that I'm back in Westwood on the top of Stevenson's, but as I look out from the roof and into the city that lays in front of me, I see that this city is completely different.

"This must be Tryton," I tell myself, not exactly sure if it is or not. Large skyscrapers extend from the ground below where I'm standing. Further out from beyond the skyscrapers stands a metal wall that looks similar to the one in Westwood. Whatever building I'm standing on is the tallest building in this city, as it is the only building even close to the top

of the wall, but the buildings below me are far from appearing meager compared to it.

The view from this height is truly magnificent. I'm reminded of the one place where I felt like I was ruler of everything back in Westwood, but I can undoubtedly agree that this view is much nicer.

But my peaceful behavior is suddenly interrupted by something I didn't even think existed anymore. In the distance, I see a bird flying towards me. With every flap of its wings, I'm left puzzled as to where this bird came from and what exactly it's doing here. As it gets closer, my heart begins to beat out of my chest, and I have to catch myself from lunging at the bird once it perches itself on the edge right in front of me.

A half-normal, half-robotic eagle rests in front of me and buries its beak into it's metallic wing. It then surveys me with it's piercing, bright red eye. This bird . . . It came back to me, just like I had hoped it would. Before I have time to reach out and grab it, my vision falls into a blurry spiral, and my eyes go back to black.

My eyes dart open. Both Cody and the nurse are inches away from me, with terrible looks on their faces. Once they notice that I am conscious, a sudden relief falls over both, and they slowly back away from me.

"Damn, you scared us," Cody says as he plunges himself back in his chair. "We thought you had a heart attack or something."

"I have to go," I tell Cody and the nurse. Both of them seem puzzled at my remark, and neither say anything to me, waiting for me to reaffirm. "I have to leave this room and go somewhere."

"You can't do that," the nurse commands me. "You're not allowed to leave. I still have a few questions to ask you, and we still have to run a few more tests before you can leave."

"I don't care," I sternly tell the woman. And before I give her time to respond, I get out of my bed.

23

Just listen

"**WHERE ARE YOU** going?" Cody asks me, concerned with my sudden statement to leave.

"I don't really know," I honestly tell Cody, as I'm not really sure why I want to leave. I weakly drag my feet across the wooden floors of the room. "I just need to get some fresh air."

"Mr. Foxx, I can't let you to do that," the nurse softly glares at me and beckons for me to sit back down.

"With all due respect, ma'am, you're gonna have to," I order her with some unknown authority that I didn't know I had. As I make my way across the room, I feel a sharp pain in my arm. Once I realize it's coming from an IV needle, I drag the IV stand with me to the door, turn the handle, and open it.

"You want me to come with you?" Cody asks me, sincerely wanting to go with me to make sure I'm okay.

"No, I'm fine. Just let me be alone." With that, I leave the two in my room.

The halls of the hospital floor are disgusting compared to my rather nice room. The ceramic floors look as if they haven't been mopped in decades, and the walls are reeked in a 1970s-esque, puke-green paint.

I drag myself and the IV stand across the unappealing halls of the floor without spotting a single person. Oh great, déjà vu is just what I need. I do, however, find a bathroom, and step inside of it.

My hand immediately races to my face, or what is left of it, once the lights flash on. The white gauze that's been pulling at my hair covers up nearly my entire head. Even the left side of my face, the only visible part of my identity, is flushed red and looks different than my usual appearance.

Both of my arms are wrapped in the same kind of gauze that my face is. They both start at my forearms and travel up above my elbows. My left leg is entirely concealed, and my ribs are enclosed in a thick, soft padding. When I push down on the padding on my ribs, I feel a cool liquid from the inside of it, telling me that some kind of ointment is applied to the injuries.

I look away from my afflictions and look at the purple iris in my eyes. I never fully realized how damaged I had become; how much pain I've went through in the past week until now. But one thing I did realize, and truly haven't appreciated until now, is that I've come a long way. An incredibly long and agonizing journey that not many people could have made it through.

Or maybe I'm wrong and a lot of people went through much worse than I have. I don't know. I'm not use to standing on a pedestal, so I can't help but tell myself I'm not as badass as I think I am.

I leave the bathroom and eventually make my way to a reception desk, where I find an older lady studying through a stack of papers in front of her.

"Excuse me, ma'am," I kindly ask the woman. "Is there like an observatory deck or anything on the top floor? And if so, where can I find an elevator? I've been walking around this place for a good five minutes."

The woman looks up at me and, once she recognizes me, becomes utterly stupefied.

"Jaden Foxx . . . It's Jaden Foxx . . ." she hastily hops out of her chair and eagerly extends her hand. I reluctantly shake it, surprised as to why she's so happy to see me. "You are . . . Oh my gosh, you are my hero. I am so thankful for you and all you have done for this community."

"Thanks . . ." I unconvincingly tell the woman, still wondering why she's so thrilled. "Anyway, is there an elevator around here?"

"Oh yes, what you're looking for is on the 23rd floor," she fervently informs me. "There's an elevator around the corner to the right that will take you directly to it."

"Okay. Thanks," I tell the woman, still a little unsettled about how excited she was. I make my way to the end of the hall and take a right as she says, and sure enough, there is an elevator.

I press the button, and after a few seconds, the light above the elevator chimes, and the metal doors slide open.

The elevator is absolutely beautiful inside. The floors and walls are made of pure marble, and the walls are all polished clean where I can see my reflection. Golden hand rails surround the elevator completely, and as I press the 23 on the button pad, I'm even more confused about why this hospital can't decide if it wants to be elegant or not.

The elevator speeds up to the top floor, perhaps too fast for my comfort. Once the elevator reaches the top, the door chimes and slides open simultaneously. I push my IV stand out from the elevator and follow it.

The halls on this floor are much nicer than the halls of the floor I was just on, but I disregard it. Instead, my attention is focused solely on the wall of windows directly in front of me that spread out through this entire side of the floor. I make my way down the hall, looking out the window as I do so.

The amber sunset gleams at the windows and bounces off the buildings that make up this city of Tryton. The skyscrapers are a bright white – either that or incredibly reflective – and mixes well with the sunset orange. The sight is amazing, but as I enjoy it, I feel a light poke on my right thigh, and look down to see an older man in a wheel chair being pushed by a nurse. The nurse gives me a funny look, as I think she knows I shouldn't be roaming the hospital, but the old man has an elated smile that shows his lack of teeth. The man moves his mouth to try to speak, but nothing comes out. Instead, I read his lips to see him trying to get the word 'Jaden' out of his mouth. The man looks so pleased to see me, like he's a little kid and I'm Santa Claus. I give the man a hearty smile and continue walking down the hall. As I make it to the end of the hall, I come to a door with the label "roof" on it that induces me to enter it.

I look around to make sure the nurse – or anybody, for that matter – isn't going to stop me from entering, and once I realize the nurse has her back to me and that nobody else is on the floor, I push the door in.

The door leads to a small room that's made up entirely of a staircase that leads to another door. Determined, I pick up my IV stand and steadily make my way up the stairs, step by step, until I reach the door and push it through the other side.

Once my face touches the outside breeze, chills travel down my spine. The warm, now April air brushes against my face, but I can only feel a fraction of it, as the rest is being absorbed by this gauze. Straight ahead of me and away from the building is a huge wall, exactly like the one in Westwood. The hospital nearly touches the metal wall. The top of it is eye level with me, and for the first time, I see the wall as not a boundary or restraint, but as protection.

I turn around and face the remaining part of the roof, and to my amazement, I see a helicopter resting in the middle of the area. I make my way over to the helicopter and inspect it, greatly intrigued by the complex buttons that I want to violently press right now. After admiring the helicopter, I shift my attention to the side of the building that faces the remainder of the city. Just as I had seen moments ago, the exact scenery meets me. However, this time, it's much more breathtaking in reality.

I slowly walk to the edge of the roof, which has a three-foot barrier extending up to prevent anybody from simply walking off. I place my hands on the concrete barrier and gaze at the beautiful sight before me. So relaxing and refreshing, but this isn't what I came up here for.

"Where are you, bird?" I whisper the question to myself, waiting to see it glide my way from inside the sunset. But, just as I had waited for it on the roof of Stevenson's, it doesn't happen.

"Jaden . . ."

My thoughts are interrupted from a soft voice coming from across the roof behind me. The voice is familiar, but I can't figure out who's voice it is until I turn around and see the person's slicked back, jet black hair.

"It's nice to finally meet you. My name is −"

"Grant," I finish his greeting for him.

Grant gives a soft grin as he averts his eyes to his feet. "Of course you do. I should have known you would." Grant nods his head as he talks, making me feel uncomfortable. He begins walking towards me, both his hands buried deep into his pockets, which leaves me afraid that he might pull out a weapon on me. "I'm glad you came up here. I have a lot to tell you."

"Honestly, Grant, you're not somebody I entirely want to talk to at the moment," I snap at him with hostility filling the air. I'm stuck not only thinking about the time he left me on the roof of Stevenson's as he rides off on the helicopter, but also at the time he fought my dad and called him a murderer. "I don't like people who don't like my dad, so get away from me."

"Who said I didn't like your dad?" he asks with a soft laugh. "Anthony and I have become close friends. Yeah, we had a little spat in Roaksville, but it's because of him that I'm alive today. He saved me, and I couldn't thank him more."

I'm confused. Literally, the last time I saw Grant, he was spitting out teeth that my dad knocked out of him. "What do you mean he saved you?"

"I voted to stay in Roaksville, but I eventually had no choice but to come to Tryton. When I got here, the people of this city weren't going to let me in, but your dad recognized me and convinced the citizens to accept me. Your dad is a hero."

He is a hero. That comforts me. That means that what Ryan said to the group in that flashback did affect him. But still, I'm not too fond about this Grant guy leaving me in Westwood. Sure, maybe I didn't exactly act like the friendliest guy when I met him and his crew, but the concept of him leaving me to die on that roof doesn't make me want to become buddies with the guy anytime soon. "I still don't want to talk to you."

"That's okay, you don't have to talk. Just listen to me," he calmly tells me, as if he were expecting me to respond like I had. His walk becomes brisker, and as he nears me, I can tell by the look in his eye that he's appetent about telling me whatever he needs to.

I consider listening to him and conclude that a few minutes won't hurt. Maybe he has answers that I've been looking for. "Alright," I inimically approve. "But how did you know I was going to be up here?"

"The same way that you knew to come up here," he tells me with a sharp smile that is obviously missing two teeth towards the front.

"What do you mean?" I ask him, as his answer had in no way gave me any clue as to why I'm up here. "Honestly, I'm not entirely sure why I came up here in the first place."

"Yes you do," he proclaims, as if he knows what I'm thinking better than I do. He then leans in towards me and whispers to me like he's keeping a secret from somebody. "You came up here to see the eagle."

I'm taken aback at his mention of the eagle. I thought I was the only one who even knew it existed. "How do you know about the bird? And how did you know I know about it?"

"Well, for starters, don't call her the B-word," he corrects me as he turns back to the area from where he just walked from. "Abbi! Come here girl!"

And out from behind the helicopter, an eagle flaps its wings and flits its way towards me and Grant. The eagle perches itself on Grant's shoulder, and Grant welcomes the bird by rubbing the metallic half of its head.

"This is Abbigail," Grant proudly introduces her to me. He finally pulls his hands out of his pockets, showing me that both hands are clothed in black, leather gloves. He holds a bag of sunflower kernels in one of his hands, pours a palm full of them into his opposite hand, and feeds them to the bird. "She doesn't like being called the B-word. Or the E-word, for that matter. I call her Abbi for short, but you can call her Abbigail if you want."

"Why the . . ." I begin, completely ignoring the bird's name preferences. "Why do you have this thing? Why is half of it made of metal? Why did I see your eagle back in Westwood?"

Abbigail's head perks up from her meal at the mention of the E-word and shoots me a condemning glare, and Grant rubs her claw to soothe her. "I told you not to call her the E-word. Call her Abbi or Abbigail." Grant seems completely calm, but I can't help to feel not only threatened that this bird just looked at me like it was going to devour my face, but also rattled at the whole concept of what this bird is. "You don't need to ask so many questions. You were just rescued. Take it easy for a minute. Just listen. Besides, I don't want to talk about Abbi. I want to talk to you about something much more important."

I don't even want to know what's more important than a half-robotic eagle. "Why exactly should I listen to what you have to say? You're a stranger to me. In fact, the only thing that I do know about you is that you left me to die on the roof of that building in Westwood."

"That's what I need to tell you about," Grant tries to calm me down. "Look, you don't understand that whole situation, but you will. One day, I know for a fact that you will fully understand exactly why we left you, but I'm just not sure when that day will be, so you have to trust me."

"Trust you?" I repeat him with a harsh laugh. "How am I supposed to even consider trusting you if–"

Black.

Sepia.

I definitely did not see this flashback coming. I'm getting irritated at how random these things come to me, not even to mention that I have no clue why I have them in the first place. However, I disregard all that and realize that I'm standing on a roof again. At first, I think that I'm still on the roof of the hospital in Tryton, but I am instead on the roof of Stevenson's, and about five feet to my side is a medium-sized helicopter with its vicious blades thunderously slamming wind down on me. All the doors in the back of the helicopter are wide open, exposing empty seats that I can't help but to occupy.

Once I jump in the helicopter and settle down in the seat, a man in a full body, white suit jumps in from the opposite side and slides over to where I am. Oh yeah, he can't see me. I quickly get up from my seat and jump in the copilot's chair. The pilot has a hefty oxygen mask covering his face, but it fails in comparison to the horrifying mask of the full-body suit that the man behind me is wearing.

The eyes of the mask are still connected into a 'v', just as I had remembered. The meshed mouth still forms a demonic smile, and I instantly wish that I could forget the suit again. The man in the suit, however, is grasping his arm, and the combined sound of his winces in pain and the squeals of his oxygen tank are enough for me to distinguish over the blades.

That's when I notice the man outside the helicopter, his gelled up, black hair fluttering. Why do I somehow feel that Grant is responsible for this flashback I'm having? He was just telling me about this exact moment, yet here I am experiencing it again but from a different viewpoint. I'm confused as to what to do, and the only thing I know to do is to call out to Grant and make him tell me what this whole thing is about.

"Grant!" I yell at him, although it drowns in the sound of the blades. The pilot next to me, however, hears me, and throws a startled glare at me. The man in the white, menacing suit whisks his head up and apprehensively calls out to Grant multiple times.

They see me. How? How can they see me? Nobody in any of my other flashbacks has been able to see me, so what makes this flashback any different? I become agitated, feeling like I have blown my cover that I didn't know I was trying to protect. I thought I was just observing. That's what I do in all the other flashbacks.

Grant turns around in response to the suited man, and once he spots me sitting in the copilot's seat, he rashly hops in the helicopter and closes the door behind me.

And immediately as he does so, the helicopter lifts off the roof . . .

"How did you get in here, kid?" Grant yells at me, perhaps too loud but far too excited to care. "I didn't even see you hop in. We were about to leave you back there. You gave us quite a ride, especially for Ralph here." Grant pauses to let the man in the white suit pitch in, but he remains speechless at the sight of my impossible appearance. "I'm just glad you haven't 'toned yet, we wouldn't want to lose you."

Clink.

And that . . . That's the sound of old me throwing my hammer at the helicopter to get their attention.

And Grant, Ralph, and the pilot all ignore it. They blow it off as something unimportant, because the most important thing to them is sitting in the copilot's chair.

Except for, I'm not.

"I haven't egotoned," I say to them, trying to get a few words in before I go back to my reality. "Don't give up on me. Please don't."

Grant looks at me like I'm speaking gibberish, and I'm sure Ralph's face is the same under that grisly mask, but before I have time to add on, my vision falls to a blur.

My eyes shoot open. For the first time, the back of my head does not hurt after I wake up from a flashback, and I notice that Grant is sitting cross-legged on the roof right beside me.

"I didn't give up on you," he heartily tells me.

24

The eagle

HE DIDN'T GIVE up on me.

"I'm sorry we didn't turn around right then and go back to get you," he continues on, referring back to the incident on Stevenson's roof. "For probably a full minute, we were absolutely stunned. We didn't know what had happened. We didn't even know what we were going to tell the people in Tryton. But –"

"You convinced them to come back and get me," I brainstorm out loud what sounds like the most reasonable answer. "Didn't you?"

He doesn't say anything, perhaps because he doesn't want to take responsibility for my rescue mission, but I can tell that he's the one who practically saved me.

"Thank you," I wholeheartedly oblige him as I sit up and look up at him. He gives a shy grin and nods his head as a way of accepting my thanks. There's no need for me to say more.

"I didn't expect you to have that exact flashback right then," he admits. "I thought, you know, maybe you would have it in a week or two. I know they're not planned; my flashbacks are completely random just as, I bet, yours are. I just wanted to sort of warm you up to myself so you won't hate me."

With that, he confirms what I had low key expected: that he, too, has flashbacks like mine. "What do your flashbacks do?" I ask him.

"They just put me in random moments in time," Grant fills me in. "I'm sure they have some deep meaning that I have yet to understand, but for now, everything about the flashbacks is random and makes no sense." We both chuckle, and his eagle takes the sign of happiness and rubs her head against her owner's face.

"I knew you had them, too, whenever you disappeared in that helicopter, it took me awhile to put it together, but I eventually did. I've done the same thing you did – talk in a flashback. That's what gives your cover away. The characters in your flashback can't see you unless you talk to them. As soon as you do, well . . ." he offers his eagle more seeds, but she refuses them. ". . . they react just like any regular human would when some random guy pops out of nowhere."

He extends his leathered hand to me to offer me some sunflower seeds, but I kindly refuse. He then turns his head back and tosses the rest of the kernels in his palm down his throat. "And then one day, I was sitting up here on the helicopter like I usually do, when I saw you standing close to the edge of this building. I tried to say something to you, but you disappeared before I could even get out of the helicopter." Despite his calm demeanor, I can tell he's excited to finally meet me in reality rather than through flashbacks.

I want to throw tons of questions at him, but I take his advice. Maybe this is a listening experience, not an asking experience. Besides, I have a feeling that, even though he knows more about the flashbacks than I do, he's still new to the whole reasoning behind them.

"Weird how the flashbacks work," he concludes. He slaps his hands together, shaking off the kernel dust from his gloves and goes to stand up. "It's like a time-traveling ability that no one wants."

"Do other people have them?" I try to hold the question back, but I blurt it out to stop him before he walks off. "If so, do they have them the same way we do?"

"To the best of my knowledge, me and you are the only ones

who have them," he tells me, relieved that I asked him. "There may be others in Tryton that have these flashbacks. Hell, there may be even more kids like you outside these walls that have flashbacks. But I have yet to find another person who randomly passes out just like we do during them. And, trust me, if it were to happen in this city, everybody would know about it. I had a flashback while I was walking down the street one day, and before I even woke up, the news had spread like wildfire across the city that I had egotoned. I'm telling you, news in this city spreads, so if someone else were to experience these flashbacks, everyone would know about it."

"Did they know you had a flashback," I ask him, "or did they just think you passed out?"

"Well, I told them that I was fine, and it was just from exhaustion, but people insisted I go to the hospital." I can tell he feels a little awkward reliving this moment, but he continues. "It's happened a few times after that, but luckily I've been in private during those moments. As far as I know, you and I are the only people who even know these flashbacks exist."

"Dang," I say, not sure how I should respond to the fact that we're the only two with these flashbacks. I instead decide to change the subject altogether. "Well, tell me about the bi . . . I mean, Abbigail. Why is she all . . . robotic?"

Instead of answering me, Grant lifts his arm, and Abbigail takes that as a sign to leave her perch and glide over to me. The eagle lands on the floor of the roof directly in front of me, then waddles her way closer to me, like a dog would as it tried to warm itself up to someone new.

The eagle, err . . . Abbigail looks just like she did when I got a close-up shot of her in Westwood. I carefully lift my hand to her metallic wing, and flinch once my fingers come in contact with the warm metal. This is so strange. Out of all the crazy things that has happened to me this past week, I think this one takes the cake.

Abbigail inches her beak closer to my face, trying to pick up my scent. I look into the eagle's bright-red eye as it pricks through the metallic side of its head. I thought I recalled that the eye she had was green instead, but I may be wrong. As she inspects me, the metal surrounding the red eye retracts, making the eye larger. The metal then constricts around the eye, reducing the eye to a tiny red dot, all while emitting a sound that suggests that her eye is zooming in on me. She quickly turns her hand and tugs at Grant's leather glove, perhaps to get his attention to look at my cheek, but he swats her away.

"It's eye..." I brainstorm aloud, left sort of disturbed by it. "Why did it move like that?" The realization hits me immediately. I quickly look to Grant, searching for some kind of assurance of what I'm about to conclude.

"Is Abbi's eye a camera?"

Grant seems just as surprised as I am at what I said. "I didn't think it was that obvious," Grant admits to me, raising his eyebrows in admiration of my catching on.

This bird has a friggin' CAMERA as an eye? What is this thing? This thing must completely be a robot, not just half of it.

"H-How...Why..." I can't decide where to begin with the questions, so I stop myself before I stutter even more. Grant doesn't add on any additional information to me about it, and I'm left trying to grasp the concept that this bird is a robot/camera. This is crazy.

"Abbigail has come a long way," Grant tells me while rubbing the back of the bird. "Despite all these modifications, she is still a living, breathing animal."

"Why is Abbi a robot-camera-bird?" I finally decide to ask him the only question that makes sense right now. Abbi disapproves of my usage of the B-word, and as Grant calms her down, he tries to compile the best answer to my straightforward question.

"This is how we watched you," he tells me as he slides his tongue through the gap in his teeth, acting as if the information isn't anything new. At first, I'm left confused as to why he avoided my question, but then it hits me. This is how the city of Tryton watched me, followed me. When Cody mentioned that the city watched me through a camera, I was expecting some secret camera crew that hid behind the corner when I wasn't looking. I definitely was not expecting for an eagle to be the camera man.

"I installed a camera in Abbi's eye long ago," he continues on, as if putting a camera in an eagle's eye is the most mundane task there is. "I never actually used the camera, though. Abbi had went through an accident that took one of her eyes. I just needed an eye the size of hers to replace it, and I luckily found one that I could also convert into a camera. I control when her eye is recording and when it isn't, and she controls the zooming in and angles of the eye."

Good God he just keeps throwing more and more questions on to my list. If I still had that journal, it would be fresh out of paper right now.

"After I came back from that trip to Westwood, I told Abbi to fly back to Westwood and follow you and capture what you do, to show that you were still alive, and she did just that. I'm lucky to have such a smart companion." He places both his leathered hands on the eagle's head and gently caresses her as a sign of gratitude. Abbi, in return, gives a soft purr, much like that of a cat.

"When these people witnessed your story, your struggle, your . . . whatever it was you were doing in Westwood, these people loved it. Loved *you*, actually. Honestly, it didn't matter what you did, the people here were going to love you because you were alive. You survived this disease, which gave all these people hope that they could somehow do the same. You were their savior, and you didn't even know it."

I think back to the receptionist and the old man in the wheelchair I met on the way to the roof. That explains both of their affectionate behavior. These people look at me like a hero, even like a celebrity.

"I don't know what to say," I tell him, feeling awkward with this new celebrity status that I just found out I have. "What if I don't want to be these people's only hope?"

"Too late," he affirms to me. "I know you have questions and doubts about this place. You probably don't even know anything about Tryton, you've only been here a day. But there are millions of people in this city, all idolizing *you*. So you have to stay positive for them. No more burning houses down when you get sad."

"Dang, now what am I supposed to do with all these Molotovs I brought with me from Westwood?" I facetiously ask him, and we both give off laughs that cut through the silent, dusk air. Despite the weirdness of this bird, despite the strange connection Grant and I have, I like the company. Very unique company, at that, but still company. As our laughs slowly fade, I ask him another question. "What else did Abbigail watch me do?"

"Well, you had two rats, which was very surprising to us because, before that, we thought Abbigail was the only surviving animal," he tells me. The mention of Scar and Scat makes me feel guilty for leaving them on the roof, and I wish they were here with me right now.

"Abbigail then captured our rescue attempt of you, which is when we discovered that wolves also somehow survived, as well." I want to correct him, telling him that those were household dogs that had just become incredibly deranged instead. "This was huge to us," he continues. "This suggests that there may still be some remaining species that are immune to the virus just like you are. There's a Tryton helicopter search team and we've went to, I think, eleven of the fifty states. The only surviving members we found were all in the city of Westwood at one point." He acts like he just discovered the most essential piece of evidence to a murder case. His enthusiasm suggests just how desperate they actually were to find any living creature outside of Tryton.

"Abbigail also captured a lot of you talking to yourself," Grants concludes. Thinking back to Westwood, to after Grant left on the helicopter, and I don't recall visibly talking aloud to myself one bit.

"What are you talking about?" I insist, wondering why he's accusing me of something I never did. I mean, the moment after the car crash is a giant blur to me, but that was before Grant came to visit me at Stevenson's.

"You know exactly what I'm talking about," he tells me with a smile. "You yelled on that roof and at that liquor store for an hour. You acted like there was somebody there, and who knows, maybe there was, and Abbigail didn't capture them, but it looked very much like you were talking to yourself like some maniac."

He's talking about when I met the talking Grim. Of course. The Grim said that nobody else can see him, only the ones who have egotoned and I have that privilege. I'm afraid if I mention the concept of faceless humans who appear out of thin air to Grant, they may lock me up in an insane asylum my first day here. "Yeah," I agree, unconvincingly, "I must have been crazy then. I don't really remember it."

"That's ok, you're safe and healthy in Tryton," he assures me. "Or, at least, we think you are." He gives off a soft chuckle, and I force myself to give one, as well. "You better head back to your room," he insists to me, "before Jenkins begins looking for you."

"Who is Jenkins?" I ask him, as the familiar name that Cody mentioned earlier still doesn't tell me anything about him.

"Oh, he's quite a character," he assures me with a snicker, but I take it as more of a warning. "You'll know what I mean eventually. Maybe not today, maybe not tomorrow, but if you stay in this city long enough, you'll know exactly what I mean.

"But seriously, Jaden, you might want to head back to your room," he repeats himself. I pull my IV stand across the roof and to the door that I had walked through about an hour earlier. I pull the door open, and, before going through it, look back at Grant one more time.

"Thanks again," I call to him.

"No problem," he raises his hand to me as his eagle raises her normal wing to me at the same time. "I'll be up here if you need me. Just keep that in mind."

I give a soft nod and begin walking back down the stairway.

25

Trophies

I MAKE MY way down the hall to the elevator and head back to my floor. As the elevator zooms down to my floor, I hear someone in the elevator singing next to me, despite nobody else being in there with me. Before I begin to freak out, I see his reflection suddenly appear in the marble elevator door.

"Juuuust the two of us. . ." I see the blue shirt/orange bowtie combination of the talking Grim pop up beside me. "We can make it if we tryyyyyy, just the two of us. . ."

"I thought I got rid of you," I interrupt the Grim's karaoke session, still upset with how he left me last time.

". . .you and I," he softly finishes his singing, sad that I didn't welcome him with open arms. "Oh, lighten up, will you? You finally got rescued, you're finally getting answers, and now you finally get to reunite with your favorite Grim and yet you still have something to bitch about."

"Excuse me if I'm not totally thrilled with the fact that you're still following me around," I respond.

"If you're gonna throw a pouting party every time you see me from here on out, you better get your tissues ready. This is the first time I've been able to catch you one-to-one since we took this vacation to Tryton, I just wanted to check in on you and make sure you don't forget to send a postcard to our Grims in Westwood."

"This isn't a vacation," I tell him, irritated that he still views this as some sort of game.

"Uhh, yeah it is," he tells me as he looks at his reflection to straighten his bowtie. "I finally have more than one person's death to foresee. Do you know how many people in this city are going to die in, like, the next year? It's awesome! Plus, I've gotten this brand new bowtie. I had to stay with my original color, though. Didn't want to spice things up too much."

"Look, if you're not going to tell me any answers as to how I'm still alive or how this whole ordeal pans out, then leave," I bark at him. "I don't want you wasting my time."

"Jesus, kid," he retaliates with just as much hostility in his voice as I had, "my job was to get you to this city without you tripping over your own feet off a cliff, and I succeeded. And now that you're here, you're still asking questions like we're playing Jeopardy. Seriously, for once in your life, quit asking so many damn questions. Do what that Grant guy said and shut the hell up and listen. Besides, you're wanting all the answers and the prequel isn't even over yet. Chill out."

I let his words settle, trying to find a way that he's wrong but I can't come up with a viable reason.

"And don't think you're getting rid of me anytime soon," he continues on in a much more encouraging tone. "You're the only person who isn't half-passed insane that can see me, so I need a friend to talk to every now and then. But, I've had my fun for now. You're at your stop and the same fangirling receptionist is waiting to take this elevator, so I'll leave you alone."

And as soon as he swipes his eyebrow to disappear, the elevator comes to a stop and chimes. The door slides open, showing me the same receptionist that I smile lightly to and walk by before she can ask me anything. The Grim is right. Maybe I should chill out.

Eh, but what does he know. He doesn't even have a damn face.

I didn't get the number of my room when I left earlier, so I head in the general direction in where I think it is. As I search around the area for what looks like my room, I hear faint yelling coming from one of the rooms. I creep my way to the door and place my ear to it. Inside, I can hear Cody and another man throwing slurs back and forth to one another. The man, who's voice I don't recognize, is yelling at Cody about letting me leave the room. Cody, in return, continues yelling "I didn't do anything" to the man. Deciding that this is my room, I swing the door open to see what all the commotion is about.

Once the door opens, both guys stop their arguing and look at me. The unknown man, who is rather short, round, and bears a bushy mustache, looks gratified to see me. Cody, on the other hand, looks rather irritated, and I can't decide if he's angry at me or the man he was just yelling at.

"Mr. Foxx! What a pleasure to finally meet you!" the man greets me with a raspy, yet ecstatic voice. He walks over to me and extends his plump hand for me to shake, but I hesitate for a second and look at Cody to see if I should accept this man's shake or not. Cody, catching my concern, shrugs his shoulders, as a way of telling me to do what I want.

I lay my hand out to meet his, and he vigorously shakes it. "My name is Harrison Jenkins! It's an honor to finally have you here with us in Tryton! Mr. Goodwin, can you please excuse us? Me and Mr. Foxx have a lot of catching up to do." The man sounds much happier than he did before I entered the room, and looks perhaps too delighted to see me. Cody, clearly still not pleased with this man who I'm not-confidently shaking hands with, walks towards the door, and as he approaches me, I let go of the man's hand and hug Cody.

"It's glad to have you here," Cody authentically tells me as he heads towards the door. "I needed somebody in this city to keep me from going crazy."

"Well, sorry to tell you this, but I don't want anything to do with you," I jokingly tell him with a huge smile, and he returns it. Cody then turns and pulls the door open, but looks back to say something to me before he leaves.

"By the way, I want my change back. I know good and well that that meal wasn't fifty dollars."

"Sorry," I tell him, "I've spent every dime of it already."

He gives me a gratified smile and heads out the door. Once the door slams shut, Mr. Jenkins walks over to my bed and sits down on it's edge.

"It's great to see you, Jaden," Mr. Jenkins tells me with a broad smile. I ignore him, as I don't really want to talk to another stranger right now. I don't know exactly what this man wants with me, or what he's even doing in here. I've talked enough the past hour to last the next week. But, this is the man that I've heard about, so apparently Mr. Jenkins appears to be pretty important. Still, I don't want to talk to him. In fact, there's only one person I want to talk to right now.

"I want my dad," I request to Mr. Jenkins, perhaps too unwelcoming. "I don't want to talk to anyone else but him."

"Well, Anthony is tending to patients at the moment," Mr. Jenkins assures me. "As soon as he gets done with them, he will be here for you." Mr. Jenkins gets up from my bed and walks over to the doorway of the bathroom. "I know you want to talk to him, but he's a busy man. Being the chief physician comes with a busy schedule."

I ignore how obnoxiously close the man is to me and perk up at his comment. "Chief physician, you say?" I ask him as I make my way past him and walk over to my bed. Cody mentioned earlier, but I want to hear this man explain it to me.

"Oh, yes sir," Mr. Jenkins tells me as he rubs his mustache. "The top doctor that Tryton has to offer. Anthony has been a huge asset to this hospital and this city, for that matter. He's made tremendous contributions to Tryton, and we honestly wouldn't have made it as far without him."

"That's good," I say with a proud smile. Despite the fact that Dad was nothing more than a nurse in Westwood, it makes me proud that he is essential to this city. But, the fact that he is the 'chief physician' without any seriously relevant experience leaves me worried with what the conditions the people of Tryton are in and the desperate need Tryton has for a doctor. However, I diverge from that subject for now. "So, what was that argument between you and my friend all about?"

"Oh, that disagreement between me and Mr. Goodwin? It was nothing really," Mr. Jenkins tells me. I can tell he's lying; he's just really good at playing it off. This man's worry-free attitude aggravates me, reminding me of a certain Grim I met a few days ago.

I get a good, up-close look at the man for the first time. His humorously bushy, gray mustache along with the man's bowling ball-esque figure gives him a wacky appearance, but just by glancing at his face, I can tell that the man has been through a lot. The roughness in his eyes tells me that he has seen far more than anyone would want to see, and even one of his ears has an ugly scar. Despite the man's awkward-yet-intimidating appearance, I still decide that I don't believe him. I can't decide if it is annoyance or distrust, but one of those characteristics gleam from him.

"That argument was definitely something," I unhappily tell him, "and I don't know if I really appreciate you yelling at my friend like that."

"Mr. Foxx, I don't know what you're talking about," the man says to me, acting clueless to what I'm saying. "That argument was not serious."

Okay, so now this man is lying to me to my face? My disapproval of Mr. Jenkins increases, and I try to let the Grim's words echo in my head, but my stubbornness takes over. "So what are you doing in my room anyway?" My distaste is too evident in my voice, but I don't care. Something about this man just irks me.

"Alright, kid, drop the attitude," the man's tone changes dramatically, as now he sounds far more demanding and serious. "I'm not here to baby you or sugar-coat anything. You will get plenty of that shit once you leave this hospital. I'm here to tell you what you need to know."

"And what exactly is that?" I'm not pleased with the way this man just walks up in here and throws two different faces at me, so I make sure he notices my displeasure. "Why exactly are you barging into rooms like you—"

"Own the place? Because I do." He finishes my sentence, which impressively shuts me up. "I'm the mayor of the city that just so happened to save your miserable life. If it weren't for me, you would still be in Westwood driving into buildings and burning houses."

I'm impelled into an awkward silence as a response. The man is right, this city did save my life. Still, the fact that he's bringing up my time in Westwood offends me.

"Now," he breaks the silence with a stern whisper, "are you going to listen to me, or are you going to pretend to be Mr. Know-It-All?"

I respond with a simple nod.

"I'm sure you know by now that you are a well-adored celebrity in this city," Mr. Jenkins sternly says. "The citizens of Tryton are actually waiting, chomping at the bit for you to be released from the hospital, just so they can see you in the living flesh. Which, for all I know, you could've just went to the bottom floor of the building and roamed the streets a second ago. Never mind, none of that is important at the moment. The main point is, you have given many of these people hope, when, in all honesty, they shouldn't have any.

"With that said, that can become a hindrance. You alone are the single most important specimen to the studies of fighting a solution for this disease."

"Wait, there still isn't a cure for this thing?" I ask him, as a part of me was hoping they had found one by now, but another part of me was pretty confident that they hadn't.

"No," he says, as if the question pestered him. "Now, we call this disease the Cozmin Disease. Us finding you will help a whole lot in finding a cure, plus it gives the people of Tryton hope in returning back to their normal lives. Once we introduce you to the city, they should really feel more . . ."

"Introduce me?" I ask the man. "So you guys have already made a schedule with what ya'll are going to do with me without even talking to me first? And I want to know why exactly I am the one who gets the title of 'most important specimen'? Yes, I survived this 'Cozmin' thing, but why am I the one who's supposed to be your guinea pig?"

"Mr. Foxx, it'd be wise to shut your mouth," the man furiously commands me. I unwillingly do as he says and wait for him to say something. He leans in towards me until I can smell his breath inches from my face.

"I didn't ask to be here," he whispers in my face, all while keeping eye contact with me. "I didn't ask to be the leader of this place. I didn't ask to have to do the things that I've done. I didn't even ask to still be alive at this point. And, I can assure you, I sure as hell didn't ask to be sitting here, talking to an eighteen-year-old brat, who thinks he knows everything about a subject he clearly knows nothing about. I didn't ask for this, and neither did you, so quit blaming me for your issues."

He pauses and turns his eyes to the bed.

"You really want to know why you're the 'most important specimen' left?" he begins, still maintaining a harsh whisper. He looks up from the bed to look me in the face. "It's because you're all that was left.

"You know what Cozmin has done? It spread across the entire

globe in a little over a month, wiping out nearly the entire human race. Not just the United States. Every continent and every country was infected. We've estimated that the survival rate is somewhere around 1% of what the world's population was. Despite the fact that the Cozmin Disease was first discovered in the United States, we still had by far the most survivors of any other country. The U.S. was lucky because we came up with the solution of putting up filtering metal walls to keep the Cozmin out from our cities. But even with the walls, there is only one other surviving city like Tryton in this country. *One.*" The emphasis he puts on the word 'one' tells me that the number should be higher.

Mr. Jenkins backs away from my face and sits back in his chair, folding his hands behind his head to get comfortable. "There are only two people to have experienced the full force of the Cozmin Disease first hand and survived to tell the story. The other man came crawling to our walls about four weeks after the disease had fully spread, but that's fairly understandable. There was bound to be at least one guy make it to us after we put our walls up, and he just so happened to be four weeks late. But that was only four weeks. Then there's you. Here you come, six months after Cozmin had taken over, and your only injuries are those that you gave to yourself. Like you're somehow immune to the virus."

I become paralyzed by what he just said. Am I immune? How can I be? How could I have survived the past six months without any treatment? I'm no longer curious for answers. I'm scared to find them.

"Whether you like it or not, whether you know it or not, you are the only hope the human race has left. And I know for a fact that that is something you didn't ask for."

Mr. Jenkins stands up from his chair as a soft knock comes from the door. A nurse peeks her head in, and before she can say anything, Mr. Jenkins talks to me.

"You're going to be sent for testing," Mr. Jenkins tells me as he switches back into his original, chipper tone. "These tests are not only to make sure all your organs are functioning properly, but also to find out if there is anything abnormal throughout your systems. There is something important in your body; we just have to find it." The shift in his tone from hostile to friendly frustrates me. There's something about this man. Something I can't exactly figure out. Whatever it . . .

Black.

My eyes are staring into darkness for awhile until I'm suddenly placed into a sepia world.

I look up and see a giant wall. It looks just the wall at Westwood, only much, much taller. The wall seems to stretch up to the clouds, and it resembles more of an infinite skyscraper. An awestruck look crosses over my face as the immensity of the wall amazes me, but as Grant's words echo in the back of my mind, I make sure not to say a word. As my eyes travel downward from the peak of the wall, I see a giant door directly in front of me. On both sides are two hefty men grabbing chains that dangle to the sides of the door. The men heave on the chains, causing the door to slowly rise. As I watch the men tug at the chains, I hear a man's voice come from directly beside me.

"I'm still not so sure about this, Anthony," I turn to my right to see the fat Mr. Jenkins standing next to me, unaware that I'm in clear sight beside him. I follow the direction of his eyes to see my dad standing to the left of me. "We shouldn't even have to talk to these people, there's no more room in this city. And what if they're not doctors like we've been looking for?"

"We can't just ignore these people," my dad calmly replies to him. "They might be doctors or somebody we can really use. But, just keep in mind, even though we may appear crowded, there's always room for people. If these people are doctors that would be great, but we can't punish them if they're not. The human race is fading, so we need as many living people that we can have."

"Right," Mr. Jenkins says with a loud pant, feeling a little more

relaxed from my dad's response. As the door opens, the men beckon for Mr. Jenkins to enter, and he takes one more look at my dad before he heads in that direction. I, too, look back as I follow the fat man, and for a brief second, my dad looks directly through my eyes.

I know he can't see me, but I wish he did. I really want to talk to him again.

Mr. Jenkins and his two henchmen cover their mouths and noses with surgical masks as they proceed to the large door. The two huge men tug on the chains dangling close to the door, lifting it up for them to pass through. We find ourselves in a small room with another large door directly in front of us. A single light dangles from the ceiling of the room, and a table with four chairs surrounding it plays as the only decorations. As Mr. Jenkins takes a seat at the nearest chair, the muscular men finish with the door we just entered, and rush over to another identical door we are facing. However, this time, the door is only lifted a foot off the ground.

"Crawl under," Mr. Jenkins calls out from under his mask to whoever is on the outside. Suddenly, a man's head extends from under the metal door, and the buff men pull him out from the door and stand him up. As soon as the man gets to his feet, they shut the door behind them.

The man has an oxygen mask clutched over his face and an oxygen tank strapped to his back with the hose running to the mask.

"Is it safe to breathe?" The man calls out with a voice I've heard before.

"One second," Mr. Jenkins responds. "Gerard, Keaton, shut the door and hit the button."

As soon as the words are spoken, one of the men closes the barely ajar door, while the other man punches a button next to the door we entered in. The single, dangling light above begins flashing red as a sucking sound fills the room, resembling that of a vacuum. This lasts for about ten seconds, then the red flashing light shines green and the vacuum sound stops. With that, Mr. Jenkins takes his mask off his face, while Gerard and Keaton keep theirs on.

"Now it is," Mr. Jenkins tells the man.

The man, with relief, throws the mask off his face and tosses it on the table in front of him, revealing the rest of his face.

Mr. Armstrong.

"Look," Mr. Armstrong begins, "you've got to help us. We've been running from the Cozmin for about a week. We can't find any shelter, nowhere is safe anymore except this place. We have an entire city that needs help and this is the only safety we can make it to. Were running low on oxygen, so there's no way we can make it to the other cities. I know that ya'll have just put these walls up, but we need—"

"Do any of your people have any medical knowledge or experience in the medical field?" Mr. Jenkins interrupts Mr. Armstrong's reasoning and asks a question that seemed to have been scripted down as the first question anyway.

Mr. Armstrong pauses for a moment, considering his answer. "No, we don't, but we have plenty of able bodies who can learn and—"

"How many are with you?" Mr. Jenkins quickly gets bored with Mr. Armstrong's response and firmly presses him.

"Uhh, there's about thirty of us," he answers with desperation filling his voice. "They're not with us now, though, they're back in Mississippi. I have two more people with me outside, and if you accept us, we're planning on going back to get them. We need your help. There are—"

"Mississippi you say?" Jenkins says as he suddenly grows interested. "What part of Mississippi?"

"We, uhm," Mr. Armstrong begins, clearly not expecting the question but glad that Mr. Jenkins is listening to him. "We, me and the other thirty people, are in Roaksville right now, but I was originally the mayor of Westwood, Mississippi. I have leadership skills, I can contribute and help the city out in any way possible."

Mr. Jenkins gives a soft grin at Mr. Armstrong's words, but I don't think its due to Mr. Armstrong's begs. "Westwood, ya say? Do you know Anthony?"

I'm just as confused as Mr. Armstrong is as to why my dad is being brought into this conversation, but Mr. Armstrong perks up. "Foxx? Are you talking about Anthony Foxx?"

"Yeah, him," Mr. Jenkins says as he softly pinches his mustache.

"Yes, I know him! Me and him were very good friends! We practically ran Roaksville together! Is he here, too? His group and my group had actually began heading to Tryton, but we got separated somehow. It's good to hear that he got here safely!" Mr. Armstrong is beaming, ecstatic that my dad is here and perhaps even more excited that my dad may have indirectly saved his life.

Mr. Jenkins looks at the floor for a few seconds and then lifts and shakes his head simultaneously.

"Sorry, we can't take you and your people."

Mr. Armstrong's mood immediately plummets. "What? No, why? Why? Is it because I know Anthony? Look, if I have to avoid Anthony in order to bring my people in, I will. If you want me to stay away from any leadership roles like I mentioned earlier, I will. But please, you can't reject us."

"Sorry," Mr. Jenkins pretends like he gives the offer thought, but I can tell he has made up his mind. "The city has already reached full capacity. We can't possibly fit more people in here."

"Yes you can," Mr. Armstrong says quickly, clearly scared that he won't be able to persuade the man. "We will help in any way possible. We have able bodies, we can—"

"Look," Mr. Jenkins tells Mr. Armstrong, sounding impatient, "I can't tell you how many people come in here saying that exact thing. And I've taken some of them in, but instead of helping, they mooch off of our success. They contribute nothing and live a laid-back life in the protection of Tryton. Therefore, I have quit taking requests for 'able bodies'. I'm incredibly sorry, sir."

"That won't be us, I promise! Please, you have to listen to me!" Mr. Armstrong's words are moving so fast that they sound like they're slurring together. "Please listen! I have kids out there, women and children!

Babies! You can't send us out to die? You have to help us! Please, we're begging you!"

"Sir, my mind has been made. Gerard, Keaton, escort this man out." Jenkins puts his surgical mask back on as the men raise the door up about three feet and go to grab Mr. Armstrong.

"No, no please, no!" Mr. Armstrong's voice gradually gets louder. "NO! GET YOUR HANDS OFF OF ME! NO! GUYS! HE SAID NO! HE'S NOT TAKING US!"

He's clearly directing his last yells to people outside. As the men each grab one of Mr. Armstrong's shoulders, the two people Mr. Armstrong mentioned earlier crawl out from under the door. Once they stand up and see that the air is breathable, the people rip their masks and tanks off and toss them on the floor.

Ryan.

Scarlett.

"Get off of him!" Ryan tries to pull Mr. Armstrong from out of the grip of one of the men, but the man backhands Ryan, sending him onto the floor.

"No!" I hear Scarlett let out a cry at the sight of Ryan being knocked to the ground. I'm left in utter shock at what is going on. I can't move. My mouth remains agape as I can't comprehend what's happening.

"How could you do this to us?" Scarlett screams at Mr. Jenkins. The sound of her voice in distress rips my heart apart. I want to help her, to take her in, but I know I can't. I can't even move at this point. I'm motionless.

"Look, missy," the urge to punch Jenkins for that remark flows through-out me, but I can't do anything. "Tryton is full. Life is hard enough with all the people we have now. You don't know what it's like in these walls."

"And you don't know what it's like outside these walls, you coward!" Ryan yells from the floor across the room.

Jenkins directs his eyes to Ryan and struts toward him with a rage like I've never seen. "Don't you DARE call me a coward!" Jenkins falls to his knees and pulls Ryan up towards him by his shirt, then proceeds to punch Ryan in the face repeatedly.

Mr. Armstrong struggles to get away from the men, but to no avail. Scarlett rushes towards Jenkins, trying to pull him off of Ryan. As for me, I remain standing still, traumatized.

Jenkins continues, blow after blow, while Scarlett tries to pull him off. Finally, she reaches in her pocket and pulls out a pocket knife.

As Scarlett flicks the knife open and raises her arm, Jenkins stops beating Ryan and turns his attention to her. He raises an arm to defend his face, and his forearm meets her shoulder. The strike misses Jenkins's face, but scrapes him on his right ear.

"Ahh! Stupid girl!" He grabs his ear with one hand and slaps Scarlett with the other, knocking her to the ground, as well. "Take them out! Do it!"

Keaton and Gerard quickly toss Mr. Armstrong out the crawlspace and drag an unconscious Ryan and damaged Scarlett out with him. As the two men begin to shut the door, Mr. Jenkins reaches down and grabs the three masks that were left behind.

"Ungrateful sons of bitches," Jenkins roars to no one in particular as he shakes Ryan's blood off his knuckles. "Lucky we didn't kill them. We should have. But we will just let the Cozmin take care of that." He gives a sneer to their masks that are now resting in his arms, admiring them as if they were trophies. Jenkins beckons for the men to raise the door leading back into the city, leaving my friends to their death.

They made it this far. So close.

The world spins out of sight, and I regain my focus in normal coloring.

"Jaden? Jaden, can you hear me?" I hear the disgusting, fake voice of Jenkins.

I slightly open my eyes to see the fat man's face close to mine, inspecting me to see if I were dead.

"Are you okay?" he asks me. "You had us worried there for a second."

The man backs away from my face and turns to talk to the nurse. As he's talking to her, I get a full glimpse of his ear. Scarred and battered. The only remaining impression of Scarlett and Ryan is the scar left imprinted on his ear.

"Nurse," Jenkins says to the woman at the door, "take him to go get tested." He turns and looks me in my eyes. "Jaden, the doctors are just going to run some tests on you. You'll be fine."

I don't answer him. I scold the man, trying my best to hold in my animosity, to hold in my urge to somehow kill this man with the few seconds I have left with him right now.

He becomes surprised at how I respond to him. For a second, I think that he knows what I just saw. I hope he does, I really do. I want him to say something, give me some reason to rip his throat open. But he doesn't react how I want him to. He doesn't recognize my anger. He gives me a slight smirk, pats me on the shoulder, and exits the room.

A coward. He doesn't even want to look at me anymore. Coward. That's all he is. As he walks through the door, he turns around one last time and looks at me with a gleam in his eye.

"Oh, and Jaden, welcome to Tryton."

CPSIA information can be obtained
at www.ICGtesting.com
Printed in the USA
FFOW02n1809010418
46128503-47190FF